# Until You

## FELICITY SNOW

# Acknowledgments

To my amazing beta readers, Hawthorne Gray, Donatella Coluzzi, Amanda Martin, and Karla A.C. I couldn't have done this without you. To my street team for all your help and support in spreading the word about Paul and Charlie's story, thank you so much. And to my editor, Jen Sharon for her dedication.

"You are the best thing I never planned."

UNKNOWN

# CHAPTER
*One*

## PAUL

Shit, I'm exhausted. The sun is dipping behind the trees now but it's been hot and humid all day. My yellow long-sleeved T-shirt clings to me, and I take my hard hat off, wiping at my brow as I let out a breath. My muscles ache and the arthritis in my knee is acting up again. God, when did I get so old? I'm not ancient, but some days I feel like it with all the new ailments my body has inflicted upon me, and the work I do doesn't help.

Honestly, I love working with my hands, and I love being outside regardless of the weather. I couldn't stand being at a desk all day or dealing with customers. I love machinery, I love seeing a project come together, and I have amazing coworkers.

Sometimes I think I'm getting too old for this, though. My lower back aches, my neck is sore and my hands are cramped. I'll definitely be icing my knee when I get home, and then probably taking a nice warm bath. God, that sounds wonderful. I sigh just thinking about it.

"Hey," one of my coworkers, Carlos, says as he slaps me on the shoulder. He's several inches shorter than me with short black hair and dark eyes. I'd guess he's in his early forties. His Spanish accent is there when he speaks but it's mild since he's lived here in Georgia most of his life. "You ready to get out of here? Some of us are meeting up for burgers and drinks in a bit if you want to join." We met a little over four years ago when I moved across town to start over and we started working together, and he's always been friendly, tried to make me feel like a part of the team.

My stomach growls at the mere mention of food, and honestly a drink sounds amazing, so I nod. I'm filthy, however, and I'm under no illusions about how I smell, so I'll be heading home first to bathe and change before I join the rest of my coworkers.

Carlos smiles and waves as I pull away from the site where we're working on a new fire station. My drive home is short, thankfully, and I make it in only ten minutes because we worked past rush hour. It was a solid ten hour day. My feet ache and I can't wait to get out of my grungy work boots.

Arriving home, I step out of my truck, wincing at the pain in my knee as I make my way up the front steps to my ranch-style home. It's older but in great shape. Small, with only two bedrooms and a single living area and bathroom, but it works for me. It's in a more rural area, tucked back off the road, surrounded by trees, no neighbors close by, which I prefer. I like my privacy. I'm not big on people, and ever since my divorce I haven't needed much space. Not to mention, the bigger the house, the bigger the emptiness.

My heart feels heavy with the reminder of how much laughter and merriment used to fill my home when my wife and son were around. The family meals, the game nights, watching movies together; dinner parties with friends, holiday gatherings, and sleep overs, delicious food, music playing constantly, and the sound of our son's laughter echoing off the walls as he chatted and played games with his friends, or sat in front of the television. The smiles of my wife and son were the best part of my day when I walked through the door. Now silence greets me. Some days I don't mind it, yet other days it's the loudest thing of all.

I turn the music on on my iPhone to distract myself and keep from wallowing in self-pity. After all, it's no one's fault but my own that I'm alone.

Once in the bathroom, I undress and toss my dirty clothes in the hamper. I relieve myself, then wash my hands and examine my reflection in the mirror as the bath water runs. I've had people tell me I need to get out and start dating again. That I'm plenty young and handsome enough. I'm in decent shape despite not being to the gym as often as I should be. My job helps with that.

It's been five years since my divorce and losing my son, but I'm not sure I'm ready for a relationship. That would mean opening myself up to someone, airing all my dirty laundry, and I don't think I can do that, trust someone with my mistakes and failures. Not when they still keep me up at night.

I run my hand through my gray hair. It's got splashes of white mixed in as well. And although I'm not crazy about the color at my age, at least my hair is thick and full. My fingers brush over my thick stubble. I've never had trouble growing a beard, though I do think it's time for a shave. Rachel used to love it when I shaved. She liked my beard too, but she said the softness of my cheeks after shaving was a huge turn on for her. It was an almost sure-fire way to get her into bed.

My cock perks up at the thought of sex, and I glance down at it, nestled in a thatch of equally gray pubes. I'm not huge, but I'm decent-sized. Six inches maybe? I don't know, I've never measured. Not that it matters when I have no one around to appreciate it. Though I honestly never liked how much of a guy's confidence in his sexual ability was attributed to the size of his dick, or why society has to make men feel inferior for being smaller. It's not like it's a choice. It is what it is. And as far as I'm concerned it's not the size that matters,

3

it's what you do with it. Ironic, considering I haven't done anything with mine in a long ass time.

My phone vibrates on the counter and I peer down as the screen lights up. It's a text from Rachel.

**Rachel: lunch tomorrow?**

**Me: Yeah, where?**

**Rachel: same place as always, noon**

**Me: sounds good see you then**

I sigh and shut the water off before sliding into the oversized garden bathtub. Even though it's a single bathroom, it's a good-sized one. It's got a shower large enough for two and a tub big enough for my six-foot-two-inch frame.

I moan as the heat seeps into my muscles, surrounding me as I sink lower, until I'm fully seated. If I had time for a longer bath I'd use bubbles, and candles. God, I love the smell of a good candle, the crackling sound as the flame licks the wick. The woodsy scents are my favorite. They remind me of being a kid and playing in the forest in my backyard, running through the creeks, building that treehouse with my dad when I was twelve, and making applesauce and apple pies with my mom. Sitting in the same treehouse and playing truth or dare with my best friends and sleeping under the stars. Then having a son of my own and building similar memories with him. A firepit in the backyard, roasting hotdogs and marshmallows, telling ghost stories to him and his friends as they ate Rachel's rice krispy treats. I see his smile in my mind and a tear slides down my cheek.

God, I miss him. I wonder if the pain of his loss will ever go away. The ache, the longing, the guilt. Somehow I don't think it will, and I'm not even sure it should. I'm not sure I want it to.

I feel another tear sliding down my cheek and wipe it away, feeling like a weight is sitting on my chest. I will myself to relax as I rest my head against the bathtub pillow I bought myself a couple of months ago, taking deep breaths in and out like my therapist taught me to. It's been five years but

4

there are days the grief is still so acute it feels like I'm losing him all over again. I wonder if it would be any easier to deal with if I didn't feel responsible.

After fifteen minutes I decide it's time to get ready to meet my coworkers, so I unplug the drain and climb out. My mind is driving me crazy anyway, and I need a distraction.

I dry myself off and hang up the towel before walking naked through the hall towards my bedroom. My knee is still bothering me but the heat from the bath helped some. I'll take some painkillers and ice it later tonight.

I dress in jeans and a simple gray T-shirt and slide on my socks and oxfords. Then I proceed to do something with my hair which mainly consists of running some styling gel through it, blow drying it and calling it a day. I grab my keys and wallet and head out to my truck.

It takes less than ten minutes for me to reach our usual hang out. I park and head inside. Carlos and a few other coworkers are gathered around the bar. I join them and order a beer.

I'm not super close with my coworkers, but we get along well enough and I enjoy spending time with them outside of work. They're decent people, some married, some not, but all loyal and trustworthy. Of all my coworkers, Carlos is definitely the one I'm the closest to, though I still don't know if I'd consider him a friend. Not sure I really have any of those.

There's a football game playing on the tv above the bar and between that and the music playing, it's raucous and rowdy as all get out in here. But what can I expect on a Friday night?

Being an introvert, I'm not big on crowds. They exhaust me and I get overwhelmed easily, even more so since I've been a bachelor, but I'll stay for an hour or so, hang out, talk, and then head home.

I'm getting better at socializing. Up until a year ago I was pretty much a hermit. But it wasn't healthy and I knew I was depressed. I had to make some changes and start living my life again as best I could. Easier said than done, but, baby steps.

"Hey, ten o'clock," one of my other coworkers, Aaron, says, gesturing with a nod across the bar.

I turn my head to find an incredibly attractive woman eyeing me. She has long brown hair that falls in waves over her shoulders and a fair complexion. She's wearing a form-fitting green dress that stops a few inches above her knees and is showing off her cleavage. Her friends sit with her and cast glances at my friends and me before turning back to her and whispering.

"She's been staring at you since you walked in," Carlos says, and nudges me.

I just take a sip of my beer and turn back to the game. I honestly don't know shit about football, nor do I care to learn, but it seems far more interesting to me than trying to make small talk, or even worse, flirt.

"Are you serious?" Aaron gapes at me. "You're not gonna go over there?"

I shrug. "Not tonight."

"Dude, she's fucking you with her eyes." Carlos laughs a little. "You have to go say hi at least."

I shake my head. "I'm good, guys."

"Damn, what a waste." Aaron bites his lip and glances over at the woman. "Fuck it." He takes a long swig of his drink and then sets it on the bar before striding over to the woman and her friends.

Carlos and I watch, smiling and shaking our heads.

"He's got balls, I'll give him that," Carlos says, then turns back to me.

"Hey, you okay?" he asks.

"Sure," I reply with another shrug.

"Well, you know you can talk to me, if you want to. I'm not trying to push you into anything, I promise. I just want you to be happy."

I nod, but I think I gave up on happiness a long time ago.

6

―――――

A little over an hour later I say goodnight to my coworkers and head for the door. I stuck to soda after my initial beer so I wouldn't have to worry about driving home.

The warm air hits me as I step outside. It's September in Georgia which means it's humid and muggy. I reach for my keys in my pants pocket, but get distracted by what sounds like a scuffle from around the corner in the alleyway. I make my way over and am horrified to see three men in their mid to late twenties messing with a slightly younger looking man. They have him pressed up against the wall and one punches the younger man in the stomach while the other two hold him.

"Hey!" I growl. "What the hell is going on here?"

The three men pause and the one who just landed the punch backs away, but the other two don't let go of the younger one. As I step closer, I see that there's blood dripping from his nose and his face is bruised, the beginnings of a black eye forming already. He's filthy from head to toe, in a hoodie and jeans that are clearly three sizes too big for him, but despite the fact that he's obviously in pain, there's mischief in his eyes.

"I'm fine, grandpa," he wheezes.

"Hear that?" one of the other guys says. "He's fine."

"Get the fuck out of here before I call the cops," I say.

"We're not going anywhere until we get our money back," the same guy as before replies with a snarl.

I sigh and turn to the boy pressed up against the wall, his thick red hair falling across his forehead. He smirks and shrugs. He's so much smaller than these guys I can't believe he managed to withstand anything they doled out.

"You stole from them?"

"Genius deduction, old man."

Okay, smart aleck. "Wanna give them their money back?" I use my Dad voice, making sure he knows it's not a question.

7

"Can't. Already spent it."

"So, you see, this is payback," the guy who was punching him says. He's sporting a backwards baseball cap and has tanned skin and a thick gold chain around his neck. He's about to lay into the redhead again when I step forward and grab his arm.

"Stop," I say. "Look, whatever he stole I'll repay you."

All four of the guys' eyes widen, but especially the redhead's.

"You got two hundred dollars on you, old man?" Backwards Cap says.

I sigh. Barely. I pull out my wallet and thumb through it, grabbing a handful of twenties and a one hundred dollar bill.

"Let him go first," I say, and they exchange glances before pulling Redhead away from the wall and shoving him forward so that he practically falls into my arms. He rights himself immediately and scowls at me before he hurries off. I rub my hand across my forehead and hand the money over. "Nice doing business with you, gramps." Backwards Cap salutes me before he and his buddies wander off.

I step around the corner and start to make my way to my car when I hear, "I had it under control, you know?" I turn and see Redhead leaning against the front of the bar I just stepped out of. Now that he's in better lighting and I'm a little closer I realize just how young he is. He can't be a day over nineteen. Blood has dripped onto his hoodie, his red hair is caked in dirt and grime, his hands are filthy, and the blood on his face is starting to dry. It's obviously been a while since he showered or washed his clothes.

"You're welcome," I say, and he snorts.

"Never asked for your help."

"Well, I'm nice like that." I look him over once again and then ask, "Where are your parents? You live nearby? You in school somewhere?"

He shakes his head but doesn't say anything.

"You got somewhere to sleep?"

His eyebrows furrow. "What is this?" he spits, "twenty questions?"

I ignore him. "Someone I can call? Anything? You shouldn't be out here on your own."

"Yeah, thanks," he retorts. "I'll get on that."

I sigh. "Come on." I gesture with my head for him to follow me. He just stares at me like I've lost my mind.

"Yeah, no thanks, gramps. I'm good. Got everything under control, like I said."

"I'd hate to see what out of control looks like then." He glares at me.

"Fuck off."

I sigh. "Look, I've got a guest room in my house that no one's using, so you might as well come with me. You can shower, get some food, and I'll get you some pain killers and some ice." I'm making it sound like it's only a one time thing I'm offering him, but I'm hoping if I can convince him to come with me, I can also convince him to stay. I hate the idea of him being out here alone and vulnerable. And I hate to think about what he's probably had to subject himself to to survive out here. It makes me sick.

"I don't take handouts," he replies, and I'm beginning to think the scowl on his face is permanent.

"Fine. If you don't want to come home with me, at least let me get you some stuff from the drug store."

He narrows his eyes at me. "Why?"

"Because you're hurt and I don't like the idea of you being in pain. Especially if you are sleeping god knows where. Those wounds could get infected if you aren't careful and we both know you don't have money for a doctor."

He eyes me, the expression on his face softening for a brief second before it hardens again, the furrow in his eyebrows returning. "I just met you. Why the fuck do you give a crap about me?"

I don't tell him the truth, the real reason why I'm doing

this, why I feel so compelled to help him, because if I did there is no way he'd come with me.

"I just do," I say. "Take it or leave it."

To my relief he nods, but then he's pointing a finger at me. "Touch me and I will jump out of the car while it's still moving."

I hold up my hands, indicating that I will not be laying a hand on him, and I hate that that's something I have to assure him of, that it's something he feels compelled to warn me about.

I lead him to my truck and open the passenger side door for him. He glances at me and climbs in. I go around to the driver's side and get in.

"Seatbelt," I say. He rolls his eyes at me, but buckles in anyway. He's silent as he stares out of the window on the short drive to the nearby Walgreens.

When we get there, I park and turn off the car, then turn to him. He's a little pale, and I really wish he would come home with me and let me take care of him, but I can't say I blame him. He seems to have plenty of reasons for not trusting people. "I'll um, I'll be right back. Probably best if you wait here." I don't think there's much chance of him running off when he's already come this far, and I don't want him walking through the store in his current condition.

He just nods and stares out the window some more. I head into the store and grab a first aid kit, some snacks, Gatorade, and a clean T-shirt and hoodie that are closer to his size than the one he's wearing. I also grab some socks, hand sanitizer, wipes, water, and a small package of washcloths. Then I search for a toothbrush, toothpaste and some deodorant before getting a backpack for him to put everything in. He might have one stashed somewhere but I don't want to take the chance that he'll have to leave any of these things behind because he doesn't have a way to carry them.

I check out and head back to the truck. When I hand him the bag and the backpack his eyes widen.

"What the fuck, grandpa, I didn't ask for all this."

"Maybe not but you need it." He glares at me again. Then he's peering into the bag and I see his face go even more pale. "Why the hell are there condoms in here?"

"Just in case. I know people in your situation get desperate sometimes and I don't like the idea of you not having protection."

He's staring at me now and I hold my hand out. "First aid kit," I say. Without hesitation, he reaches into the bag and pulls it out. I take it and open it. Then I pull out a water bottle, and holding the door open, I soak the washcloth and then squeeze it out. I turn back to him and use it to wipe the blood and dirt from his face as gently as I can. Then I get a clean washcloth and do the same thing, this time applying it to the cut on his lower lip. He doesn't wince or squirm once.

I finish with some Neosporin and a bandage over the cut on his forehead. It's only after all the blood and dirt are gone that I realize how striking he is. His hair is still dirty and he doesn't smell the greatest, but his eyes are the greenest I've ever seen and his skin is incredibly fair. With all the dirt gone you can see the freckles sparsely scattered across his nose and cheeks. His red hair is shorter on the sides and longer on top and his bottom lip is quite a bit fuller than his top. It suits him.

"You should probably change shirts," I say. He does without hesitation and my chest constricts when I see not only the bruises on his abdomen, but how incredibly thin he is. God, you can practically see his ribs.

He slides on the T-shirt and hoodie I got him and then his eyes meet mine.

"I'll just take these home and get rid of them, if that's okay," I say, grabbing the discarded bloody shirts.

He nods and then wraps his arms around himself. It's killing me to leave him out here when I have everything he needs at home, but I can't make him come with me, no matter how much I want to.

11

"You sure you don't want to take me up on that offer of a warm bed?" I ask. He seems to be considering it for a moment but then shakes his head.

"I'm good." It's barely a whisper. He takes the backpack and the plastic bag in hand. I reach over and shove the first aid kit and washcloths back in and he chuckles a little. "Thanks, gramps." He turns and reaches for the door handle, but I speak before he can leave.

"You have a phone?" He nods and I'm surprised when he unlocks it and hands it to me. I type in my number and address and hand it back to him. "Just in case," I say. "My offer is always open."

To my surprise he actually takes it and types something, a name no doubt, probably something like 'old man', then shoves it in his pants pocket. "There's some instant cold packs in the first aid kit, you should probably use them on your ribs." He nods and steps out of the truck. "Take care of yourself," I add. He shuts the door and walks away, and I drive away with a sick feeling in the pit of my stomach.

It's only when I arrive back home and step inside, greeted by the silence once again, that I realize I never got his name.

# CHAPTER
## *Two*

## PAUL

When I arrive at the small Cuban cafe the next afternoon, my ex-wife greets me with a kiss on the cheek. We stand in line to order, then take our numbers as we make our way to our usual booth near one of the windows.

"You look nice," she says. I'm wearing jeans and a long-sleeved gray Henley since it's a little colder out today than normal. My chest tightens as I think of the boy from last night and how he must have been freezing sleeping outside. I really hope he found somewhere to sleep that wasn't an alleyway or a sidewalk. I haven't been able to get him out of my head all day, and I didn't sleep very well last night either, because I was worried about him. Part of me, a really freaking big part of me wants to track him down and make sure he's okay, but I have no way of knowing where he is. I just hope he can stay out of too much trouble.

"Thank you," I say. "So do you." She's got her dark hair in a ponytail and is wearing skinny jeans and a black sweater that I don't think I've seen on her before. Her boots are black as well and she's got large silver hoop earrings in her ears.

"Thank you." She gives me a warm smile.

13

"How are you?" We both ask at the same time and then laugh. It does me good to hear her laugh. It's not measured or forced, but genuine and carefree, and it warms my insides. Even though our marriage didn't work out, she's still my best friend, and seeing her happy gives me joy.

"How's the wedding planning coming?" I ask as our food is delivered, and we both dive in.

"Good," she says, her smile brightening. "Colin is ready for it to be over with, I think." She chuckles at the mention of her fiancé. I've met him a few times and he's a good guy. Very patient, somewhat stern, but kind, and I know he loves Rachel. He's been married once before too, but his wife passed away early on and they never had kids. Rachel and he met about a year and half ago and got engaged six months ago. The wedding is in two months, and since her father and mother passed away a while back, she's having me walk her down the aisle. It's a bit untraditional, having your ex-husband give you away to your future husband, we know, but it works for us.

"So what's new with you?" she asks. "You been getting out at all?"

"Yeah, actually," I tell her. "Just went out last night with some friends from work." She beams. "I uh, I had kind of an interesting experience, too."

She raises an eyebrow. "Oh?"

I nod. "I ran into a homeless kid, and, well, I helped him out a little."

Her other eyebrow shoots up. "Oh. That was nice of you."

I shrug. "I wanted to do more. He wouldn't let me."

Her gaze softens. "Paul, I'm all for you helping people in need, but are you sure you aren't doing it because of Trey? Trying to make up for what happened?"

"No, of course not. But it doesn't matter, does it? The boy needed help regardless. And I already know that nothing I do will make up for what happened to Trey."

She nods, her eyes filling with tears, and I reach over to

14

take her hand and give it a squeeze. She wipes her eyes with her other hand and sniffles. "I'm sorry."

I shake my head. "Don't be sorry." She takes a deep breath and gives me a small smile.

We continue to eat and she updates me on life as a real estate agent. I tell her how the fire station is coming along, and then she hits me with, "So, are you seeing anyone?"

I groan. "No."

She sighs. "Paul, I hate that you are alone. Have you tried? You're a great guy, there's no reason for you to be without someone."

"There's every reason," I tell her. "I don't want to be with someone."

She eyes me. "Look, I get that it's hard. Trust me. I didn't think anyone could love me enough to see past my mistakes either. But then I met Colin. He showed me that I was worthy of a second chance. And so are you."

I shake my head and bite my lip. She squeezes my hand. "Well, when you change your mind, there's some nice single women I know from work that I can introduce you to."

I sigh and change the subject.

We talk a little bit more about the wedding and I leave thirty minutes later, saying goodbye with a kiss to her cheek this time. "Say hi to Colin for me," I tell her.

"I will," she says, and we part ways.

———

It's a week later and I'm sitting on my sofa drinking my tea and reading, when I hear a knock on my door. It's after ten pm and I have no idea who would be knocking at this hour, or honestly, who would be knocking, period. I'm not exactly popular.

Standing, I make my way to the door and peek through the peephole. My breath leaves me when I see the red-haired

15

boy from the other day on my front porch. Did he walk the whole way here? Fuck.

I unlock the door and fling it open. He blinks at me as he sways slightly, his hand on the door jamb. Is he drunk? Or high? Or both? Shit.

"Evening, gramps," he slurs. His pupils are dilated and his eyes bloodshot. His forehead is sweat-slicked and his face flushed. Fuck, what the hell is he on?

"Get in here," I say, and grab his arm, yanking him inside before closing the door behind him.

The minute he steps inside, he vomits on the floor and then blinks at it like he isn't sure how it got there. I grab his arm and drag him over to the kitchen where I push him down on a chair before reaching under the kitchen sink and sliding on rubber gloves, then grabbing the paper towels and some of my disinfectant spray before moving to clean up the mess. At least it landed on the tiled entryway and not on my carpet. As it is I have to hold back my gag reflex as I work.

"Nice place, pops," he says, gazing around, his eyes lidded. His hiccups loudly and then belches.

I toss the soiled paper towels in the trash and immediately take it out to the garage. When I return he's still at the table, his hand in front of his face, staring at it like an infant discovering their fingers for the first time. Fuck, he is plastered.

I grab another paper towel and get it damp, then make my way over to him and reach for his face to wipe off the vomit. He jerks back as soon as my hand moves in his direction.

"Hey, easy," I say. "I just want to clean you off." To my relief, he sits still and lets me clean his face, his green eyes locked on me. I toss that paper towel in the trash and then grab a glass and fill it with water and bring it to him.

He blinks at it for a while before his gaze meets mine. "You are awfully nice for an old guy," he slurs. He takes the water and downs it, placing the glass back on the table. "That was refreshing. Is there more?"

"Yes, I haven't run out of water yet." I get him another glass and hand it to him.

"What are you doing here?" I ask."And what the hell are you on?"

He waves his hand at me, making a "Pfft," sound. "It doesn't matter." He reaches into his pocket and pulls out a wad of cash and slaps it on the table. My eyes widen.

"What the hell is that?" A sick feeling builds in my stomach.

"Your money," he replies.

"What?" The sick feeling in my stomach only builds and my temples heat. "What did you do to get this?" I take his chin in my hand and force him to look at me. He blinks again.

"I didn't steal it," he says, and pulls out of my grip. "I earned it fair and square."

I clench my teeth. That's exactly what I'm afraid of. "What did you do?"

"It's not so much what, as who," he says, and then giggles and burps again.

"Fuck," I snarl at him. "You idiot, that money was a gift. You didn't have to…" I run my hands through my hair. "I didn't *want* you to pay me back. Especially not like that."

He frowns. "I don't like owing anyone, and like I said, I don't take handouts."

"So you fucking sold yourself to get me my money? You really think that's what I'd want?"

He stands, and sways again. "It's all there, minus the money I had to use to pay for an Uber. I'll let myself out." He moves unsteadily towards the door but I grab his arm. He jerks away from me so fast he stumbles and lands on his ass.

"Asshole," he snarls.

"Shit, I didn't mean to hurt you," I say. I reach for him again out of instinct, but he holds his hands up and backs away.

"Look, I'm not trying to scare you or hurt you," I tell him. "I just wanted to help you up. You seem a little unsteady."

"I'm fine," he says, and pushes himself to his feet, tottering.

"Stay," I blurt out before he can take a step.

"What?"

"I don't want you to go back out there. You're drunk and obviously on something, and you need rest and for someone to watch over you. Please stay."

"I don't do—"

"Handouts," I interrupt. "I know. Tell you what, if you are feeling well enough in the morning, I'll let you cook breakfast. How's that?"

He blinks again and then nods and I feel the knots in my stomach loosen a little. I'm still mortified that he slept with a total stranger to pay me back, though. What the hell was he thinking? My blood boils at the thought of someone taking advantage of him, him feeling like he doesn't have a choice, like he has to resort to prostitution because he's so convinced he can't let anyone do something nice for him.

"Down the hall," I say, gesturing. "This way." He walks in front of me and it's only then that I realize something is missing.

"Where's the stuff I got you?"

"Outside," he mumbles.

"Bedroom is on the right," I say. "Second door. First door is the bathroom."

He stops just outside the second door and I go in front of him, turning the light on. It's not much but it's got a queen-sized bed, a nightstand, a dresser, and a chair in the corner, plus a closet.

"It's all yours," I say, and gesture with my hand for him to go inside. He just stands there for a long moment, taking the room in, and then glances at me before stepping over the threshold and making his way over to the bed. He sits on it like it's made of porcelain or something, and runs his hand over the comforter. I swear I hear his breath hitch, but when his eyes meet mine again his face is stoic.

"You should sleep," I say. "I'll bring you some pajamas." He doesn't say anything, so I go down the hall to my bedroom and grab a sleep shirt of mine for him to wear. It's going to be huge on him. I'm guessing he's around five-foot-five, and all of one hundred and twenty pounds soaking wet. Oh well. At least the shirt is comfortable and clean.

I make my way back across the hall and hand him the shirt. He takes it from where he's still seated on the edge of the bed. It's almost as if he's afraid to move or touch anything.

"I'll leave you to change," I say, and disappear again.

Fifteen minutes later, after I've grabbed the backpack from the front porch and finished loading the dishwasher, I still haven't heard a peep from him, so I stop by the door and listen for a moment, then say, "Hello, is everything okay in there? Do you need anything?" There's no response, so I open the door slowly and peek inside. A small smile crosses my face when I see him tucked under the blue comforter, fast asleep, his mouth parted slightly and his hands situated under the thick pillow. God, he must be exhausted. I step inside and grab his dirty clothes to wash them, then turn off the light and shut the door behind me.

As I change into my own pajamas and climb into bed, I have one thought on my mind. I hope I can get him to stay longer than one night, because the idea of him being out there again, knowing what could and probably will happen to him, is enough to gut me. I couldn't save my son. I'm hoping I can save him.

# CHAPTER
*Three*

## CHARLIE

I wake to the sun shining in my face and I'm incredibly confused when I realize I've slept through the night. No noise, no shivering, no rock hard ground underneath me, no being afraid. Not even one of my usual nightmares. Instead I'm laying in the most comfortable bed I've ever slept in, surrounded by thick plush blankets and a soft pillow. The room smells fresh, unlike me. I fucking reek. How long has it been since I showered? I don't think I want to answer that.

I groan as my head throbs painfully, and when I blink open my eyes, I notice some pain relievers and a glass of water on the nightstand. He must have put them there either last night after I passed out or early this morning.

I still can't believe I let myself sleep over at a complete stranger's house. But after the night I'd had, it sounded pretty great. One night is fine. I just won't make a habit of it. I'll be on my way after breakfast and a shower.

I down the pills and the glass of water before pulling the comforter back. I blink down at myself when I realize what I'm wearing. My head is fuzzy with memories from the previous night, but I do recall the other man lending me his T-shirt. It's practically a dress on me. Well, a very short dress that barely covers my bum. It's insanely comfortable though, and it has his scent. A mix of pine and citrus.

I stand and run my fingers through my hair. Glancing across the room, I see my backpack resting on the chair near the closet. I can't for the life of me figure this guy out. Why on earth he helped me at all, why he's letting me stay here and not expecting anything in return.

Except for breakfast. Shoot, I was supposed to make breakfast.

I tear out of the room and down the hall to the open kitchen and living room area and skid to a stop, standing there in my oversized shirt and socks.

"Good morning," he says with a slight chuckle when he glances over at me. "Did you sleep well?" And all I can think is, damn, Grandpa is fine. He's wearing tight jeans that accentuate his amazing ass and a snug-fitting T-shirt that shows off his biceps and toned upper body. Fuck, who knew an old guy could be this hot? Gotta be something wrong with him, though, right? If he's single? Maybe he's a total dick. But he hasn't been anything but kind to me so far.

"I, uh, yeah," I stammer, and I notice his gaze lingering on my bare legs for a split second before he glances away, his cheeks flushed. I bite my lip. Was he just checking me out? I've got some kind of mixed feelings about that. Maybe I shouldn't since I was just doing the exact same thing to him, but I've had way too many people use me for my body, and while it was my choice, it was also because I felt like I didn't have a choice, and I'm tired of feeling like an object or a fucking toy. Still, he hasn't made any advances, only cared for me so far. And the expression on his face just now wasn't one of lust, more embarrassment.

I narrow my eyes at him. "I thought I was supposed to make breakfast. We had a deal."

"I'm sorry," he says genuinely. "I meant to let you, but it

21

was getting late and I was hungry, and I didn't want to wake you. You needed rest."

I want to growl at him, be angry with him. But his words are so thoughtful and so sincere, I just can't bring myself to be upset. I know I should thank him, but words won't come out. He seems to sense my internal conflict and comes to my rescue.

"You like waffles?" I nod, my mouth watering. I can't remember the last time I had a homemade waffle.

"Sit," he says, and gestures to the small kitchen table. I do and he places a large plate with a warm waffle on it in front of me, along with a fork. Then he brings over syrup, sliced strawberries, blueberries, peaches, and whipped cream. Shit. I don't even know where to start. My stomach growls so loudly I know he must have heard it but he doesn't say anything.

He glances back at me from his place at the counter where he's making a second waffle. "Dig in."

"You feeling okay?" he asks a few minutes later as he sits across from me. My waffle is almost gone, I've inhaled it so fast. He glances at my plate and I swallow another bite, my cheeks flushed. Shit, am I being rude? I don't know. Am I eating too fast, being messy, chewing loudly?

"Is something wrong?" I say.

"Not at all," he replies, with a slight chuckle. "You just seem hungry. I'm glad you're enjoying it. Here." Before I can say anything he's sliding his plate over to me with a soft smile on his face.

I shake my head. "I'm not taking your food."

"I don't have a shortage of waffle mix. I can make another." He gestures to the plate with his head. "Eat. I'm making bacon and eggs, too. You want some coffee? It'll probably help with your hangover."

I sigh. I hate nice people. Especially stubborn, nice people. I pull the plate to me as he stands and heads back to the counter to turn on the Keurig.

"Coffee?" he asks again, and I nod.

22

"Yes, please," I get out over a mouthful of waffle. He chuckles and I flush again. What is it about this guy? He's fucking old enough to be my dad, I'm pretty sure, but I'm finding myself drawn to him. He's incredibly sweet and generous, and he tolerates my sarcasm well, which is a bonus, because it's about ninety percent of my personality.

I find myself staring at his back side as he moves around the kitchen. It's quite a nice view. For an old guy, I mean.

"How old are you?" I blurt. I've never been one to mince words. Gets me in trouble sometimes, but somehow I don't think he'll mind my bluntness.

There's that chuckle again. It's deep and warm and it makes my stomach fill with butterflies. "Old enough I pass for a grandpa, apparently," he says, turning to look at me, a small smile gracing his lips.

I bite my lip and wait, curious.

"I'm forty-six," he says, and I whistle.

"Damn, even older than I thought," I joke, and he gives me the finger, making me laugh. His smile widens and I think it might be the sexiest thing I've ever seen. Other than his ass, of course. Shit, am I perving over a guy old enough to be my dad? Well, my dad was never this good-looking, that's for damn sure. This guy, whatever-his-name-is could be a model. Maybe he is a model. I should ask.

"What do you do?" I say as he brings me a mug filled with hot coffee and places cream and sugar in front of me.

He laughs. "Your turn for twenty questions, I see."

I shrug. "I feel I graced your house with my presence, and you owe me."

"I see." His blue eyes twinkle. Fuck, are we flirting? He can't possibly be flirting with me. A) I'm like barely an adult, and two, I'm a homeless fucking whore. There's no way he'd be interested in me.

"I'll make you a deal," he says. "I'll answer anything you want, but in return you have to answer one of my questions."

I'm not sure I like this, but it only seems fair. As long as he doesn't get too personal. "Okay," I say.

"What's your name?"

"As first questions go, that's kind of cliche, don't you think? A bit on the nose? A little boring?"

He chuckles and shakes his head. "It's the thing I want to know the most."

My gaze lingers on him for a second before I say, "Charlie. My name is Charlie."

He raises an eyebrow. "Is that your real name?" he inquires, mirth in his voice.

"Yes." I can't help but laugh a little. God, he's cute. "Want me to prove it? I think it might be on the label of my underwear."

He laughs and shakes his head again as he sips his coffee. I noticed he didn't put any sugar in it, or cream. Eww. How can anyone drink their coffee black? Is there a point? As far as I'm concerned the whole point of coffee is for the creamer. "No thanks," he says. "I believe you."

"Your turn to answer my question," I remind him. "What do you do?"

"Construction." Ooh, that explains the excellent shape he's in. Those biceps are glorious, let me just say.

"How old are you?" he asks, and I'm not surprised. I knew it was coming sooner or later.

"Nineteen," I say, then follow up with, "What's your name?"

"Paul," he tells me. "Paul Richards."

I nod. He looks like a Paul.

"So, what are you gonna let me do since you didn't let me cook breakfast?" I'm ready to be done with the questions. It might lead to things I'm not ready to discuss.

He looks at me for a second and then around at the messy kitchen. "You can do clean up. Unload and load the dishwasher, and wash the pans."

I nod and stand, and I'm pretty extra sure I catch his eyes roaming over my bare legs again. Why does it not bother me?

"If you want to shower there's towels and washcloths in the hall closet and you can use my soap and shampoo. It's pretty nice stuff. I have some extra razors if you need one."

I grimace because I can't believe he's had to handle being in the vicinity of my stench for as long as he has. "Yeah, I think I'll do that," I say. "Thanks."

"Of course. I'll put your clothes in your room for you. They should be done in the dryer by now."

Shit, he washed my shitty clothes, too? Fuck, why does he have to be sweet as hell and fucking gorgeous? It's gonna suck to leave here. I've only been in this man's home for approximately sixteen hours, but I already feel more seen and heard, more loved and accepted and cared for than I ever felt living under my parents' roof.

I make my way down the hall and grab a fluffy white towel and washcloth. God, they're so plush I want to curl up in them. I know they will feel like heaven on my bare skin. Shit, do I have a fluffy towel kink? Is that a thing?

I make my way into the bathroom and close the door before starting the water and going pee. That coffee is really going through me, along with the water I had, and I just realized I haven't peed since last night before I got here.

I strip and step into the shower. I practically moan as the warm water cascades over me, relaxing my muscles and relieving tension. I wash my hair with his shampoo like he said to, and it smells amazing. I can tell this stuff aint cheap and there's maybe a little part of me that's smiling at the thought of smelling like him. I scrub and rinse, and then just stay in the flow of the water for a while. I don't know when I'll get my next shower and I want to enjoy this as much as I can. I don't want to run up his water bill, though, so I shut the water off and step out after a few minutes. I grab the fluffy towel and use it to dry my hair first, before my body. Then I wrap it around my waist and get a good look at myself in the mirror.

Ugh. I'm freakishly skinny. My skin is pale, my eyes are still somewhat bloodshot and I'm feeling ridiculously tired suddenly, and a little nauseated. Crawling back under the covers in the extra bedroom and sleeping for a few more hours sounds amazing. But I'm supposed to be getting out of here, after I clean the kitchen. I can't believe last night I had to convince myself to stay and now I'm trying to convince myself to leave.

I make my way out of the bathroom and towards the bedroom. I sit on the edge of the bed for a moment, telling myself I'll get up in just a second. I notice that the sheets are a different color and I realize he must have changed them while I was in the shower. Thank God. They smell so much better now. I slip out of the towel and climb under the covers, pulling them up and over my naked body.

*I'll just lay down for a minute*, I tell myself.

## PAUL

God, what the hell is wrong with me? I was fucking checking out a nineteen-year-old. When I saw him standing there in my T-shirt it did something to me. My chest constricted and my fucking cock twitched. He looked so cute in it, his red hair a mess, his socks still on, and his legs, I don't think I've ever thought the word *pretty* about a guy's legs before, but there's just no other word to describe them. Slender, and pale, and why on earth did I have visions of grabbing onto them, running my hands over them? Nipping and biting them? Oh my god, I'm disgusting. He's a kid. *A fucking kid!* Younger than my son would be if he were still alive and I'm lusting after him. God, I've reached a new low.

I've never had thoughts like this about another guy, so why the hell am I now, and about someone who is way too

26

young for me? How mortified would he be if he knew where my mind has been?

Speaking of which, where the hell is he? He finished with his shower twenty minutes ago and I haven't seen him since. Is he okay?

I make my way down the hall to his bedroom. The door is shut and it's quiet on the other side again. I knock softly. "Charlie?" I say. Why does it feel so amazing to now have his name on my lips?

There's no answer so I open the door. A soft smile forms on my lips when I see him passed out in bed again. Good, I want him to rest. I step in and grab the damp towel on the floor before leaving and closing the door behind me. It only then occurs to me that he was probably naked under those blankets. Why do I like that idea so much? His naked body on my sheets?

Fuck. Not going there. *He's nineteen, he's nineteen, he's nineteen*, I repeat to myself so it gets lodged in my brain.

I take the towel back to the bathroom and hang it up on a hook behind the door. I consider doing the clean up in the kitchen, but since I already took over one of his chores, I decide to leave it, even though the mess unsettles me.

I curl up on the sofa and turn the television on, a blanket draped over me, and before I know it I'm fast asleep too.

I wake to the sound of the dishwasher being loaded and the sink running. I grunt, and for a brief second wonder who the hell is in my kitchen, before remembering Charlie.

"Bout time," he says. "If I had to bang the dishes around any louder I was gonna break something. I've been in here slamming cabinets and everything and you were just snoring away, grandpa."

I smirk at him as I sit up. "I don't snore."

"Well it was either that or you have an elephant giving birth somewhere in your house," he replies.

"Very funny." I stand and run a hand through my hair. Do I really sound like an elephant in labor?

"I took a video if you want to hear yourself," he says, as if reading my mind. He whips his phone out of his back pocket. I stare at him because he can't be serious. Who does that at a stranger's house? Charlie, that's who. My Charlie. Fuck, I'm in way over my head. He hasn't even been here twenty four hours and I'm labeling him mine? And the thing is, the longer he stays, the less I want him to leave. Mostly because I hate the idea of him being back out there, but also because he's fun to have around, and he keeps me from feeling so desperately lonely. I like that I woke up to noise for a change, instead of silence.

He turns the video on and holds it out for me to see before I can even answer him, like he's sure I'll want to hear myself snoring, or he just doesn't care because it's too damn funny to him, which seems more likely. You know what though, if my snoring is what makes him laugh and smile, I'll take it. I'll snore like a million pregnant elephants to see him happy.

"I could hear you all the way from my room when I woke up," he says, and chuckles as I watch, his phone camera making its way down the hall towards the living room, my very unsophisticated noises getting louder and louder the closer he gets. God Almighty this is mortifying. I'm making whistling noises through my nose and everything, and I am loud as fuck. Was I this bad when Rachel and I were married? She complained some, but I thought she was exaggerating. She must have been a frickin' saint to put up with this.

"All right, I think that's enough," I say, and reach out to stop the video. He jerks his phone away and I reach for it again as he moves it behind his back, and then the next thing I know he's running and I'm chasing him as he laughs, moving through the kitchen, around the island, and back to the living room. He circles around the coffee table, and the video is still playing. He's laughing so hard he can barely move anymore and I'm chuckling too, as he collapses on the couch and I follow. I sigh with relief when the video finally stops, but then Charlie grins at me and holds his phone in

28

front of his face. He sticks his tongue out of the side of his mouth and his eyes dance as he presses play again, and I groan. "I'm thinking of making it my ringtone," he says.

He laughs as I reach for it one more time, this time kneeling on the couch and hovering over him. He reaches his arms above his head, the phone out of reach yet again, smiling at me, and I swallow when I realize how close we are, and the position we're in. I've got my hands on either side of the arm rest where his head is resting, my leg between his on the sofa, my other leg pressed against the back cushion, and my face is only a few inches from his. And now he's gazing at me, his breathing heavy, and his laughter forgotten.

I clear my throat and sit up, backing away. He sits up as well and stops the video. The atmosphere in the room seems to have changed rather abruptly and I try to lighten it.

"You, uh, you had lunch?" I ask, and stand, running my fingers through my hair again.

He shakes his head. "You don't need to feed me again. I'll finish up in the kitchen and be out of your way."

My heart sinks. He can't leave. I have to convince him to stay. But I know he doesn't want something for nothing.

"Stay and eat lunch with me." My gaze meets his. "Please." His green eyes stare back at me for a long moment and I can't help but wonder what he's thinking. But then he simply nods. I want to squeal in excitement but I rein in my exuberance and just smile.

"I don't have a lot. But we can have sandwiches, if that's okay?"

"That sounds amazing." We work around each other in the kitchen, me making our lunch, and him finishing with the dishwasher and the pots and pans. It's silent but peaceful, and I can't help but love having him here next to me. It feels good to be making food for more than one person and sharing my home with someone. I've missed this.

"Oh, um," I say, as I see him putting the bowls in the top rack. "Those go in the bottom."

He eyes me. "Do they?" There's a small smirk playing at the corner of his mouth.

I flush. I know I can be quite particular about how the dishwasher is loaded. Hell, I can be quite particular about a lot of things. I've come to accept it after this long as one of my wonderful quirks, but I know it can be irritating for other people.

The smirk turns into a grin. "Well, I wouldn't want them to get confused." He grabs the bowls and moves them to the bottom rack. He winks at me when he's finished and I feel my cheeks heat. What is happening to me?

After washing and drying his hands, he joins me at the table where I've placed out turkey and cheese sandwiches. He's dressed in his old clothes again, baggy jeans and the T-shirt and hoodie I got him last week.

"Shit, I forgot to ask if you were allergic to anything," I say. He just smiles.

"I'm a big boy, gramps. If I was allergic to something I'd tell you." He takes a bite and says through a mouthful of food, "The only thing I'm allergic to is shitty people."

My face heats and my stomach tightens. I suddenly don't feel so hungry anymore. Sure, I'm helping him out now, but if he knew about my past, what would he say? Fuck, he'd hate me. And he'd have every right to. I fucking hate myself.

"You okay?" he says, taking another large bite out of his sandwich. I give him a smile that I'm hoping doesn't appear as forced as it feels.

"Yeah, I'm good." I begin to eat and decide the best way to get rid of this feeling is to distract myself again. I've been working on forgiving myself, but I think it's a lost cause. Even the therapy Rachel and I did together and individually didn't make me feel loads better about what happened. We failed our son. The one person we were supposed to be there for and love unconditionally, and we lost everything as a result. Him, each other. How can I possibly forgive myself for that?

I clear my throat as I swallow a bite of sandwich, then take a sip of water. "How long have you been on your own?" I ask him.

There's a pause, but then he says, "Eight months."

"I'm sorry," is all I can think to say.

"It's okay." He fidgets with the string on his hoodie. "It's better this way."

I gape at him. "You can't mean that. Selling yourself, doing drugs, stealing and getting beat up, starving half to death, that's better than life with your parents? Did you even graduate high school?"

His jaw clenches and my face heats. I can tell when I've overstepped, and this is one of those times.

"Look, I didn't—" I start, but he drops his sandwich and scoots out of his chair.

"Where are you going?" I ask as he walks past me.

"To get my things." He storms down the hallway and I growl before standing and going after him.

"Stop," I say, as he enters the spare room and reaches for his bag. But he doesn't stop. He picks it up and swings it over his shoulder before heading back to where I stand, blocking the doorway.

"Move." He stares me in the face, defiance in his green eyes.

"No."

He juts his chin out and glares harder. "I thought you were different, but you are the same as everyone else. The same as my parents. Just a judgmental prick. I've had enough shame and guilt from them and I don't need it from you too, so get the fuck out of my way."

"No," I repeat, my gaze hard. He tries to push past me but I just move my arm and block him again. He's pinned against the wall now and he's scowling at me. Fuck, this boy is infuriating. What is it about him that makes me want to gnaw my own arm off and at the same time grab him and hold him close, feel him melt against me? How can I have only known

31

him for a little over a day and yet have the most intense desire to kiss him?

I swallow. It would be better if he left. Better for me, for sure, because I need to get these messed up thoughts out of my head before they destroy me. But I can't let him go. Along with the need to be with him, to be close to him, is an equally intense desire to protect him.

"I'm sorry," I say, my gaze never leaving his. "You're right. I shouldn't have said those things. I shouldn't have assumed anything. I shouldn't have judged you. I've had enough life experience to know that parents aren't always right. And if you left you must have had a good reason. I'm sorry that you were in that position, because you never should have been. You should never have felt like you were safer alone or on the streets than you were at home. Please don't go."

His gaze softens. I reach up without really thinking and brush a strand of hair away from his forehead. God, his hair is soft. My cock twitches when I hear his breath hitch and I step back.

He shakes his head. "Deal is over, I did what we agreed on, and you have done enough for me. It's time I left anyway." He straightens and hikes his backpack up on his shoulder again, but to my surprise he doesn't race out of the door.

"Let's make another deal," I say quickly. He raises an eyebrow at me. "Can you cook?" He nods. "Stay here, sleep here, eat here, do your laundry here. This will be your home for as long as you need it to be. And in return, you do the cooking and cleaning, laundry, grocery shopping and meal planning and prep. I help you out, you help me out."

There's that smirk again. "Yes, this place is a mess. I think I saw a magazine on the coffee table that was sideways."

I smirk back. Little shit. "You staying or what?" I try not to give away how desperate I am for him to say yes. If he leaves, I'll spend every second of every day worrying about him and every spare minute I have driving around trying to find him and make sure he's okay. "If it'll make you feel better I can be more of a slob to give you something to do."

"Can you?" A smile graces his lips as he crosses his arms over his chest.

No, probably not. Just leaving the mess out on the counter after breakfast was killing me. "If it gets you to stay I can." I don't miss the way his cheeks flush, and he bites that plump bottom lip. God, he's pretty. Such delicate features, and I never noticed how long his eyelashes were until I was closer to him, or the freckles on his adorable ears.

"Trial basis," he says, and I raise an eyebrow at him. "I'll stay for one month under those conditions and we'll see how it goes. If either of us is unhappy at the end of the month, I'll leave."

I smile. "And if we're not unhappy?"

He flushes again. "Then we'll go from there."

"A few conditions first. While you're here, there are some rules." He narrows his eyes and I hold up my fingers. "No drugs, no alcohol, and no selling yourself to earn cash. You need anything, you tell me." I hold my hand out to him but then make sure his gaze is locked with mine before I repeat, "Anything."

He hesitates, but then nods, and takes my hand. We shake. His hands are significantly smaller than mine, and his skin is so light and fair, the contrast between us is a little surreal, but there's something about it that feels right, good. And I can't wipe the smile from my face, because he's staying.

There's a pause before he speaks again, his gaze darting to the floor. "I'm not a junkie, you know. I know I was stoned last night but that's just because..." he swallows and his voice is softer when he speaks next. I notice his hands are trembling slightly and he tucks them into the sleeves of his hoodie, wrapping his arms around himself. "I only did it when I was getting fucked. It made it easier."

Fuck, what was this kid going through at home that the better alternative was life on the streets and prostitution?

33

# CHAPTER

*Four*

## CHARLIE

I'm staying. For a month, anyway. We'll see what happens after that. He might regret his decision in twenty-four hours, let alone a month. But I'm determined to do my part around here. If there was one thing my parents did do well it was teaching me to cook and clean, so I'm confident I can handle it. Since it's only my second night here and my first night with our arrangement, we ordered pizza, and he said I could start with cooking tomorrow. It's only dinner since he said he'd be in charge of his own breakfast as he gets up pretty early a lot of mornings and doesn't want me to have to do the same. Apparently he also has smoothies for breakfast most mornings. Shock and awe. And he says they are a little complicated so he'll make them himself. Apparently the waffles this morning were a special treat for me. I think he's trying to fatten me up.

We've finished the pizza, and the old man even splurged for soda. It's been ages since I've had either and I ate so much, I don't think I've ever been this full. I let out a loud belch from where I'm sitting across from him in the living room and he chuckles.

He's got the electric fireplace going, so it's giving the room an incredibly cozy vibe and I'm loving it. He even grabbed a blanket for me from his stash next to the couch and I've curled up under it, my legs dangling over the side of the oversized plush armchair I'm in. There's a small side table next to me with a mug of hot chocolate on it, complete with marshmallows. He was making some for himself and asked me if I wanted a cup. I don't think anyone's ever done that for me before.

His living room is small but cozy. The brown leather sofa and this chair are the only places to sit, but they are decent sized. There's a coffee table where the magazines rest, immaculately stacked and organized. There's a few photos and some fake plants on top of the mantle, and not a speck of dust can be found up there, which isn't surprising given the level of organization and cleanliness that is the rest of his house. Above the mantle is a giant clock. The curtains over the window are a soft beige and match the throw pillows.

Paul gave me his wifi password and I've spent some time on my phone browsing the internet, but I'm bored now and the magazines on his coffee table do not look appealing, unless I want to read about building muscle strength and endurance, how to have the best sex at age forty, or the symptoms of an erectile dysfunction. No thanks.

"You got anything to read besides these?" I ask, and he glances up from his book, pulling his glasses down his nose. I can't help but chuckle because he looks like the quintessential old person that way. An old person who is in incredible shape and sexy as fuck in glasses when they aren't perched on the edge of his nose like a little old librarian. You know, if you're into that sort of thing.

"What?" he says.

"You got something else I can read?" I repeat.

"Oh, yeah, sorry," he apologizes. "I should have offered. I have a bookshelf in my bedroom you can take a peak at and see if anything sparks your interest."

I get up and head down the hall towards his room. When I step inside and turn the light on, my breath catches in my throat. Holy fucking shit. I was picturing a little bookshelf stashed in the corner with maybe ten books on it, but this bookshelf is gorgeous and it takes up an entire wall in his room. Fuck, it is the wall. I blink as I step closer. There must be a couple hundred books on here. And he's got them categorized. Of course he does.

I shake my head and laugh a little as I peruse the shelves. He's got everything from biographies, to nonfiction, fiction, historical, mystery, poetry, fantasy, science-fiction, a couple of westerns and even some romance. It's straight romance though, which isn't really my thing, so I grab one of the westerns with the sexy cowboy on the front and bring it back to the living room.

"Find anything you liked?" he asks as I take my seat back on the chair.

"Um, maybe, we'll see." I show him the book and he nods.

"It's a good one," he says. "If you do like it, it's a series, so there's three more after that."

I sigh. "Great. Does it end on a cliffhanger?"

He chuckles. "Read it and find out."

I stick my tongue out at him like the mature adult I am and start to read.

"What types of books do you normally go for?" he asks a moment later.

"Oh, um, it doesn't matter," I deflect. "This is fine."

"What kind?" he asks again, more seriously and I have a feeling he's not going to let up.

My cheeks heat as I answer, "Romance."

He's blushing and I feel like a complete moron for admitting that to someone who's almost a total stranger. I'm waiting for the judgemental comments when he says, "There's a few of those in there. Did you see them?"

I nod, my face growing even hotter. "I prefer gay romance," I admit.

36

He bites his lip and I have a feeling it's to hide his grin. But a smile is a hell of a lot better than being told I'm a sick pervert and there's something wrong with me, which is what my parents said when they found the stash of mm romance books in my room. They grounded me for a month and forbade me from going to the library again, even confiscated my card and my phone.

The first thing I purchased for myself when I left home was a cheap smartphone and a tracfone card to go with it. Sure it meant sucking a few dicks to get the cash, but if that's what it meant to get me out of my parents' house and earn me my freedom, it was worth it to me. Anything to leave that suffocating, abusive environment. I only use the data when I absolutely have to, since I can get internet access at the local McDonald's or library, but I want to have it if I need it. It's my only connection to the outside world and feels like a lifeline to me, and that's important. It keeps me sane, and I feel like having a phone is also a safety issue. Unfortunately, while my phone does give me access to wifi, there's no books on it.

"Shut up," I mumble.

"What's your favorite?" he asks, and I stare at him, stunned. Is he actually trying to start a conversation with me about gay romance books?

I clear my throat. "Oh, um, I don't really have a favorite," I say. "I like sweet stories, I guess, and I love if they have mental health representation in them. That always draws me in. Coming of age is cool. I'm not really into the sports ones or the single dads. Can't really relate. But I like fantasy, and cowboys." I gesture to the book I'm holding. I could go on for an eternity about the different mm books I like and the different tropes that are my favorite but I have a feeling he's not interested in all that, so I don't.

He nods and goes back to his book. Some historical some-thing or other that looks like it's about as much fun as an enema.

We read in silence for about an hour before he sets his

book aside, takes off his glasses and rubs at his eyes. My eyes catch onto the small sliver of skin that shows between the bottom of his shirt and the top of his pants when he stretches and I glance away as soon as I realize what I'm doing, hoping he didn't notice. It's really hard to get the image of that happy trail out of my head, though. And that cute as fuck belly button, that I'm pretty sure is an outie.

He stands and then winces, flexing his right knee. It cracks loudly.

"You okay?" I ask.

"Yeah," he says, laughing a little, though I can tell he's in pain. "Old people problems. Don't worry about it."

He brings his glass to the kitchen and puts it in the dishwasher. "I'm gonna head to bed," he says, stopping in front of my chair. "If you wouldn't mind putting your glass in the dishwasher and starting it before you go to bed, that would be great. The soap's already in there so just press the start button."

I nod. "Goodnight."

"Goodnight, Charlie," he says, giving me a warm smile.

I don't think I've ever liked the sound of my name more.

## PAUL

It's ten o'clock the next morning when I knock on Charlie's door. I've been up since seven thirty, had breakfast, showered, and dressed for the day. On any normal day I'd let him sleep as late as he wanted, but I'm too excited to wait any longer. I laid awake after going to bed last night, thinking about what he said about the books he likes to read, and a few other things, and I have plans for him today that don't involve him sleeping the day away.

"Charlie, sweetheart, are you awake?" It's not until the endearment has left my tongue that I realize I've said it, and I slap a hand over my mouth and then wince. Shit. That wasn't okay. I can't be giving him pet names. But it felt so natural. Maybe he didn't hear it?

"Yes, darling, I'm awake," he grumbles, and I'm relieved at the sarcasm in his voice. At least he's not grossed out by my slip up.

"Can I come in?" I ask, and he mumbles something that I'm pretty sure is code for "yes" so I open the door slowly. I practically swallow my tongue when I see him sitting up on the side of the bed, the blankets discarded, my oversized T-shirt hanging off of one of his shoulders and pooled at the top of his legs, giving me a full view of his gorgeous thighs. Fuck, is there a part of his body that isn't covered in freckles? I suck in a breath and he rubs his eyes, blinking at me. God, does he have any idea what he's doing to me? I can't fucking breathe.

"Morning, Papa Bear," he says, one eye open as he runs a hand through his tousled red waves and grins at me.

I blink. What did he call me? And why the hell did I like it so much? I clear my throat and attempt a normal response, but it's fucking difficult with him still sitting there like that, all rumpled and sexy as hell. God, that shoulder. I want to sink my teeth into it, leave my mark on the freckles there. I want to fucking claim him. Oh my god, what's wrong with me? Three days ago a relationship was the last thing I wanted. I never saw myself being with anyone again, let alone a fucking nineteen-year-old. And a male. How can I be as old as I am and just now be finding myself attracted to someone of the same sex?

"Well, it's better than grandpa," I manage, and he laughs. I'll never tell him how much better. Shit I'm standing here for a reason but I can't for the life of me remember what it is anymore.

He groans and yawns, then stretches, giving me a view of his underwear, and the outline of his cock. It looks perfect, too. The perfect size for Charlie. I wonder if there's freckles on it. What the fuck? I shouldn't be analyzing his dick. Where are these thoughts coming from? Someone help me.

"You okay?" he asks, snapping me out of my daze, and I realize my gaze has been lingering on his dick this entire time. Oh my god, I'm a fucking pervert. But when I lift my head and meet his gaze, Charlie is smirking at me.

"I thought you might like to run some errands with me," I say. "There's a couple of places I'd like to take you."

He side-eyes me, but then stands, and if I thought him sitting there was bad, him standing and sauntering across the room, that adorable little ass barely covered and his shoulder still on display, is ten times worse. I blow out a breath and turn to face the wall, but not before he bends over to pick up his clothes and I get an eye-full of his rear and thighs. Oh, god, I'm going to hell. I mean, I was already going to hell, but now I definitely am.

"You gonna get out of my way and let me shower, or what?" I hear, and turn to see him standing there, that smirk ever prevalent.

"Sorry," I say, and step aside. I most definitely do not stare at his ass again as he walks down the hall.

Fifteen minutes later he's dressed and running his fingers through his hair as he steps into the living room.

"Breakfast?" I say, and he nods. "Help yourself. There's cereal and toast and some fruit. Bowls are—" I start to say, but he opens the correct cupboard before I can finish and grins at me. I smile back, a warmth spreading through my chest at knowing how familiar he is with my kitchen already, and how at home he feels rooting through the pantry and the refrigerator. He makes coffee for himself without asking, and I love it.

Twenty minutes later, he slides on his worn, tattered sneakers and I grab my keys and wallet before we head outside. We climb into the truck and pull out of the dirt driveway.

"Can I ask you something?" I say once we're on the road, driving through town.

"Maybe," he says.

40

"If you have been on your own for this long, who has been cutting your hair?"

"Oh, um, there's a barber downtown who gives free haircuts to the homeless once a month. There were a couple times I couldn't make it 'cause of transportation issues or whatever, but he's super cool."

I nod. "That is cool." I pause before saying, "All this time, were you ever in a shelter?"

He wrings his hands together. "I tried, but it didn't work out. I got harassed by some of the other guys the very first night and I didn't exactly feel safe, so I never went back."

Shit. My stomach clenches. "And what about school? Did you finish?"

He bites his lip and shakes his head.

"Would you like to?"

He nods vigorously and I smile.

"Well, let's talk about that later," I say. "We're almost there."

He peers out the window and I hear a breathless, "Oh," escape his lips as we pull into the parking lot of the local library.

"What are we doing here?" he asks.

"Checking out some books," I tell him, "any that you want." I swear I see him tearing up. Gosh, this boy. Under all that sarcasm and tough demeanor he's really very soft and sweet, and I think he's dying to be loved and cared for, to be accepted for who he is. I intend to give him that to the best of my ability.

"Come on." I step out of the truck and he joins me on the sidewalk.

"Go nuts, sweetheart," I whisper in his ear once we're inside, my hand on the small of his back, and his eyes light up so beautifully. "And by nuts I mean, you have a max of twenty-five books and five magazines because that's all they'll let me check out at a time."

He chuckles. "That should be doable." He heads for the

lgbtq section right away. I want to follow him but I feel like maybe I should let him have his privacy, so I wander instead.

Half an hour later, he's standing next to me with a stack of a dozen or so books and a few magazines, and blushing beautifully.

"Good?" I ask, and he nods. We take them to the self check-out and scan my card and the books. I can't help but think that if he stays longer than a month, maybe we can think about getting him his own card. "You can get books on your phone if you download the library app," I tell him. "There's a limit of ten but I don't use it much 'cause I prefer paperbacks, so you can use my information. Audiobooks, too."

He nods, a wide smile across his beautiful face.

"Where to next?" he says as we head outside again and climb back into the truck.

I hesitate because I'm not sure he'll approve of where I want to take him next. "I was hoping you would let me buy you some clothes," I tell him. I know if I try to trick him into anything it won't go well, so I'm laying it all out there before we make the trip to the mall. He's got nothing but what he's wearing right now, and he can't keep wearing those pants. The holes have holes, and they are clearly way too big. I'm pretty sure if I put them through another wash cycle they'll just fall apart. He has to need underwear too, and he most definitely needs new shoes.

"That wasn't part of our agreement," he says, his expression sour.

"The agreement was you take care of the house and I take care of you," I tell him. Not the exact words we used, but it's the same idea. "I promise I won't go overboard, just what you need. You have to have something to wear while your clothes are washed at the minimum, and my stuff is way too big for you." He flushes and I hope I haven't hurt or embarrassed him. I didn't mean to.

"Okay," he says eventually. He seems a little uncomfortable the entire way to the mall, and I don't know why, but he's fidgeting with the string on his hoodie again and chewing on his bottom lip.

I turn into the Macy's parking lot and his eyes go wide. "You're buying me clothes here?" he says. "But, it's really expensive. We could just go to WalMart. I don't need—"

"Yes, and then you would need new clothes again in a few months. This way they will last."

He sighs but seems to relent. "While we're on the subject of money, I don't know how you've been paying for your phone this whole time," I add, and he flushes crimson, his gaze darting to his lap, "but assuming it was neither safe nor legal, that will be my responsibility now, too. Just give me the details and I'll take care of it."

I expect him to argue with me, and he opens his mouth like maybe he's about to, but then he simply bites his lip and nods, still fidgeting with that hoodie string, before he turns and takes in the view out the window again.

"Ready?" I ask, and he nods. Climbing out we make our way inside. I'm hoping they don't judge him for his current attire. At least it's clean, and so is he.

We head over to the men's section and I let him browse for jeans and T-shirts. He's significantly less enthusiastic about this than he was about the trip to the library, his shoulders slumped and his beautiful smile gone, and I wonder again if I've said or done something to upset him. Maybe he's worried about the money?

"I'll be right back," he says, rather morosely, and takes a few things into the fitting room. He comes back a few minutes later with two pairs of jeans in his arms and a few shirts—two casual and one button up. They all seem decent to me but he still seems unhappy.

"Hey," I say, taking his chin in my hand gently and forcing his gaze to mine. "What's wrong?" I'm glad to see he's become more comfortable with my touches in such a short period of time. He's not jerking away, or glaring at me or telling me to back off.

He blinks at me, then shakes his head. "Nothing," he whispers, but I see tears filling his eyes.

"Charlie, talk to me," I plead. "Did I hurt you?" he shakes his head again and a tear slides down his cheek. It guts me to see him crying. "Then what is it?"

"I'm sorry," he says, his chest heaving. "This just isn't me."

I blink. "What isn't you?" I move my hands and wipe the tears from his cheeks with my thumbs. He trembles under my touch and closes his eyes.

"These," he says, opening his eyes and holding the clothes up. "They aren't me."

"Then what is? You can get whatever you want."

He glances across the store, his green eyes filled with longing, but then his gaze is back to the floor, his cheeks flushed. I turn my head in the direction he was looking and my eyes widen slightly when I see the junior girl's section. Oh. I don't mind at all, I just have never been in this situation before. And I hate that I just assumed he'd want more pants and T-shirts. If skirts, dresses, and rompers is what he wants then that's what he'll get.

"Hey," I say, "look at me." He does and I rest my hands on his shoulders, smiling at him. "Anything you want," I reiterate. He doesn't move so I grab the clothes he's still holding on to and set them aside, then take his hand and pull him across the aisle to the section he was eyeing. His eyes light up like a child in a candy store. My sweet Charlie.

"You don't mind?" he says, glancing at me.

"Not a bit. You do you, sweetheart." God, the endearments keep flying out of me, but I can't help it, and he doesn't seem to mind.

He flips through the racks for a while, his smile back, and then heads to the dressing room with his arms full. I follow him and wait on a chair seated just outside.

"Papa Bear?" I hear a minute later, and it takes me a second to realize that's me. I turn and my jaw drops. Charlie is wearing black, slim-fitting, high-waist pants with a very big bow in the center, situated right under his belly button. Two additional bows adorn the tapered ankles. For a shirt he's wearing a white, long-sleeve, crop-top sweater that criss-crosses in the front and falls off of his shoulders. There's about two inches of abdomen peeking out between the top of his pants and the bottom of his shirt. I can't help but think that the only thing that would make his outfit even more stunning is high heels. They would look amazing with his slender, elegant body. Fuck, I can't tear my gaze away, and my mouth is watering. My heart feels like it's about to leap out of my chest. I had no idea that feminine clothes could be so striking on a young man, but Charlie is perfection in these.

"I look okay?" he asks, and my gaze finally meets his eyes. He's fully alive, and happy. His green eyes sparkle. They're divine, as is the smile that adorns his face. Oh, my heart.

"Yeah," is all I manage to croak out, and he fucking giggles, his hand moving up to cover his mouth as his cheeks turn rosy. It's the cutest thing I've ever seen or heard. I smile widely.

"Wanna see more?" he asks, swaying his hips slightly, the excitement evident in his voice. I swallow and nod. Boy, do I ever. He's so fucking pretty. Is it wrong that I want to see more? That I'm enjoying myself? Enjoying him? God, I don't know. It's been so long since I've felt any kind of joy that I don't want to examine it too much.

He scampers off to his dressing room again and I wait, feeling jittery and unbelievably excited to see what he'll have on next. But I'm not sure anything can compare to the first outfit. Then he steps out in something a little bit more casual than the last outfit but equally as adorable. White skinny jeans with holes in the knees and a tie dye cropped hoodie with ribbon laced through each arm and tied in a bow at the wrists. God, that little sliver of tummy is driving me crazy. I want my mouth on it more than I've ever wanted anything in my life. Why is he so goddamn tempting?

It was never my intention to get turned on from this mini fashion show, but my cock didn't get that memo apparently. "You look beautiful," I tell him, and he must sense my sincerity because his face lights up again. "I think after this, we should get you some shoes, and maybe some underwear, too."

"Go on," I say, waving him off casually. "Let's see the rest."

He beams at me and hurries off again, and I try to will my cock to behave itself. I keep my legs crossed when he comes back out, and I almost moan at the sight of him in a pleated black and red skirt and a cropped black sweatshirt.

"Stunning," I say, my voice surprisingly low, and his cheeks pinken. His gaze meets mine again and he winks at me. Fucking hell, is he flirting? Does he know the effect he's having on me? And he's encouraging it? Is he as attracted to me as I am to him?

I clear my throat. "How many more do you have?" I ask, my voice at least sounding normal this time.

"A few. A dress, a couple more pants, and one more skirt."

"Don't show me those." He frowns, but I quickly add, "Let me be surprised when you wear them at home." That brings a wide smile to his face and he nods.

Ten minutes later he's out of the fitting room with his clothes draped over his arm, once again in his old jeans and T-shirt combo and worn out sneakers. God, it's so weird to see him dressed like that now, and I understand completely what he meant when he said those clothes weren't him. After seeing him in the other pieces, I can't imagine him in anything else. He was born to wear feminine bottoms and crop tops.

"Let me," I say and hold my arms out for the clothes. They aren't light and he's a string bean. Besides that I kind of like the idea of carrying his clothes for him.

He smirks at me but hands them over. "Where to next, Papa Bear?" he says, sliding his hand through my arm.

"You decide," I tell him. "Shoes or underwear."

"Underwear." I struggle to hold all of his clothes over one arm as he pulls me towards the men's underwear section. I'm a little surprised we're here, actually and I don't hesitate to say something.

"Are you sure this is what you want?"

He turns to me and raises an eyebrow, his eyes dancing. "You think I'd look better in something else?"

My cheeks heat and I almost growl at him for being such a brat. He knows exactly what he's doing. "You know, you can carry these yourself," I gesture to the pile of clothes in my arms, and he laughs.

"These are fine," he says with a shrug. "It's just underwear."

I narrow my eyes. "But is that what you want?"

He bites his lip. "It's fine."

"Charlie?"

He sighs. "Papa Bear, it's fine. I like the more feminine stuff, but it's more expensive and I don't need you spending all your money on me."

"What if I want to? What if I like spoiling you?"

He smiles and nudges me. "You wanna be my sugar daddy now?" I flush, shaking my head at him.

"Why don't we wait a bit, huh? Get these for now, and if we decide I'm staying we can revisit the fancy panties?" he suggests. "Besides, if we really want to do it right, we need to get panties that are made for men. The women's panties don't fit right. No room for everything." He smiles at me again and grabs a package of mixed color briefs. "I'll need these anyway. Practical underwear is good, too."

I sigh, because I want to give Charlie everything. And I don't want to wait, but I won't push him. "Okay," I say, then we head for the shoes.

There's more customers in the store now than there were

thirty minutes ago, probably because of church letting out. There's a handful of people in the shoe section other than us, but that's it. Still, it's enough to make me a little nervous. I don't want anyone saying something to him that will take away that breathtaking smile. And I hate that people feel the need to judge others for something just because they don't understand it or think it's "normal." What is normal, anyway? The only reason we subscribe to the whole concept of what is for boys and what is for girls is because that is what society has taught us, and I hate that for him. I hate it for everyone who feels pressured to be anything other than their authentic self. Everyone should feel free to dress how they like and enjoy the things they like without fear of judgment or being shamed or bullied.

I'm honestly feeling nervous myself about what people who walk by us are thinking when they see me holding what are supposed to be clothes for a teenage girl, and Charlie sauntering towards me in a very sexy black heel that will go perfectly with his black pants and white off-the-shoulder sweater, and I hate myself for it. I've come a long way when it comes to being accepting, having an open mind, and there not being any such thing as boy's and girl's attire, but I'm still learning and I definitely still struggle with what other people will think, even though I don't want to.

I don't know if he hasn't noticed any of the glances, or if he has and is just ignoring them, but I'll be damned if I let anyone make him feel like less than the amazing person he is because of his choice of wardrobe. So when the middle-aged woman in the same aisle gives him a judgmental stare and then glances at me like I'm a lousy parent for letting my son dress in women's shoes, I just say to Charlie as loud as I can, "You look amazing, sweetheart."

"Thanks, Papa Bear," he says, and the woman's eyes widen. I just give Charlie the biggest smile as he slides out of the dress shoes and searches for some sneakers. He finds some cute white Keds with blue stripes on the side that sparkle. They are so him, and they will compliment his pleated skirt outfit perfectly.

When did I start to care about this stuff so much? I never gave a crap about fashion or going clothes shopping with my wife. I mean, there were certain outfits she had that I liked to see her in more than others, and I enjoyed it when she did her mini fashion shows for me, although, let's face it, that was more because I got to see her take her clothes off repeatedly, but I would never choose to go shopping with her for a new wardrobe. Yet somehow with Charlie, it feels completely natural, and I'm enjoying myself. I feel like I could do this for hours and not get bored. Maybe it's just him? Who the hell knows, but I decide I'm not going to question it anymore and just go with the flow.

"I think you might need one more pair," I say. "Maybe boots?"

He grins at me and a minute later he's sauntering towards me again in a pair of adorable brown ankle boots, his hips swaying. I can't wait to see what they will look like with his new clothes because even now they're incredible. God, how is he not a model? He can work a pair of shoes. I'd watch him all fucking day. Did that sound the tiniest bit creepy? Fuck, I'm so screwed up right now. I feel like I shouldn't be enjoying this nearly as much as I am, but why? He's enjoying it too. We're both happy, and we're not hurting anyone, though by the way the lady next to us is shaking her head, you'd think we'd committed a crime just by being here.

Charlie turns when he is within about three feet of me and saunters back down the aisle, giving me the perfect view of his cute little tushy. The woman from earlier is glaring at me and I wave at her, making her scowl and mutter something under her breath. I don't hear it but I have a feeling Charlie must have because his face pales as he slides his old sneakers back on. His handsome face is downcast as he walks over to me with the shoes in hand.

"Hey," I say. "Look at me." He sniffles and wipes at his

nose with the sleeve of his hoodie before his eyes meet mine, and I could just throat punch that woman for making my boy cry. My boy. God that sounds so wonderful. How can I think of him like that when this is only the second day that I've had the privilege of knowing him? I don't know, but he's crawled inside my heart and I can't let go. I don't want to let go. "I don't know what she said, but it doesn't matter. Did you have a good time today?"

He nods.

"And do you like what you found?"

He nods again.

"Then that's all that matters. Don't let anyone take that away from you. Don't let anyone tell you who to be, beautiful boy." I press a kiss to his forehead and it feels so right. I hear his intake of breath, and he relaxes at my touch.

A smile forms on his face and my chest constricts with how beautiful it is. Pride swells in me knowing that I was the one to put it there. I promise I'll do anything to make him happy. Anything.

# CHAPTER
## *Five*

## CHARLIE

"You hungry?" Paul asks as we make our way out of Macy's. I'm so unbelievably giddy about all my new clothes that I can't keep the smile from my face. The way he supported and encouraged me in there meant the world to me. My parents never would have let me buy those clothes. Okay, except for the underwear. But "girls" clothes, never, and my mom would have never even let me try on high heels even for fun, let alone purchase them. Paul not only allowed it but encouraged it. I've never felt that kind of support and acceptance my entire life. The bitch in the shoe aisle needs to get the stick out of her ass, but I'm trying to focus less on what she said, *"Disgusting perverts. What is this world coming to?"* and more on what Paul said. He's right. I have a right to wear what I want and I won't let anyone take that from me anymore. Not my parents, and certainly not a total stranger.

"Yeah," I say, "starving." He smiles at me and we make our way to the food court, but before we get in line, he turns to me.

"You wanna change?" he asks, holding the bags out to me.

I smile and nod. I'm dying to get out of these tacky, too-big-for-me clothes and into something that makes me feel like myself.

I take the bags and head for the bathrooms. I decide on the family restroom because it's bigger and because guys' bathrooms are disgusting. Not to mention there can be some real jerks in there who might not appreciate my attire and decide to harass me for it, or worse. I'm not in the mood to deal with that today.

I slip inside and strip out of my jeans, T-shirt, and hoodie, and into my skinny jeans and a black and white striped cropped T-shirt. I wish I wasn't quite so skinny. You can practically see my ribs, but the shirt covers all but my belly button and about an inch above it, so unless I raise my arms above my head no one can see my ribs anyway.

I slide my new Keds on and try to decide what to do with my old clothes. I toss the jeans and shoes in the trash but hang on to the T-shirt and hoodie, and place them in the Macy's bag with the new things. They aren't my go-to style but they still fit, and besides that, Paul got them for me, so I can't bring myself to get rid of them.

Taking one last peak at myself in the mirror, I run a hand through my red curls, and then out of habit because I'm in a bathroom, I wash my hands before stepping out into the crazy bustle of the mall once more.

My pulse skyrockets when the burly, bearded man lurking outside the men's room grins at me, his gaze raking me over, eyes gleaming. I've seen that look way too many times. I try to side-step him, but he cuts in front of me and grins down at me. "You're a pretty thing," he says, backing me against the wall. "Where you headed, pretty boy? You here alone?"

I swallow. I can't breathe. I'm frozen stiff, which is the only explanation for me not batting his hand away when he reaches up and brushes his finger over my cheek. I'm mortified when tears spring to my eyes, but then the man is flying away from me, and his back hits the opposite wall. The large man blinks as Paul steps into his line of vision, his eyes going wide.

"No, he's not here alone," Paul growls. "And if you so much as glance in his direction again, I will break every bone in your body." Holy hell, I think my cock twitched at that. Papa Bear can be fierce when he wants to be, and he's doing it for me. Fuck, that's hot. I'm trembling when he turns to me and the other man scampers off.

"Fuck, are you okay?" he asks, and I don't think twice before I fall into his arms, shaking, as the tears slide down my cheeks. "I'm so sorry, Charlie." His arms come around me, holding me tight. "Did he hurt you?"

I shake my head. "I'm okay." His big strong hands rub up and down my back. I can feel his T-shirt against the expanse of my bare skin. It's warm and soft, and it comforts me somehow.

"I should have come with you," he says, and I can hear how upset he is with himself.

"It's okay," I assure him. He pulls back and his crystal blue eyes lock with mine.

"It's not okay." He wipes my tears. "Nobody has the right to treat you like that, Charlie. Nobody. Do you hear me?" More tears come and I nod, falling back into his embrace. People are moving around us and the music is playing through the speakers, the conversations in the food court carrying through the open space, but all I hear is the sound of his heartbeat.

"Do you want to leave?" he asks me. I shake my head.

"No. I do that and he wins. I won't let that happen. I'm fine. Really." My gaze meets his again. "Thank you."

He gives me a soft smile and brushes the hair away from my eyes. "Always." His lips press to my forehead. God, I want to melt into this man, let him hold me and feel his lips against my skin for an eternity. I didn't think I'd ever want anyone to touch me again after my parents and my time on the streets, but his touches are different; gentle, kind, and tender. I've never had that before. Like he actually cares for me.

"You look wonderful, by the way," he tells me, and I blush. My cheeks heat even more, and I'm sure I'm the color of a tomato when he steps back and holds his hand out to me. I don't hesitate to take it. Then he reaches over and grabs the bags from my other hand, and I don't mind at all. I'm more than willing to let him treat me like a princess. Just give me a tiara and call me Cinderella. Or maybe Belle. I like her better.

My heart beats wildly when he links our fingers together and squeezes.

We stand in line at the Chinese place, holding hands the entire time, until Paul has to pay. We're getting some looks, and I honestly don't know if they are approving or reproving, but I don't care. I'm happier than I've ever been and I feel safe.

We take our number to our table and wait for our food, as we sit down across from each other. Paul sets the bags on the chair next to him instead of on the floor.

"I wanted to apologize," he starts off, making eye contact with me, and my eyebrow quirks. What does he have to be sorry for? "I never asked you what your pronouns are, I just assumed. I assumed a lot of things, Charlie, and I'm sorry. I saw you in those jeans and that hoodie and I just figured that that's what you would go for. I didn't even ask if you preferred something different or what your style was and I've been referring to you as he and him in my head this whole time. I'm still learning, so if I say or do something that upsets you, please correct me and please forgive me?"

Oh my god, is he for real? I want to cry. This man is beyond precious. "They are," I say, "he/him I mean. I identify as male. I just like to dress more feminine and feel pretty. But it means a lot that you are asking. So thank you." He smiles and nods.

"When was the last time you went shopping?" he asks, "or went to a mall?"

"Honestly, I don't really remember the last time," I say, taking in my surroundings. My gaze meets his. "My parents didn't really let me get out much, so thank you for this."

"My pleasure," he replies. "I think after lunch we should stop somewhere else and get you some pajamas and lounge clothes. Maybe some sweats?"

I nod. "Fine. But I'm keeping the T-shirt." His face turns the most adorable shade of red and he scratches behind his ear, making me grin. He's so fun to mess with. But seriously though, he's never getting that T-shirt back.

A young woman from the Chinese place approaches our table and sets our meals in front of us with a warm smile on her face. Then she turns to me and in accented English says, "I really like your outfit. It looks great on you."

God, am I crying again? Fuck, I hope not, but there's some sort of liquid filling my eyes and making it difficult to see. "Thank you," I whisper.

She nods. "Let me know if you need anything else," she says, and then walks away.

"Charlie?" Paul says after a moment of us just enjoying our food.

My stomach clenches because he sounds serious and I don't know if I want to do serious right now. "You don't have to tell me if you don't want to, or aren't ready, but I never did get the story of why you left home. I'd like to know. Not so I can judge you, I promise. I'm done with that. I just want to know you better, and understand your story."

I let out a breath and poke at my food a little. "My home life wasn't the greatest," I say. By that I mean it was fucking awful. I don't think a day went by where I wasn't berated or abused either physically, mentally, or emotionally. I won't go into details about that, though. I don't want his pity. "My parents had some views on things and I didn't measure up to their expectations. They never let me be myself."

"How so?" he asks.

I shrug. "They stifled me. Forced me to do things I didn't

55

want to do, dress the way they wanted me to dress and not how I felt most like myself because it didn't fit their image of what a man should be. They told me who I was allowed to date and not date. They made it very clear to me when I started showing interest in more feminine things like skirts, and jewelry and makeup, that those things weren't appropriate for boys. I came home from a birthday party in second grade and showed my mom my nails because I thought they were so pretty, and she yelled at me until I cried and then took the polish off and called the girl's parents and yelled at them. I was mortified, and I felt so much shame and confusion. I didn't understand then how some things were for girls and some things were for boys, that we couldn't just like what we liked and it didn't have anything to do with our gender. But they made it clear that I had done something wrong just by liking the way something looked on me. That it was wrong for me to be or feel pretty.

"They made me play sports even though I hated them and was terrible, and then my dad would get mad at me for not trying hard enough." I leave out the part where he would hit me when I didn't do as well as he thought I should and how he told me I was a disgrace to the sport and to men in general.

"I wanted to take dance classes but those were too feminine, so I couldn't. I felt suffocated. My entire life under their roof was a lie and I would never have the freedom to be myself if I stayed. So I left. I had to. I couldn't take it anymore." Tears are falling down my cheeks again, and I sniffle as Paul reaches across the table to take my hand. He gives it a gentle squeeze.

"Charlie," he says, the empathy evident in his voice. "I'm so sorry, sweetheart."

Somehow, hearing him call me that, any term of endearment from him, calms me, warms me, makes me feel loved and wanted. I've never been wanted before, at least not in a good way. Only by men who wanted my body. I hate that that is a part of my life and I feel sick whenever I think about it.

It's humiliating. But as bad as it was, as much as I hated doing it, selling myself, letting those men touch me, I would do it all again if it meant being out of that house. Honestly, if I hadn't left I probably wouldn't be alive right now, either because my dad would have beat me to death or I would have fucking killed myself. At least the choices I made on the street were my choices to make, and no one was telling me how to live and who to be, just to make themselves feel better, or beating the shit out of me because they caught me wearing makeup or because I didn't perform well enough in a stupid soccer game I never wanted to be involved in in the first place.

I sniffle and wipe my eyes, my lunch forgotten on my plate. "They never would have done any of the things you did today," I tell him. "Let me try on those clothes, or shoes, and they certainly wouldn't have bought them. They would have been standing there with that lady in the shoe aisle, glaring at me like I was a pervert."

"Then there would have been three idiots instead of one," Paul says, and I laugh a little.

"Thank you," I say, and realize he's still holding my hand. And he doesn't let go. Even after I've picked up my fork and started eating again, and even after we're both finished with our food, he keeps his hand in mine as we stand, and he takes the bags in his other hand, linking our fingers together once again as we head out to the car.

Is it too soon to fall in love? Because I'm starting to think I'm dangerously close.

———

When we get home, Paul carries my bags inside for me and I can't help but grin at the fact that he's treating me like a china doll, like I'm so frail and dainty. But honestly I kind of like it. He doesn't think I'm weak or incapable, he's just caring for me. And I think it's good for him, having someone to care for.

I don't know his history, but I did see a few photos in his house of a woman and a young teenage boy, and I wonder where they are now. He's not wearing a ring and they haven't been around since I've been here. I'm guessing his wife either passed away or they got divorced. I'm more curious about the boy, who I'm assuming is his son. He looks to only be about sixteen or so in the pictures, and he never gets older than that. If he were away at college or married and on his own, surely they'd have more updated photos. It's a mystery, but not one I feel safe diving into right now. He deserves his privacy, same as me.

"I'll bring these to your room, huh?" he says, as we step inside and he shuts the door.

I nod as I slide my shoes off, leaving them by the front door. Paul grins and I wish I knew what he was thinking as he heads down the hall. A minute later he's shouting my name, his voice laced with anger and panic. I turn as he makes his way back towards me and shoves the box of condoms in my face—the ones he bought me just last week.

"These haven't even been opened," he says, his jaw tight and his face red.

My eyes narrow and I snatch the box out of his hand. "Were you digging through my stuff?" I'm more embarrassed than upset, but I try not to show it.

"They fell out of your backpack when I set the other bags down," he explains. "You told me you slept with someone the other night, but that is a full box." He gestures to it, and I can't decide if there's more anger or concern in his voice. But I'm not used to anyone being concerned about me.

"So?" I try to deflect.

He runs a hand through his hair. "Fuck, Charlie, did he have one?"

"Who?" I say, even though I know exactly what he's talking about.

"Don't play dumb with me," he almost shouts, and I

58

flinch. "This is serious, Charlie. Did he have one?" My cheeks flame and I shake my head.

His eyes get wider than I thought possible and he fucking snarls, his nostrils flaring.

"It's no big deal," I say, waving him off with a smile. "I'm fine."

"God damn you, Charlie, what the fuck were you thinking? Why would you do that? I got those for you for a reason. Do you have any idea how dangerous that is?"

I narrow my eyes at him because now I'm pissed. "I'm fully aware of the risk, thank you, and I don't need you parenting me or berating me."

He sighs, his anger dissipating and an expression of hurt washing over his handsome features. "I'm not trying to berate you," he says earnestly. "I just care about you and I don't want you to get sick. I couldn't..." he glances down and then back up at me, scrubbing a hand over his face. "I don't want anything to happen to you."

I blink at him because how can someone who's known me for only a few days care for me enough to make sure I'm being safe when it comes to sex? The fact that he's having this conversation with me means he's more invested in me than my own parents were. And he's not making it about the ethics or morals of sex with strangers or sex outside of marriage or anything else but my safety.

I swallow. "They pay more if you let them go bareback," I say in barely a whisper. I hate telling him this, and my gaze shifts to the floor as I stuff my hands in my pockets and shuffle my foot. The next thing I know he's taking my chin in his hand and bringing my gaze back to his. I would say he's forcing me, but he really isn't. I go willingly.

"Please," he says, as tears fill his eyes, making my breath catch in my throat. "Please don't do that again. It makes me sick to think of you putting yourself at risk, especially knowing you did it to make money to pay me back. I never wanted that. I will never want that. Please—"

I step forward and wrap my arms around his neck before he says any more. He's tall enough that I have to stand on my tiptoes. His arms come around me, holding me to him. "I'm sorry," I say. "I'm sorry." Shit, now I'm crying. His arms tighten around me and I breathe in his scent. God, it feels so good to be held, his arms encasing me as I draw on his warmth and comfort.

My breath hitches when I feel his lips brush against the side of my face, and my heart skips a beat.

"Promise me," he whispers, his warm breath ghosting over my ear, his arms tightening around me even more until I think he might crack my ribs. Let's face it, there's not much of me there.

I pull back and peer at him. God, he looks wrecked, and not in the fun way. "I promise," I say, and I mean it more than I've ever meant anything in my entire life. Seeing him like this, the pain he's in, I can't cause that again. It's just hard for me to believe that anything I do could cause him pain. Because that would mean I mean something to him, that my actions and words matter to him. That I matter to him.

My gaze lowers to his lips for the briefest of seconds before I reach up and press a kiss to his cheek. I taste the salt from his tears there and feel his chest heave against mine ever so slightly.

"Was it just this one?" he asks, rubbing my arm with his big, rough hand, and I can't lie to him, so I shake my head.

He nods, and sniffles. "We need to take you to get tested," he says matter-of-factly. "Tomorrow."

I bite my lip. I'm not overly fond of the idea, but he's right. I've been risky and I should get checked out. I don't have symptoms of any STIs that I'm aware of, but that doesn't mean I don't have any. I've been with my share of guys in the past several months. Probably half didn't use a condom, and I was so stoned to try and ignore what was happening to me that I might be off on that number too. "Okay," I say, and he leans over and presses another kiss to my hair.

"Can we watch something, or…?" I trail off because I wonder if he's too upset with me to want to be around me right now. He nods, though, and heads into the kitchen to get a snack, and I follow. He grabs an orange while I head for the pantry and grab Pop Tarts. I'm relieved to see him crack a smile when I tear them open and take a huge bite without toasting them. What? They're better this way, and I'm impatient.

He takes his spot on the couch, lying down like usual. A big part of me wants to join him on the couch and maybe even snuggle up next to him, but I worry that maybe that will be taking things a little too far, so I plop myself down on the chair instead. It doesn't feel right though. I'm aching to be close to him. Maybe because we just had a really intense conversation and it was kind of…intimate. I don't want to be separated right now, not even by a coffee table.

Screw it. I get up from the chair, and taking my blanket with me I make my way over to the couch and nudge his leg with my foot. "Scoot over." His blue eyes meet mine and I can tell he's a little stunned at first, but then he sits up and makes room for me, a smile on his face as I sit next to him. I'm not quite in his lap but I'm as close as you can get without actually being. I love that he doesn't hesitate to put his arm around me as I curl into his side. He's only eaten a slice of his orange but it's left sitting on the plate that he has for it, because of course he has a plate for a fucking orange. Oh, Papa Bear. My heart swells because I know he must be hungry, but he's using his hand to grip my shoulder instead of peeling his orange, and for some reason it makes me really stinking happy.

"What are we watching?" I ask as he makes his way through Netflix.

He lands on *Diehard* and I groan. He gapes at me. "You don't like my man, Bruce?"

I laugh. "Does someone have a crush?"

He shrugs. "I dare you to find a man on this earth who doesn't have a crush on that man."

I raise my hand. "Okay, that's it. Get out," he says, and I laugh, throwing a pillow at him.

He returns the gesture and then asks, "What do you want to watch?"

I take the remote and start searching. I grin widely when I find what I'm looking for. To my surprise he doesn't balk like I'm expecting. "No complaints?"

He shrugs.

"I don't know if you know this or not but there won't be any guns blazing or things catching on fire and blowing up in *Pride and Prejudice*," I inform him.

He smirks at me. "I'm aware."

"You've seen it?"

"Seen it and enjoyed it." I raise my eyebrows. Why does that surprise me? It really shouldn't.

"You like chick flicks?" I ask.

"Not many. But this one, yes."

"What are the others?"

He smiles. "You know if you don't stop talking we're going to miss it."

I smile back and nudge him. "They have these fancy things now called remotes that let you rewind, you know. Just tell me."

"*Runaway Bride, You've Got Mail, Ever After, While You Were Sleeping, Thirteen Going on Thirty*, and this one. There might be a few more but I can't think of them right now."

I nod, then rest my head against his shoulder as the movie plays. The warmth of his body seeps into me, and for the first time in a long time I feel at peace.

# CHAPTER
## *Six*

## PAUL

Charlie falls asleep on my shoulder while we're watching tv. It makes it a little awkward when I have to get up and use the bathroom, but I manage to slide out from under him and rest his head on the couch while I go do my business. I sit back on the couch when I return to the living room, lifting his legs and sitting down with his feet in my lap. I don't think I ever noticed how dainty his feet are, and the thought of his cute little toes being painted makes me smile. I don't have any nail polish in the house but I'd be more than happy to get some for him if he wanted it. Hell, I'd kneel at his feet and paint his toenails for him. All he'd have to do is smile at me. Shit, this boy has me wrapped around his little finger already.

My fingers ache to touch his feet, his toes, massage them with my hands. Then I think of having his toes in my mouth, licking and sucking on them, making him moan and look at me with his eyes glazed over, his mouth parted, and oh god, I'm getting hard. Shit, I can't have an erection with his feet on my lap. Fuck. I bite my lip and close my eyes, willing myself to think of something vile and disgusting.

Then I hear a groan, and Charlie shifts. I don't even think,

I just shove his legs away and leap off the couch like my pants are on fire. If he feels me being even a little bit hard against his feet I will be mortified, and fucking hell, so will he.

"Papa Bear?" he says, rubbing his eyes and then gazing up at me all sleepy and adorable. "What's wrong?"

"Nothing," I lie, my chest constricting. "Just, uh, gotta make dinner now."

"I didn't realize it was that urgent," he says, giving me a sassy smirk, and of course my cock twitches when I'd just talked it down. Fuck, why does he have this effect on me? I fucking hate it. And I fucking love it. His sass is just as sexy as the rest of him. Fuck, I can't think that. I can't. He's a kid. Fuck, fuck, fuck.

"Papa Bear?" he says again, his brows furrowed. "You sure you're okay?"

No, no I'm not. I'm a forty-six-year-old man having completely inappropriate thoughts about a boy who's barely legal, and it shouldn't affect me like that when he calls me Papa Bear. But I love it. It makes me feel like I belong to him, and he belongs to me. And I love that idea more than I should.

"Besides," he says, pulling away the blanket he's been under and standing up—he stretches his arms over his head and I get an even better view of his abdomen when his crop-top rides up. "I'm making dinner, remember?"

Oh, right, I guess I forgot that in all my horniness and guilt. "Yeah, right," I say, running a hand through my hair. "I'm gonna go take a shower, then."

I head down the hall and into the bathroom. I strip and turn the water on, then step under the shower head.

I have to use every bit of self-control I have to not jerk off to thoughts of that boy.

———

64

We eat our dinner in relative silence and I feel like it's my fault. He's done nothing wrong, but I can't figure out what to say and I worry he knows why I'm acting so differently. Maybe I should have jerked off in the shower, because now I'm grumpy and horny instead of just horny. I took a cold ass shower to try and make myself calm down, which worked until I came back out and saw Charlie in the kitchen. Those jeans accentuated his ass so perfectly, and the few inches of skin I got to see due to his crop top, oh god. It was even better when he stood on tiptoes to reach something from one of the high up shelves and his shirt rode up a little bit more, his stomach sinking in. Every part of me wanted to race over there and drag him into my arms and press my lips to that pale skin. He looked so fucking pretty. Apparently my dick thought so too, because it perked right back up, and I'm trying to hide my hard on while we eat.

My suspicions are confirmed when he says, "Did I do something wrong?"

He sounds more angry than hurt. "No," I tell him, trying to sound casual. "Of course not."

He returns his gaze to his food but he doesn't eat, just picks at it with his fork. Honestly it's delicious. Just spaghetti and meatballs, but they are the best I've ever had. "You're lying," he says, and I jerk my head up to face him again.

"No, I'm not. I promise."

"Then why does it feel like I'm being ignored and avoided?" His gaze darkens as he scowls at me. "You spent an extra long time in the shower, and then another fifteen minutes in your room, and you haven't said a word to me since you got out here. If I did something I want to know."

"Charlie," I tell him gently but sternly. "I need you to trust me. You haven't done anything. I'm sorry if I gave you that impression. I didn't mean to. I guess I've just been lost in my own head is all, okay? But you are fine. We're fine. If you do something that I don't like, I will tell you. Got it?"

He locks eyes with me for a moment, as if studying me, before he nods.

"Thank you for making dinner," I say. "It's really good."

He gives me a soft smile. "Thank you."

We clean up together, and it feels like things are back to normal between us. He's smiling and wiggling his hips as he hums a Lady Gaga tune and loads the dishwasher while I clean the pots and pans. My cock is soft again, thank goodness.

"You dance?" he asks, swaying even more and holding his arms up a little as he makes his way over to me. He sets down the glass he's carrying and grips my arm, turning me to face him. Dirty water drips from my hand onto the floor and he just laughs when my eyes widen.

"Look at the mess you made," he chides playfully, and every part of me wants to reach around him and smack that sassy ass. Instead I toss him a towel and he chuckles as he cleans up the mess, then steps towards me again and slides his hand in mine, his other hand gripping my arm and bringing it around his waist. Fuck, I can't breathe. Electricity shoots up my arm as soon as his bare skin connects with my hand, and I have to not get any closer to him because there goes my hard on again.

"Charlie," I whisper, and swallow. He just smiles at me and takes the lead as we move, very ungracefully across the kitchen floor, my heart beating wildly the entire time. I'm so terrified, and so fucking turned on, but he's smiling so big I can't stop. And he feels so good in my arms. I will myself to be okay, to just enjoy it, the way he feels, the way he moves, the way he's gazing at me. I don't miss how his eyes lower and linger on my lips for the briefest of moments. I tell myself I imagined it even though I know I didn't, because if he wants the same things I do, this is going to erupt into something so big and terrible we'll never get through it unscathed. One of us has to be able to say no.

"You're not bad, Papa Bear," he says softly, a warm smile

on his face as he stops his movement. "We should go out dancing sometime."

I blink at him. "Dancing?"

"Yeah, you know at a bar or a club?"

"Yeah, maybe," I say, still trying to calm my racing heart. "Sure." I don't know why the fuck I'm agreeing, because I've never been dancing in my life. Well, okay, maybe in my twenties, but that was a lifetime ago. I'm pretty sure my body can't move like that anymore. Charlie would be embarrassed to pieces, dancing with me in public.

He smirks at me and then we're back to loading the dishes and washing as if nothing ever happened.

I head to bed early that night. Partly because I'm exhausted and have work in the morning, plus I'm taking Charlie to get tested, but more so because my mind and my body need a break from him. I have to not look at him or talk to him because when I do my cock reacts.

I can't want him the way I do. I can't.

———

"Charlie?" I ask, knocking on his door the next morning. "Time to get up."

I hear him grumble on the other side of the door. "Two more minutes."

I sigh, but decide a couple more minutes won't hurt. If he does have any STIs, finding out about them a couple of minutes later isn't going to matter. I'm just anxious for him to see someone and find out what he might be dealing with, if anything. Even if he is, I know there's treatment, and above everything, if he finds out he has anything—especially anything serious—I want to be there for him.

I make us both a cup of coffee and grab a package of Pop Tarts for him. I don't put them in the toaster because I noticed he likes them better that way.

A couple of minutes later he stumbles into the kitchen, his

red hair a tousled mess and his eyes blinking like he's trying to figure out what he's doing awake. He's dressed in sweats and a T-shirt that we got on our shopping trip, and he's positively adorable. He makes his way to the coffee on the counter, and pours about a tablespoon of sugar into it before opening the refrigerator for the cream.

"Want some coffee with your creamer?" I tease him when he keeps pouring it until the coffee is almost white. He grins at me and I can't help but smile back. I hand him the Pop Tarts and he pecks me on the cheek.

"Thanks, Papa Bear," he says. My face heats as I bite my lip. Jesus, this boy will be my undoing.

"Can you eat on the way?" I say, eager to get going, but also because I don't want to be super late getting into work.

"Okay." He pours his coffee into a to-go cup and snaps the lid on, holding the Pop Tarts, wrapper still on, between his teeth.

"You don't want to do something with your hair?" I say, gesturing to the unruly mop. I think it's fucking adorable, but I'm not sure he'd agree.

He shrugs. "It's the Dr. I don't care. I've looked worse than this before."

I chuckle. "Suit yourself." I grab my keys before we head out to the truck.

"How far is it?" he asks as he eats and sips his coffee.

"Ten minutes or so. You okay?"

"A little nervous," he admits, and I'm glad to hear him opening up to me.

"Listen, whatever we find out, I'm here for you, okay?" I assure him. I don't realize my hand is resting on his leg until he glances down to where it sits on his thigh, and I immediately pull it away. "Sorry," I mutter, but he just grins at me.

"I know," he says. "Thank you."

I nod. "When I get home, after dinner, I thought we could talk more about you getting your GED, if that's something you still want. Maybe you could do some research on it after you get back home?"

"Okay," he nods, seeming eager, and I'm glad. Charlie seems like a bright kid. I'd hate for all that potential to be wasted, and it would give him something to focus on and work towards. I'm worried he'll get bored and lonely staying home all day and I want him to have things to keep his mind engaged and active.

We arrive at the medical office shortly and climb out, heading into the waiting room. Charlie signs in and we sit next to each other as we wait for his name to be called.

"I assume you want to go in alone," I say. I can't imagine he would want me with him but I figure I should mention it just in case.

"I think that's a good idea. I wouldn't want you getting a hard on when they make me drop my pants." He waggles his eyebrows.

My skin heats and I'm sure my face is scarlet. Fucking Charlie, why does he have to do that?

"Charlie Morrison," the nurse calls, and he stands. He holds his hand out to me and I squeeze it, my flush returning.

"See you later, alligator." He winks at me and I give him a reassuring smile. At least I hope it's reassuring, but I can't help the tightness that seeps into my chest as he disappears through the door and I'm no longer with him. God, why am I such a fucking wreck? I'm aching to be back there with him, holding his hand, holding him. My leg bounces up and down and I keep running my fingers through my hair. I get my phone out to give myself something to do while I wait, but nothing is holding my attention. All of my thoughts are on that boy. That adorable, sweet, sarcastic, smart-mouthed, beautiful, pain-in-my-ass boy.

Fuck, why do I feel like this? Why do I care for him so much and why do I feel so drawn to him? It's fucking irritating.

"Hey," I hear his voice and jerk my head up, and I can't

69

help myself. I stand and take him in my arms, hugging him tightly. He lets out a chuckle and I pull away.

"Worried?" he says, raising an eyebrow.

"Of course not," I reply. "You just seemed like you needed a hug is all."

"Sorry it took so long," he says. "I waited in the room for the HIV results cuz they said it would only take twenty minutes."

"They tested you for HIV?" My chest is constricting again. But he seems fine. Surely if he had tested positive he wouldn't be this upbeat.

"Yeah, doc thought it was for the best when I told him my history and everything."

"And?" I feel like I'm waiting on bated breath here.

"I'm negative, for that," he says, and l breath a sigh of relief. "Still waiting for the results for the others. They said it could take up to ten days, and they'll call me. If I haven't heard from them by next Friday I should call."

I nod and drape my arm over his shoulder. Getting tested for STIs is never fun, and I'm proud of him for being responsible and doing the right thing, for himself and his future partners. I'm hoping after the life he's been dealt and the shitty people he's let touch him, that he can still have a healthy and fulfilling sex life. He seems pretty positive and has a fairly sunshiny personality, but that stuff's got to affect you no matter how much you pretend otherwise.

"You should be proud of yourself," I tell him and press a kiss to the side of his head as we make our way to the parking lot.

He beams at me. "Thanks, Papa Bear."

I ruffle his hair if only for an excuse to touch it, and we climb back into the truck.

"Be safe," I say, pulling into the dirt driveway and putting the truck in park. "Call or text me if you need anything."

"Sure thing," he says, and pecks me on the cheek.

I remind myself to get an extra key made so he can have

his own, but for now I give him mine. I won't need it because he'll be here waiting for me when I get home. And that thought has me smiling the entire way to work.

———

"Hey, you seem happy," Carlos says when he sees me. I didn't even realize I'd been smiling while I was working, but now that he's mentioning it, I am quite a bit more upbeat than usual. I can't believe it but I actually blush, and of course he grins even wider at me. "You finally get some action?" he asks, clapping me on the shoulder.

I roll my eyes. "Of course you would think that is the only possible reason for me to be smiling."

"No, but it's the best one."

I can't help it. I laugh. "If you must know, no, I didn't get any action. I actually have someone staying with me for a while who needs some help, and I'm enjoying having the company, and doing something for someone else."

"Oh, I see. I'm guessing it's not a gorgeous woman?"

"No." *It's a gorgeous nineteen-year-old boy.* "He's a kid I ran into that night at the bar, down on his luck. I'm helping him get back on his feet."

"You took in a total stranger?" he asks, his eyes widening, and I don't know if it's a *I can't believe how amazing you are*, or a *I can't believe how stupid you are*, look.

"Yeah," I shrug.

"Well, good for you, man. I hope it works out for both of you. Just be careful, huh?"

I nod.

His eyes flit over my face for a moment longer as if trying to decipher something before he nods again and goes back to work.

I'm more than ready for the day to be over when six o'clock finally rolls around. I can't believe how quickly I jump into my truck and peel out of the work site, knowing that there will be someone waiting for me when I get home. The idea that not only do I not have to cook dinner, but I don't have to eat alone, spurs me on. Charlie is a wonderful cook and I can't wait to see what he's made. I'm fucking starving.

When I get home, I park and turn the truck off. It's getting dark now, and just the fact that I can see a light on inside makes my heart swell. Shit, it's been a long time since I came home to anything but an empty and quiet house. This is what it's supposed to be like. I can't believe I have this again, because I don't deserve to. But somehow, this boy has come into my life, and made it so much better in such a short amount of time.

I climb out and make my way up the steps to the front door. The smell of garlic and lemon hits me before I even open it, and I groan. Music fills my ears when I step inside and breathe in the heavenly scent wafting from the kitchen. The music is playing so loudly I don't think he can hear me, but I don't mind one bit.

I take my work boots off before placing my hat on top of them. I can't believe how happy it makes me to see his shoes on the mat by the door. A reminder that I'm not alone, that someone shares this house with me now.

I find more reminders as I make my way through the house, like the book left open on the coffee table and the glass next to it, filled part way with orange juice. The wrapper from the Pop Tarts he must have had earlier and the banana peel he didn't throw away. I don't even care, because it means he's here, making himself at home, so he can be messy if he wants to be, and I'll enjoy every minute of it.

I make my way to the kitchen and a smile splits my face when I see him bopping his head and swinging his hips to the music playing from his phone. It's steady and upbeat and seems to suit his personality perfectly.

He's wearing a pleated skirt, which must be one of the ones I asked him not to try on for me. This one is black with fucking roses on it. Only Charlie could make roses adorable.

He's wearing another crop top. It's black with mesh sleeves and a hood, and he's so fucking cute. My hands ache to grip his mid-section and feel his skin under mine again.

I sigh loudly and he turns to face me, a bright smile crossing his face, his green eyes lighting up. He reaches over and turns the volume down on the music. "Hey, Papa Bear. How long have you been standing there?"

"Not long." I smile back at him. He steps towards me but I back away. He frowns, the sparkle in his eyes dimming.

"I do not smell good," I explain, my hands up. His smile returns as he bites his lip and looks me over.

"Dinner's almost ready. Go shower. It'll be waiting when you get out."

I nod and head down the hall, hearing the music rise in volume again. I shake my head fondly as I enter the bathroom and shut the door. I smile when I see his toothbrush and tube of toothpaste there and a shaver on the counter that isn't mine, along with his deodorant. There's no organization to the items whatsoever. They're just taking over the sink. I'm so used to living by myself and having everything in order all the time that I'm surprised it doesn't annoy me, but it does the opposite. Happiness blooms in my chest at the thought of sharing my bathroom with someone else. I also notice that the bathroom hamper is empty, which means Charlie must have done laundry. Why do I have butterflies fluttering around in my stomach at the thought of his clothes being mixed in with mine?

I strip and step into the shower. Ten minutes later I'm in my room, dressing in clean sweats and a white T-shirt. I notice that Charlie has stacked my folded clothes neatly on my bed and another grin splits my face. I put the clothes away before heading back to Charlie in the kitchen.

"God, that smells amazing," I tell him as he sets the plates on the table, and I make my way over, running a hand through my damp hair. He gives me that dazzling smile again and I don't miss the way his gaze lingers for just a moment on the sliver of skin peeking out when my shirt rises ever so slightly.

"It's garlic and lemon chicken with mashed potatoes and green beans," he tells me. "I hope you like it. It's one of my favorites."

"Thank you for doing this," I say as we sit.

"I like cooking," he replies as we dig in. "And I like feeling useful."

"Thanks for doing the laundry, too," I add. "I hate folding clothes."

He grins at me. "Sorry I didn't put them away. I wasn't sure if I should be doing that part or not. You might not want me peeking around in your underwear drawer."

I laugh. "I don't mind. If you've folded them I don't think you putting them away is any weirder."

He chuckles. "I'll put them away next time, then. If I do it wrong you can tell me."

I nod. "Did you have a good day?" I ask, and then moan around the bite of chicken I just put in my mouth. God, it's delicious. He smiles and blushes.

"It was fine. I looked into the GED stuff," he says around a mouthful of food, and I almost laugh because his cheek is so big he reminds me of a chipmunk. But it does me good to see him eating.

"Oh? And?"

"I can take courses online at my own pace, or in person, but I think I'd prefer online. Looks like it takes about three months or so, depending on what pace you go at, so I don't think I should start any courses until the trial period is over. I don't want to be part way through and have to quit."

I swallow. Just thinking about him leaving makes me uneasy and honestly, depressed. "I'm perfectly happy with you being here," I tell him rather quickly. "And I'm happy to pay for you to do something that will improve your quality of life."

He gives me a soft smile. "You might not feel that way in a few weeks."

"Yes I will." I say the words without hesitation. *Please don't leave me.*

"What do you want to do when you get it?" I ask. I make sure to say when and not if. He's going to get his GED because I won't have it any other way. The world needs what he has to offer. And he needs to know that he is capable.

He smiles again and his cheeks turn pink. He seems elated that someone asked him what he wants to do with his life, and it makes me think it was something his parents never did. Did they have any interest in their son?

"I really like kids," he says, and I can't hide my smile because I just know Charlie would be amazing with kids in any setting. He's lively and vivacious, caring, thoughtful, fun, but he can be stern and take charge when he needs to, too. "I've thought about being a teacher, maybe for preschool kids or elementary age. Or I could be a nanny, too. That's less schooling," he chuckles.

"You'd be amazing at either one," I tell him, and his eyes dance. God, this kid needs more praise, more encouragement. He deserves to believe in himself, and to know that others believe in him, too.

"How was your day?" he asks, and I realize how good it feels to have someone ask me that. It's been a really long time. I'm so used to just coming home and eating dinner in front of the television, alone after I shower, and not talking to anyone until work the next day. Rachel asks me how work is, but that's only once a month when we meet up for lunch.

"It was good," I say with a smile. *Coming home to you made it even better.*

"Oh, and sorry about the mess in the bathroom. I didn't really know where to put my stuff. I can keep it in my room if that's better."

"No," I say, maybe a little too quickly, and his eyes widen. He gives me a grin like he knows why I told him no, and I flush. "I uh," I clear my throat. "I mean, I don't mind your stuff being in there. Why don't I clean out a drawer for you and you can put everything but your toothbrush in there? I'm sure I have a bunch of stuff in there that doesn't need to be."

"Okay." He's still giving me that knowing look and I turn my gaze to my meal and keep eating.

A few minutes later, when we've both finished our meals, our plates scraped clean, I say, "Why don't I clean up since you did the cooking?"

"Why don't we both do it? You worked all day, and I'm sure you are tired," he replies. "I don't mind."

"Okay." We scoot around each other just like the night before, only this time when Charlie turns music on, and I've placed my plate in the dishwasher, he takes my hand and I don't hesitate. I take him in my arms and we move across the kitchen floor. At one point he steps back, still holding my hand, and twirls, his skirt billowing out around his thighs, before he comes back to me, his smile wide. I don't know for how long we dance but I can tell he's in his element. This is everything Charlie was meant to be—carefree and happy, and smiling that radiant smile. God, I'm addicted to him.

"Sorry, you probably want to get off your feet," he says. And while my feet are sore, I'd dance all day with Charlie if it kept that smile on his face, even if my feet were bleeding at the end.

"I don't mind." I look into his eyes. "I just wish I wasn't so terrible at it."

"You're not terrible. You haven't stepped on my feet yet." He grins at me.

"Just give it time," I say, and he giggles.

"Okay, let's finish so we can watch a movie." He pecks me on the cheek a minute later before pulling out of my arms. I almost whine at the loss of his slender, warm body against mine.

We load the last of the dishes and start the dishwasher. Charlie tells me he'll wash the pans tomorrow, and even though it's hard to leave the mess, I relent. He needs to feel useful and I need to learn to let go. Besides, he's had enough of people trying to control him, and giving him orders. Dirty pans never killed anyone, right?

I take my spot on the sofa and turn on *Friends*, and Charlie joins me, curled into my side with his fuzzy brown blanket. He seems to have gotten quite attached to said object. It's one Rachel gifted me when we were married and I never used it much, but it seems to suit Charlie, and I'm glad it's being enjoyed. I put my arm around him and let him rest his head against my shoulder, drinking in the scent of my shampoo on his hair and feeling it tickle my cheek and chin. It really is incredibly soft. My fingers ache to run through it, but I keep my hand on his shoulder and do my best not to bury my face in his succulent waves.

Charlie laughs at something Phoebe says on the television and it's so genuine and unfiltered that I can't help squeezing him to my side and pressing my lips to his hair. His laughter is like medicine to my soul. He reaches his head up and presses a kiss to my cheek, smiling at me, before resting his head back on my shoulder.

I get frustrated only five minutes later when my back and shoulder are aching because I don't want to move, or switch positions, but I don't think I have much choice. I slide my arm away from him and rotate my shoulder as he lifts his head. I arch my back and groan, then rub my shoulder and try to stretch a little.

"You okay?" he asks.

"Just sore," I reply. "Comes with the job. And being old."

"I can give you a massage," he offers.

God, having Charlie's hands on me sounds like the most exquisite torture. But I'm not sure that's such a good idea. My cock is already half hard just from having him close to me.

"Come on." He stands up. "Let's move to your bed. It won't work so well on the couch."

I stand and follow him down the hall, even though every part of my brain is telling me not to do this.

"Take off your shirt and lie on your stomach," he directs once we're in my room. I do as he says and I almost gasp when I feel him climb on top of me and straddle my hips, his ass touching mine. Holy shit, this was so not a good idea.

I rest my head on my forearms and let out a deep breath, as his small hands begin to work the muscles in my back, kneading and massaging, loosening up areas I didn't even realize were so damn tight. His hands are strong, but gentle, and so soft. He finds a trigger point on my shoulder blade and I wince when he applies a steady pressure.

"You okay?" I nod and grunt.

"Yeah, peachy," I reply, and he laughs, which makes his body move against mine. Oh god, why did I enjoy that so much? I'm a sick, sick man.

He keeps applying pressure until I feel the trigger point give, and I sigh in relief. But my body begins to betray me as he moves further down my back, using the heels of his hands, and I feel my cock harden. His thumbs press into the small of my back, just above the waistband of my sweats, and I groan. It feels so good, and I'm horrified that I'm so aroused. Shit, I can't let him see me like this.

"Relax," he tells me. "You're tensing up again."

I let out a breath and close my eyes, willing myself to relax. That's the whole point of this, after all. I tell myself this isn't sexual and he's just trying to help me feel better and that I need to get a fucking grip.

"That's better," he says. I feel his hands move up my back again. "I can do more if you want."

I shake my head, because I need to be finished so I can calm my dick down and not think about how it feels to have Charlie sitting on top of me in that cute as fuck outfit, his hands all over my bare skin.

"Good?" he asks, rubbing my shoulders a little and then the base of my neck.

I nod. "Thank you."

"Of course." He climbs off of me and stands up. "Ready to watch more *Friends*?"

"In a minute," I hope beyond hope that he doesn't catch on to why I'm not getting up right away, and chalks it up to me just being super relaxed.

He smiles. "I'll go make some popcorn," he says, and then leaves the room.

I sigh and roll over, staring down at my very hard dick and willing it to behave itself. "You are causing problems," I tell it. "Be good. He's not for us." I lie there for a moment longer and think of vomit and diarrhea so I can get my erection to deflate. Fortunately it does the trick, but not so fortunately it makes me not really want the popcorn Charlie made for us. He doesn't seem phased by it and just grins and shoves a huge handful into his mouth. I watch as it falls all over his lap.

"You need a dog," he tells me.

"And why is that?"

"They're like natural vacuum cleaners." He says it like it's the obvious answer. "No cleaning up the food you spill. You just let them do it and everyone is happy."

"Yes, until the dog needs a stomach pump," I reply, and he laughs.

He's sitting with his legs tucked under him now, in the corner of the sofa, and I miss him being next to me, but glancing over and seeing his adorable bare knees peeking out from underneath his pleated skirt, along with that cute as fuck belly button, it's almost worth it.

I have an ache in my chest that night as I lie in bed, because I don't fucking know what to do about this insane attraction I have for him. I've never felt this way about a guy before. I've never felt this way about anyone before, not even my wife. The need, the utter desire I feel for Charlie is overwhelming.

I'm so fucking ashamed, and tears start to slide down my

cheeks as my body trembles. After everything with Trey, after losing him, after all the conversations we had, after I treated him the way I did, here I am, wanting a boy who is twenty-seven years my junior. And even if it were okay for something to happen between us, I don't deserve it. Not after I destroyed my son. And if Charlie ever found out, he'd fucking hate me. And he'd have every right to, because what I did was unforgivable.

# CHAPTER
## *Seven*

## PAUL

When Saturday rolls around, I decide to take Charlie out to brunch. I would take him out to breakfast, but he never wakes up before nine. Not that I mind. I'm sure he's catching up on all the sleep he didn't get living on the streets. Even before that, I can't imagine he slept well at home, given the circumstances. The fact that I can provide him a safe and peaceful place to lay his head down every night is my greatest reward. And one I probably don't deserve. I still don't know how I managed to be lucky enough to have him fall into my life, but I swear I won't ruin this. He deserves this, someone taking care of him, looking out for him, providing for him, letting him know that he is worthy and good, and I will not screw it up. Even if it means I have to deny myself the one thing in five years that has brought me joy.

"I'm ready," he says, entering the living room. I turn from where I'm sitting on the couch. He's dressed in the snug-fitting white jeans and the tie-dye crop-top sweatshirt he showed me at the mall with the ribbons through the sleeves, his Keds are on his small feet, and he looks incredible.

"Great." I stand. "Let's go." I'm realizing, with it getting a little chillier out, Charlie will need a jacket, and make a mental note of it. He'll fight me on it, but whether he stays with me or not, it won't be negotiable. I won't have him freezing this winter.

I slide my own shoes on and grab my keys and wallet, and we head to the truck. I take him to a local mom and pop place that I love. I haven't been in a while because I'm embarrassed to go alone, and I never have anyone to take with me.

"This is cool, Papa Bear," he says when we pull up. The outside of the restaurant is brick that's been painted in all different breakfast foods. It's quite the sight, but I love it. Through the window we can see families with young children and elderly couples enjoying their food and chatting. Waitresses and waiters walk by.

"I hope you like it," I say. "It's my favorite breakfast place."

"Then I'm sure I'll love it," he tells me, and I grin as we get out of the truck.

I shove my hands in my pockets to keep from reaching for him. I've been less tactile with him the past few days, and I know he's noticed. I just feel like it's for the best if I have any hope of keeping things platonic between us. He frowns at me but doesn't say anything.

Fuck, I hate this. I don't want to hurt him, but I don't know what to do. God help me. I'm so crazy about him.

I open the door and the bell above it dings, signaling we're here. There's a hostess behind the counter as we approach, and she gives us a beaming smile. She's probably about Charlie's age and in college, I would guess. She has her dark hair pulled back in a ponytail and leopard print glasses frame her face. She wears the typical *Sunny's* uniform—black pants and a bright blue polo with a sun on the upper left side.

"Good morning, and welcome to *Sunny's*," she says cheerfully. "Two?"

"Yes, please." I smile back at her, and I notice Charlie grinning too, which eases a little of my guilt.

She grabs two menus and makes her way around the counter. She grins at Charlie. "I like your outfit," she says. "Mind if I ask where you got it?"

"Macy's." He beams at her. "And thank you."

She nods. "This way, gentlemen."

She takes us to a small booth across from a window and an elderly couple and sets our menus down along with some silverware. "Your server will be with you in just a moment," she says, and then wanders off.

"Good morning," a middle aged woman says when she reaches our table. It's mid morning and I'm guessing she's had a time of it already because she looks fucking worn out, but she's trying her hardest to give us a smile. Still, there's no missing the bags under her eyes and her slumped shoulders. Her dark hair is graying and her skin has a fair amount of wrinkles, making her seem older than she probably is.

"Morning, gorgeous," Charlie says, giving her a radiant smile. Her cheeks turn pink. Fucking charmer.

She smiles widely at him. "Well aren't you a sweetheart. I'm feeling better already."

"Rough morning?" he asks, then takes a peak at her nametag and adds, "Dorine?" and I can't believe how fucking wonderful he is.

"You could say that." She gives a soft smile. "Just some tough customers. Got a lousy tip from the last table and that didn't help. But enough of me complaining." She holds her pencil to her pad and glances back and forth between us. "What can I get you handsome fellows to drink?"

"I'll have coffee," I say.

"Cream and sugar?" she asks.

"Yes," Charlie pipes up, and I grin at him. "He won't use them but I most definitely will."

She laughs. "So, coffee for you, too?" she asks, and he nods. "I'll be right back." She smiles at us again and scampers off.

"You are all kinds of wonderful, you know that?" I tell him when she's gone.

He just shrugs. "She seemed like she needed cheering up. It's not a big deal."

"It was to her," I say, my eyes meeting his. "Not a lot of people would have even noticed she was struggling, let alone tried to do something about it. She came over here upset and left smiling. That matters. Don't minimize that, Charlie."

"Here you go," Dorine says when she returns a minute later with two steaming cups of coffee, creamer and sugar. "You guys ready to order?"

I can't help noticing that her smile is still there, and not forced, but genuine. I order the breakfast sampler so I can have a little bit of everything, and Charlie orders the cheesecake pancakes. Why am I not surprised?

"I'll be right back with your orders," she says, taking our menus.

"Dorine, could we have one of those children's menus?" Charlie asks, and I raise an eyebrow at him. "We need something to do while we wait," he shrugs.

She chuckles and nods. "I'll be right back." A minute later she returns with two children's menus and two sets of crayons. "There you go." She sets them down on the table. "You guys have fun." I see Charlie wink at her and she lets out another laugh before leaving us alone again.

"Better be careful or she'll want to take you home with her," I tease him.

"She can't have me," he replies. "I'm all yours." His grin is wide and my heart skips a beat. God how I wish that were true. I'd give anything to have him be mine. All mine.

"So, what gives with the kiddie menus?" I ask him.

"Play tic-tac-toe with me," he says, sliding one menu aside and then pushing the other menu towards me. He opens a packet of crayons and holds them up. "Which one?"

This is so utterly ridiculous, I can't help but smile. When was the last time I used a crayon for anything? The last time I colored? The last time I played a game on a restaurant menu? Fuck, I think Trey was a child. That was ages ago. "Green." I take it from his outstretched hand. He goes for blue and we start. There's four different tic-tac-toe boards and we tie on all but one, which Charlie wins, and then throws his arms up in the air and cheers, making everyone in the restaurant turn their heads in our direction. I laugh and cover my mouth with my hand.

"Ooh, they have a would-you-rather game on the back." Charlie wiggles in his seat. God, he's so fucking adorable. "Would you rather kiss a frog or hug a snake?" His gaze lingers on me expectantly.

"Neither," I say.

"Eh, wrong," he replies, making the buzzing sound of a game show and slapping the table. "You have to pick one."

I groan. "Seriously? This is like asking, 'would you rather be stabbed in your right eye or your left?'"

Charlie laughs loudly and I can't help but follow suit, attracting the attention of the other guests yet again. "Okay, even though I'm terrified of snakes, I'd probably pick that, because kissing a frog is gross and depending on the frog they can actually have poisonous skin, so, there." I shiver and Charlie chuckles.

"I didn't know you were afraid of snakes," he says.

I nod. "And if you ever try to scare me with a fake one I promise you it will not go well." I eye him because I know that's the type of thing he would do.

"Scary how well you know me already," he says with a smile and a twinkle in his eyes.

"What about you?"

"Probably the snake," he agrees, then peers down at the menu, ready for another one. That's when Dorine arrives with our food and sets it in front of us. My eyes bug out of my head when I see the size of Charlie's pancakes, filled with cheesecake bits and covered in strawberries and whipped cream. It looks like a diabetic coma on a plate. And Charlie is elated.

"Thank you," we both say, and Charlie stops her before she can walk away.

"Hey, Dorine, would you rather be able to slide down rainbows or jump on clouds?"

She smiles. "Probably rainbows," she says. "I'm too old to jump. You guys enjoy."

Charlie takes a few bites of his pancakes and then looks at me with his mouth full. "You want any?"

I laugh and shake my head. "No thanks."

"Darn," he pouts. "I was hoping to trade you."

I laugh again. "You could just ask."

He grins. "Can I?"

"Help yourself," I say, and he reaches across the table and snatches a piece of bacon.

"Thanks, Papa Bear," he says softly, then proceeds to devour it.

Dorine comes back a couple of times to refill our coffee and ask if we need anything else, and of course Charlie charms her with his smile and vibrant personality each time. When she leaves the check on the table for us she turns to him.

"You wouldn't be looking for a job by any chance, would you?"

Charlie's eyes widen. "Oh, um, I don't know." He glances at me. I think him having a job would be amazing but I'm not sure if he can get one without the proper papers and identification. Probably should have looked into that sooner but I was so caught up with getting him settled and the STI testing and thinking about him finishing school.

"We're hiring another waiter, and I know you would be amazing at it," Dorine tells him. "I know I'd love working with you. We could use a little sunshine around here." She glances between us. "Talk it over with your dad and if you decide to apply just come back in and see us, okay?"

We both blush but don't correct her. She gives us another smile and hurries off.

"So, what do you think, Pa, can I get a job?" Charlie teases in a terrible thick southern accent, his eyes sparkling.

"Shut up," I say, and he laughs. "It was a logical mistake."

"Can I, though?" he says, and I can tell he's excited about the idea.

"You have a license?" I ask, and he nods. "You still need a birth certificate or social security number. Have either of those on you?"

He frowns and shakes his head. "They're at my parents' house."

"Know where you were born?"

"Here," he says. "Why?"

"I think you can get a copy of your birth certificate online." His eyes light up, and I know this is something we have to do. He needs this. "We'll look into it more when we get home."

He nods, and we scoot out of the booth and head to the counter to pay. The bubbly hostess is there and Charlie gives her a big smile as we leave.

"Can we go for a walk?" he asks before we get in the car.

"Sure," I say. We get in and I drive us to a nearby park with a walking path around a beautiful lake. There's children playing on the playground nearby and ducks in the water. The weather is sunny and pleasant.

He doesn't ask before he slides his hand into mine and we stroll. I'm sure we're getting some looks and I'm tempted to remove my hand from his on principle. We shouldn't be doing this, right? But his hand feels so good in mine, so perfect. I can't let go.

Charlie finds delight in everything as we walk. The sunshine, the fresh air, the smell of freshly mowed grass and wildflowers, the ducks in the lake. We stop on the bridge and watch them for a while, and Charlie slides his hand out of mine.

A family stops nearby and watches the ducks with us; a young girl, probably five or six with wavy dark hair, along with a man and woman whom I'm assuming are her parents. The little girl looks at Charlie and he waves at her with a bright smile. She grins and waves back with only four fingers, her thumb in her mouth, and I can't help thinking Charlie would be an amazing dad some day. We stop at a bench a little while later, because my knee is hurting.

"Sorry," Charlie says as I rub the joint. "I didn't even think of that being an issue."

"It's fine," I tell him. "I can't let it keep me from living my life. And I'm enjoying being here with you."

We sit in silence for a while, and I ache to scoot him closer to me and feel his body against mine, but I resist. The little girl from earlier comes up to us a minute later and hands us each a wildflower while the grown ups she's with stand off in the distance smiling.

"Thank you very much," Charlie says. "Purple is my favorite color."

She beams at him. "Mine, too," she says in her sweet little voice. "You're very pretty."

Charlie flushes and grins. "Thank you," he says. "You're lovely, too. And you are very kind, which is even better."

"Charlotte, come on sweetheart," her mom calls, and Charlotte waves as she bounds away, her brown curls bouncing. We wave at her parents as they move along.

"Are we okay?" Charlie asks after a minute, and my chest tightens. "It's just, you haven't been as…affectionate lately and, uh, I kind of miss it." I turn to see tears in his eyes, and my heart shatters.

"Charlie," I whisper and scoot closer to him. I take him in my arms and hold him to me, his arms sliding around my waist as he sobs, his chest heaving. "My Charlie." I press a kiss to his hair and sigh again. This boy is starved for affection and TLC. And I decide right then and there that if he needs me to touch him, I will, and I'll just have to figure out how to not let it drive me insane. Or maybe I'll just go insane because it's worth it. "I'm sorry," I tell him. "I didn't mean to hurt you. I guess I'm just stressed about something and I don't know how to handle it. But it's not your fault, and we are very much okay."

He sniffles and wipes at his nose with his sleeve.

"Will it help if I go back to touching you?" I ask him, and he nods immediately.

"I don't want to make you feel uncomfortable," he adds, "but I really do miss it, and I didn't realize how much I needed it until you weren't doing it anymore. My parents were never physically affectionate with me. The only touch I've ever gotten was…" he trails off and I feel him trembling. I don't ask him to say more, because I have a feeling I know what he was going to say, and my insides boil at the thought of anyone hurting my precious boy.

"Just tell me what you need and I will give it, sweetheart," I tell him. God I feel like I've just signed my own death warrant because this may very well destroy me, but if that's what it takes for him to know he's loved and worthy, I would destroy myself a thousand times over.

I feel his hand slide into mine and he rests his head on my shoulder. "It feels longer than a week," he says.

"Hmm?" I ask, looking down at him.

"Since I came to stay with you."

I rub my hand up and down his arm and rest my cheek on his hair. "Don't regret it yet?" I tease, and he chuckles.

"Not for a second," is his reply.

*Me neither, sweet boy. Me neither.*

# CHAPTER
*Eight*

## CHARLIE

Paul and I make dinner together that evening, and he doesn't hesitate to touch my shoulder, or playfully nudge me over with his hips when I'm in his way, or press a kiss to the side of my head when I say something that makes him laugh.

After dinner we sit on the couch together, me curled up beside him with the laptop on his lap as we look up the possibility of me getting a copy of my birth certificate and applying for a job. If I can work, I'll be able to get out of the house and not be home alone all day, make money to pay for my own GED, and maybe even save up enough that I can eventually pay him back for everything. Or at least some of the things.

"It looks doable," he says as he reads, his sexy as fuck glasses perched on his nose again. "You just have to apply." He turns to me and grins. "You wanna make this happen?"

I nod. "What do I do for transportation?" I bite my lip. Paul only has the one car and it's definitely too far to walk. It might be within biking distance, though. I mention the idea to him and he frowns.

"What's wrong?" I ask as he slides his glasses off.

"I don't like the idea of you biking that far. What if something happens to you?"

I smile and squeeze his hand, then nuzzle his shoulder with my nose. I can't get over how protective he is of me and it does things to my insides.

"Maybe you can use Uber, or get a ride from someone who works there?"

"So you are okay with me getting into a car with a complete stranger but riding a bike alone is off limits?" I tease, raising an eyebrow at him.

He frowns. "Fair point." There's a pause. "Okay, look, I have a bike you can use, but only until we can afford another set of wheels. I'm gonna see what's out there."

I nod. "I can look too," I say. And I smile because he said 'we.'

I don't think I've ever been this excited about the idea of working. "You sure you are okay with this?" I ask. "It's not exactly what we agreed to. I won't be the doting house boy."

He smirks at me and I grin. "Of course I'm okay with it. I want you to be happy, Charlie, and that was more just to give you something to do, keep you occupied. I think this is a great idea."

I beam at him and press a kiss to his cheek. Then I pull the laptop away from him and get to work on getting that copy of my birth certificate. Tomorrow I'm going to go back to Sunny's and get an application.

Paul laughs and grabs his book, then sits next to me, reading while I work. I can't remember ever being this happy.

## PAUL

Three more days go by and we still don't hear about Charlie's test results. I'm nervous as fuck the entire day at work, and everyone senses it. I just don't have my head in the game today, and I'm constantly checking my phone to see if Charlie's messaged or called me, even though I have the volume turned up as loud as possible.

"Dude," Aaron says as we work on installing the cabinets in the kitchen. "What's got you so distracted today, man? You seem upset. Is everything okay?"

I sigh. "I'm fine."

"Carlos says you have someone staying with you. Is everything okay with him?" He's not asking to be nosy, I know. That isn't Aaron. He really just wants to make sure everything is okay. I'm just not sure how much I should be sharing about Charlie. I don't want to betray his trust.

"I appreciate you asking, but I don't think I should say. It's not my place."

He nods. "Okay, well, if you need anything, or if he does, you let us know?" He places his hand on my shoulder and looks me in the eyes. I nod. "Okay," he says, and claps my shoulder before we get back to work. "I've got a date so we need to hustle." He grins at me and I realize I never did find out how things went with the attractive brunette that night. Shit, Charlie's taken up all the space in my head, consumed my thoughts, and I've become a dick of a friend.

"That woman from the bar?" I ask, and he beams at me. That's a yes. "Good for you."

"It's our third date," he replies, and waggles his eyebrows. I just roll my eyes.

"Do me a favor and please don't give me the details," I tell him, and he laughs.

"If you ever get yourself back out there we can double. Or maybe even triple, with Carlos and his wife."

Why is it that the one person I can see myself going on a date with is a skinny, sassy, stubborn boy with freckles and red hair, who looks killer in a skirt?

———

"Charlie?" I call his name as soon as I step in the door. I'm desperate to see him, to know if he heard anything in the ten minutes it took me to get home. He texted me twice at work but neither were about his test results. The first was a video he took of himself licking a spoonful of peanut butter and then acting like he was going to stick said spoon back in the jar just to make me squirm. It drove me crazy, in more than one way. I never realized his tongue was that long. And I couldn't help wondering what it would feel like on my skin, in my mouth. I had gotten more than a little distracted on my lunch break, and may have also gotten a little hard. Damn him.

The second message was to ask about dinner. Pork chops or pasta? I'd texted him back that I didn't care because I was so consumed with thoughts of his test results, but then responded a little while later with, *Pasta please.*

He'd sent me a laughing emoji and a thumbs up and sent me a picture shortly after of the pasta boiling.

I hear him speaking as I make my way further into the house. When I see him he's on the phone, pacing through the living room. His face is pensive and he's biting his lip as he listens to whatever the person on the other end is saying.

"Okay. Yes, thank you," he finally says, then hangs up. His gaze meets mine.

"So?" I ask, my chest constricting. "Was that them?"

He nods. "I'm not clear," he tells me, and my heart rate spikes, my stomach dropping to the floor. "But it's not serious, either. I tested positive for chlamydia and trich, so they're putting me on antibiotics for seven days, and then they want to test me again in a few months."

God, I'm so relieved. I feel like a thousand pound weight has been lifted off my chest and I can finally breathe again. The air seems clearer. My arms ache to hold him, but I'm a filthy mess, so I resist. He doesn't hesitate, though, and a moment later he's wrapping his arms around me and burying his face in my chest. "I'm gross," I say, pushing myself away.

But he yanks me back, having none of it, and even gives me a bit of a stink eye that has me chuckling.

"Don't you fucking dare," he threatens, squeezing my middle.

My arms go around him instantly and I hold him to me, kissing the top of his head, so thankful that we didn't get worse news. We knew he didn't have HIV but there's a slew of other STIs he could have tested positive for. Antibiotics for a week is nothing. He's going to be okay. My baby will be okay. We just have to make sure he keeps getting tested on a regular basis and doesn't have unprotected sex anymore. I can't risk him getting sick, or hurt. I couldn't bear it.

"You okay?" I tilt his chin to look at me. He nods.

"I think so. I'm just glad to finally have an answer, you know?" I nod and press a kiss to his forehead.

"When can we pick up your meds?"

"Oh, um, they have a pharmacy there. I didn't know where you usually go so I said that was fine. They should be ready tomorrow."

"I can pick them up on my way home from work then."

"Or I can do it. It's not far from Sunny's," he tells me. He started there two days ago and he's been loving it. They hired him on the spot as soon as he filled out the application. The fact that he didn't have his high school diploma didn't deter them at all. The only thing he's not crazy about is the uniform, but he doesn't complain, because it's work, and I know how grateful he is for it. It's only part time but it's enough for him to keep busy, and if he stays, he'll be working on his GED too, and then he'll really have a full schedule.

My heart sinks at the thought that he only has two-and-a-half weeks before his month-long trial period is up. Surely he'll stay, right? He seems happy. I know I am. God, I hope he stays.

I kind of hate the idea of him being out there on a bike, unprotected, but I haven't found a car for him yet, and I can't very well tell him he's not allowed to ride the bike I've lent him. He'll be doing it in broad daylight, after all. He should be fine. But I do tell myself to make more of an effort to find him a vehicle. Unfortunately his work hours don't align with mine at all. His schedule is kind of all over the place because that's what they need and he's willing. Besides that, he likes the bike. He says it's refreshing, and good exercise, and I don't want to take that away from him.

He's definitely healthier than he was when he first moved in here. He's less malnourished and he's put on a little bit of weight. Although, I have noticed that he still has the bags under his eyes, and he drinks an abnormal amount of coffee. He doesn't think I notice, but I do. He's tired even when he sleeps in, and despite his cheery personality, he drags throughout the latter part of the day, always yawning as we're relaxing on the sofa after dinner. Half the time he falls asleep on my shoulder while we're watching tv in the evening and I've been carrying him to bed the last few days when it's not even ten o'clock. I tell myself it's just that he's got more on his plate now with the new job, but I don't know if that's because I don't want to have one more thing to worry about in regards to him, or because I actually believe it.

"Sounds good," I tell him, and he smiles at me. God, that smile could rival the sun in its brilliance and warmth. I press another kiss to his head and then unfurl my arms from around him. "I'll go take a shower."

We talk about work during dinner. Charlie made chili tonight and it's amazing. Just the right amount of spice. And there's cornbread muffins to go with it. He puts so much cheese on top of his I can't even see the chili underneath and it makes me laugh.

After we clean up, Charlie goes to his room to change. He returns in sweats and a T-shirt. This one is normal, no crop-top, and while he's still adorable, I'm not going to lie, I miss the crop-top. Hell, I miss the skirt.

I smile when I see that he's reading the second book in the

cowboy series he had started the first week he was here. "You liked it, huh?"

He looks at me from where he's seated on his chair, then down at his book. He grins. "Oh, yeah. It's no gay romance, but it's good. I'm totally shipping Zach and Wyatt, though. Only friends, my ass."

I give a hearty laugh and he smiles widely. "You can't tell me there were no shenanigans going on when they were stuck in that barn together overnight." He winks at me.

An hour later he's yawning and I'm having trouble keeping my eyes open as well, so we say our goodnights and head to bed.

———

Over the next week, Charlie and I don't even see much of each other. He's still making meals and leaving them in the freezer or refrigerator for me because he's gone when I get home, working the evening shift at Sunny's. It's incredibly sweet, because he really doesn't have to do it, not when he's working just as many hours in the day as I am, and is also on his feet all day. I've even found little notes on them from him that say things like "Save some for me," or "Can't wait to see you."

As much as I appreciate it though, it's not the meals I want, it's him. I miss him so damn much. I miss his presence at the dinner table, I miss his music when I enter the house, I miss our conversations and our cuddles on the couch. I miss his sass and snark. I miss seeing his shoes when I walk in the front door. The only time I do see him is when I pick him up from work, because I'm not letting him ride home in the dark on a bike no matter how much he grouses. Besides that, despite his protestations, I think he really does like showing up to drive him home. It proves that I care, and he needs that. He always has the biggest smile when he sees me through the restaurant window, regardless of the exhaustion prevalent on his features. Inevitably, he falls asleep on the short drive home, his head resting against the window frame.

My chest aches with the need to be close to him, talk to him, have his hand in mine again, and I plan to do something about it. I still haven't brought up how exhausted he seems, but I'm hoping that since he has Friday off he'll be able to sleep in, and that after I get home he'll let me take him out.

I want to spoil him, and I have just the way to do it.

# CHAPTER
## *Nine*

## CHARLIE

It doesn't surprise me that Paul has already left for work when I make my way out to the kitchen Friday morning. It's been a long week and we've barely set eyes on each other. I've tried so hard to stay awake after he picks me up so that I can talk to him, even if it's just for ten minutes. I miss him so much. But I'm always asleep before the tires hit the road. I'm so fucking exhausted. I did better last night than usual, though. No nightmares this time. They happen less now that I'm living here in general, but they still wake me several times a week. I'm always scared to go back to sleep afterwards and I end up moving out to the living room to watch *Friends* until I can't keep my eyes open anymore. I have a feeling he suspects something, given how tired I always am, but he hasn't said anything. Part of me is aching to tell him about the nightmares, crawl into his bed and ask him to hold me, but I don't. I know he cares for me but I don't want to be a burden, and he's already doing so much. Part of me feels like that would just be asking too much, and I feel like I should be handling this aspect of things on my own.

I stop in my tracks when I see a beautiful bouquet of

flowers sitting on the island. It's huge, and arranged in a lovely green glass vase. Inside are red roses and lilies, some of which have bloomed and a few that have yet to, along with purple stock and dianthus. It's absolutely breathtaking. I lean in and close my eyes, drinking in the fragrant scent. The best part is, he remembered my favorite color, from me mentioning it randomly one time. Shit, I might cry. That bastard.

Next to the flowers is a gift box wrapped in sparkling silver paper. A card with my name on it in his messy scrawl sits on top. Why does it give me goosebumps to see my name in his handwriting? I feel a shiver race down my spine as I tear open the envelope and pull out the card. I'm smiling like an idiot when I see the words in multi-colored print on the front that say "Miss You Like Crazy." I open it and there's his handwriting again. He's written a poem. Well, sort of. It's not exactly original, but I'll take it.

*My darling Charlie,*

*Roses are red (these ones anyway)*
*Lilies aren't blue*
*Please join me for dinner tonight*
*I've been missing you :(*

*Paul*

*P.s. I purchased something for you to wear tonight if you like it. If you don't I won't be offended. Well, maybe a little bit. :)*

I bite my lip and grin. Fuck, I'm crazy about him. Is this a date? I probably shouldn't assume that. God, I want it to be, though. I'd date him in a heartbeat if he asked me. I'd give anything to be his for real. To know what it felt like to kiss him, to fall asleep in his arms and wake up next to him. To have his warmth surrounding me every night and feel his steady heartbeat under mine. To have him making love to me would be the most amazing thing in the world. I haven't had the most positive experiences when it comes to sex. Okay, I haven't had a single positive experience when it comes to sex. But something tells me it could be different with him. That he could show me how good it's supposed to be. That he would treat me with the tenderness and care I deserve and yet show me passion and desire at the same time. That's all I've really wanted when it comes to sex. Something other than lust, or the person I'm with only thinking of themselves. Despite my past experiences, I know sex can be good. And I know it could be good with him.

I sigh because I have no idea if that dream will ever become a reality. I'm not even sure if he's ever had sex with a guy before. Despite our age difference, I feel so drawn to him. Not just because he's hot, and god, is he hot, but he's also incredibly sweet, and good, and kind, and he shows me every day how much he cares for me as a person, not what I can do for him, or how much power he exudes over me. He's never once tried to change me or mold me into someone else. He genuinely wants what is best for me, wants to see me be successful, and happy, and I want to give myself to him for everything that he is, and everything that he's challenging and encouraging me to be.

I put the card aside and reach for the box, pulling it to me. I'm curious as hell to see what he got me. And, I'll admit, a little nervous, too. I pull off the ribbon and bow and then tear off the sparkling silver paper. I lift the lid and move the tissue paper aside. "Oh," I say to myself. Inside is a lovely emerald green chiffon camisole, with a v-neck and matching pants. I take out the camisole and smile as I hold it against myself. It's soft and flowy and comes to just above my belly button. I set it aside and reach for the pants. When I do, my cheeks heat so much I wouldn't be surprised if they were the same color as my hair. The third item in the box is a black lace thong. I don't know where he got it but I can tell it's made for men. The thought makes me blush even deeper. On top of the panties is a note that reads,

*I know this is rather intimate and that we agreed to wait until you decided if you were staying before we bought anything like this, but I figured they would go better with your outfit than what you currently have, so please forgive me. I wanted you to feel your best.*

Well, for fuck's sake. I can't even pop a boner because that was too damn sweet to make me horny. They're lovely. Papa Bear bought me panties. I can't help the fluttering feeling in my stomach at the intimate gesture. Taking them in my hands, I realize how incredibly soft they are and I can't wait to feel them against my bare skin.

And okay, my cock does twitch a little bit. How can it not, thinking of him buying me these panties and knowing that he'll know exactly what I have on under my outfit tonight?

He did such an amazing job with everything. This outfit is not only soft and comfortable, but incredibly chic and sassy, and I fucking love it. I can already tell it will look amazing with the strappy heels he bought me at Macy's.

The only problem is, I have to wait eight hours before I can wear it. Damn. Well, I do have lots of primping to do. Not to mention I want to get an outfit ready for him. If he gets to pick out my clothes I get to pick out his. But first things first. I get my phone out and text him.

**Me: Thank you for the flowers and the outfit. My answer is yes 😊 I would love to have dinner with you tonight**

I get a text back a minute later.

**Hot old guy: Can't wait. You're welcome.**

I should probably change his name in my phone but I can't bring myself to do it. It's funny and it reminds me of when we met, and how I found myself bringing my walls down for the first time in my life because he was so kind and intriguing. And something in his eyes had told me that as desperately as I needed somewhere to belong, he needed someone to hold on to, someone to care for, someone maybe even to save. I don't know why, but something tells me we need each other. I can't seem to shake the feeling that this arrangement is turning into something more than either of us ever expected.

I spend a good amount of time doing chores around the house that have been neglected since I got my job. I iron my new outfit and I also make a grocery order to have delivered so we have food for the coming week. Then I have a couple hours of down time before I start getting ready.

I strip and step into the shower. I take my time, lathering and rinsing, washing my hair with the amazing shampoo he lets me use. I can't help but get a little turned on by the fact that I smell like him, and he smells like me.

I shave my legs because I like to, and my pits. I like the feel of smooth skin, and it will look better with my outfit. I dry off but leave the towel around my waist as I shave my face. It doesn't take long as there isn't much there. I've never been able to grow much of a beard, but that's fine with me. I've never wanted one. I lather some moisturizer on my face and body to make it extra soft and smooth, then peer at myself in the mirror. Damn, what I wouldn't give for some make up. I'd love some bling for my eyes and just a light shimmer of gloss on my lips. I'll have to wait for my first paycheck for that. Only one more week. I can manage that. I squirt some curl cream into my hand and run it through my hair, then wash my hands and make my way out of the bathroom and into my bedroom.

I slip into my thong panties and take a moment to enjoy how they look on me, admiring my ass in the mirror, and my cock. Damn, I wish I had someone who could enjoy this. Not naming any names but he's roughly six foot-two, has incredible cerulean eyes, a smile that lights up my world, an ass that won't quit, arms that make all my troubles fade away when I'm in them, and makes gray hair look sexy as fuck.

I pull the camisole and pants off the hanger they are on, and slide into them. The pants hug my hips and flare out around my ankles. There's a bow in the middle, just below my belly button. The camisole is flowy and billows out as I twirl, admiring myself once again in the mirror. I have been putting on weight, and I'm not so sickly skinny anymore. At least not so much that you can see my ribs, so this outfit is even sexier on me than it would have been three weeks ago. Both the shirt and pants are insanely soft, and I'm loving how they look and feel. I twirl once more as I take myself in in the full length mirror, and it's only when I step away that I see Paul standing just inside the bedroom door, a wide smile on his handsome face.

"Shit," I say, putting my hand to my chest and gasping. I laugh.

"I'm sorry." He steps closer, chuckling.

"You scared the hell out of me." He plants a kiss on my hair and I notice he's holding something behind his back.

He smiles. "You looked like you were having fun. I didn't want to ruin it."

"What do you think?" I glance down at my attire and then back up at him.

He tilts his head and takes me in. "Almost perfect." I squint. He moves his hand out from behind his back and shows me a small white gift bag with bright pink tissue paper poking out of the top.

"More presents?" I take it with a raised eyebrow. "What is it?"

"Open it." He seems a little nervous, but I do as he asks, and my mouth falls open. Tears fill my eyes.

"You got me makeup?" I look up at him and he blushes beautifully. Inside the bag is eyeshadow, mascara, eyeliner, and lipgloss. Shit, it's like he's read my mind. How the hell does he do that? "Thank you." I go to him and hug him, but he pushes me away and takes my chin in his hand instead. He kisses my forehead, his lips lingering longer than normal.

"I would love a hug, but I'm gross and you are divine. I'm not messing up your brand new outfit with my filth." I chuckle and go back to the makeup.

"How did you know what to get me?" I ask as I rummage through and pull everything out, opening it up and admiring it all. The color palette he got me is perfect for a redhead, and will look wonderful with my skin tone. He didn't skimp, either. This is top of the line stuff. If he goes broke because he keeps spoiling me I will never forgive him.

"I asked someone at the store. They were very knowledge-able, and quite eager to help." He smiles at me and I smile back. I can't believe he was willing to do that for me. My Papa Bear loves lavishing gifts on me.

"I'm gonna go ahead and shower, if that's okay," he says. I nod and he leaves the room.

"Oh, wait," I call, and he pokes his head back in. "I uh, I have your outfit set out on your bed." He eyes me. "You pick out my clothes, I pick out yours." He grins and leaves, a flush to his cheeks.

Twenty minutes later, he's knocking on the open door. I turn from my place on the bed where I'm resting on my side reading my latest book—a friends to lovers mm romance. My mouth practically falls open. I knew he'd look good in the clothes I picked out for him, but hot damn. Good is a major understatement. He's fucking stunning in the white button down shirt, dark wash jeans, and leather jacket. His hair is styled to perfection.

"Wow," I say, and I just barely register that he's said it, too. I blink, because he's already seen me, but then I realize it's the makeup. I bite my lip and stand as he moves towards me. He takes my hands and I swear he's giving me that look that tells me he wants to kiss me, but he won't. Ugh, this man is infuriating! Fucking kiss me, goddamn it! Would he, if he knew I wanted him to? How can he not know I want him to? I haven't exactly been subtle the past couple weeks. Or ever, really. I've wanted him since, like, day three of moving in here, and I thought I'd made it pretty obvious.

"You look amazing," he tells me, then presses his lips to my knuckles. I fucking shiver. "The makeup suits you, Charlie."

"I love it," I say. It comes out as a whisper even though I don't intend for it to. And I do love it. I applied a gold shade to my eyelids and it's got a light shimmer. The gloss on my lips is just enough to give them a light sheen and the mascara and eyeliner make my eyes pop.

"Ready?"

I nod, and he extends his elbow, which I take with a smile. He leads me to the truck, which we chuckle about because we both know it's not the ideal vehicle for our outing or for how we're dressed, but oh well, it's what we have. I'll take him and a truck any day over no him.

He opens my door for me and I slide inside, and we make our way to dinner.

## PAUL

Fuck, I feel like I've been weak in the knees ever since I saw Charlie in that incredible outfit. He's so goddamn sexy. My mouth is watering just being near him, and I can't believe I've actually been able to utter complete sentences. I've been semi hard for the last hour. And thank god I had a good excuse for pushing away from him when he went to give me a hug, because otherwise he would have felt how very much I liked his new attire. The way the thin straps show off his freckle-strewn shoulders is more enticing than I ever thought it could be. Having him on my arm tonight feels like a precious gift.

The waiter leads us to our table when we arrive at the restaurant. I didn't want to skimp on anything tonight, so we're eating fancier than I probably ever have. Not a three course meal or anything, but it's a nice place. I pull Charlie's chair out for him and he blushes adorably before he sits and I help him scoot in. I hear the tinkling of silverware and the light murmur of conversation around us. There's a lovely linen tablecloth on the table and a candle in the center. The lighting is warm and gives a romantic vibe.

When I take my seat across from him I find myself just staring. It feels like ages since I've been able to just look at him, and I miss his face. I miss that smile, and those beautiful eyes. I miss his freckles and his adorable button nose. I miss his laughter and his sarcastic remarks.

"What?" he asks, when he notices me staring at him. He sets his glass down and grins at me. "Like what you see?"

My cheeks heat but I don't play it off. He deserves to know how beautiful he is. He deserves to know what an amazing person he is and I don't want to sully that with a joke. "I like you," I tell him, and he flushes. I think my comment affected him even more than me saying something about his physical appearance.

"I…like you, too," he tells me, the words soft, and careful almost, like he's unsure if he should be saying them, and my blush deepens, until he adds, "old man," and then winks at me. I smirk, but my chest warms because it's so Charlie, and it reminds me of when we met, which is quickly becoming one of the best days of my life.

"I've missed you," I say, as I reach across the table and boldly take his hand. He smiles at me and gives my hand a squeeze.

"Me, too."

The waiter arrives just then and we order. I get us a stuffed mushroom appetizer and salmon as my main meal. Charlie orders lobster. We hand the waiter our menus and he hurries away.

"I haven't even gotten to hear how your job has been going, we've barely seen each other," I tell Charlie as my gaze meets his again, my hand falling right back into his.

"It's been going well, for the most part. I did finally tell Dorine you aren't my dad." He chuckles and I grin.

"How'd she take the news? Not too terribly, I hope."

"No, she apologized for assuming but said she wasn't surprised. She said we have too much chemistry for her to not have realized it on her own."

I blush, feeling skin prickle at the back of my neck, but I can't take my eyes off of Charlie. "Oh, I see." He tells me more about Dorine. Apparently she's a single mom with a son in college and a teenage daughter, working two jobs and just trying to make ends meet. She is, in Charlie's words "a hoot," and is always making him laugh at work. It sounds like they really enjoy each other. He seems to be making friends with his other coworkers, too, mostly middle aged women, but a few men, and a fair number of college students as well.

"I'm happy for you," I tell him, unable to keep the smile from my face. It feels so perfect, being here with him, talking to him, sharing my day with him, and hearing about his. His eyes are bright, his smile wide and his laughter is my heart's song as he listens to my stories. I tell him about how the firestation is coming along, and about the antics of my coworkers, as we eat our meals.

"Dessert?" I say, as he's finishing up his lobster.

"I know you are trying to fatten me up," he tells me, patting his stomach, "but I couldn't eat another bite."

I laugh. After paying the bill, I stand again and scoot Charlie's chair out for him. He smiles that breathtaking smile at me as I take his hand and we walk to the parking lot. We stop at the truck but I don't open the door yet.

"Thank you for coming tonight," I tell him, then reach up and stroke his cheek. His skin is so fair, and so soft. I feel him shiver at my touch. He gives me a soft smile, his eyelashes fluttering. They're long and thick, and they skate over his cheek bones when his eyes close. It's absolutely breathtaking. The makeup really does accentuate his features so perfectly. I love the way his eyes shimmer and his full lips shine.

"Of course," he says. "I'll do anything that makes it

possible for me to be with you. Besides, who could say no to such an artfully crafted poem?"

I laugh. Cheeky brat. "Go for a walk with me?" I say, stroking his cheek again. He nods.

We make our way to the same park we went to after I took him to brunch at Sunny's, and walk around the lake. Of course it's evening this time, which I think makes it even more beautiful. The stars are out and the moon shines brightly above us as we walk hand in hand. I don't think I've ever stopped and enjoyed nature as much as I do when I'm with him. Before Charlie came along I would go for walks, or runs, before my knee got bad, but it would be about getting a certain amount of steps in, or a certain number of miles. It's different with him. Better. He soaks in everything. The sound of the crickets, the fresh air, the smell of the flowers, the wind blowing through the trees and ruffling his hair. Right now he stops on the pathway and crouches down, touching a delicate purple wildflower with the tips of his small fingers. I can't help but think that it's him that brings them life rather than the other way around. That somehow his touch, his radiance, and warmth helps them grow. Charlie is like the sun. If I didn't know better, I'd say he was the sun, so full of warmth and light, bringing life to everything around him. I stoop down too, so that I'm right next to him, and pluck one of the flowers from the dirt. He smiles at me as we both stand, and I tuck the flower into his curls. It's absolutely perfect for him. My beautiful boy.

He blushes beautifully and smiles at me, but then starts to shiver. "Shit, I'm so sorry." I take my jacket off and drape it over his nearly bare shoulders. He tugs it around himself. "Do you want to keep going?" I ask. He nods and takes my hand again. We make our way to the bridge and stop there for a while, peering out at the ducks. Charlie watches them in fascination just like everything else in nature. I've learned that the word "just" doesn't seem to exist in Charlie's vocabulary.

Everything is mesmerizing. Everything is unique and precious.

"How's your knee?" he asks, bringing me out of my daze. It's only then that I realize I've been staring at him again.

"I'm fine," I say.

"Well, I'm not." He winces and starts to unbuckle his high heels. I laugh as he sinks a good three inches, but it seems right to have him back to normal height. He rubs his feet with one hand, holding his shoes in the other. "These are not for comfort, that's for sure."

I smile and step forward, scooping him up and into my arms bridal style. Charlie shrieks, but then laughs, his arms coming around my neck. The jacket falls from his shoulders, getting pinned between us. He clings to his heels as I carry him to the truck.

"I could get used to this," he says, wiggling his legs, making it even more difficult for me to carry him.

"Keep that up and I'm gonna drop you," I tell him. He grins at me and then reaches up and plants a kiss on my cheek. I know I'm blushing again, but I can't help it. This is what he does to me. "You'll have to open the door," I say once we're at the truck. He does and then turns to me.

"You're not going to set me down inside and buckle me up, too?" He says it like he's Scarlet fucking O'Hara, fluttering those insanely long eyelashes.

"You're lucky I don't drop you on your ass, smart mouth," I reply. He laughs and I set him on his feet. We climb in and make the drive home, Charlie keeping his shoes off the entire way, his bare feet up on the dash, wiggling his tiny toes. I remind myself that he needs some nail polish. I keep forgetting.

When we arrive home, I climb out of the truck quickly, hurrying around before he can step out. I open the passenger side door and he grins as I take him in my arms again. "Don't get used to this," I say as I carry him to the door. "I just don't want you to hurt your feet on the gravel."

"Okay." The grin never leaves his face and I roll my eyes. I set him down once we're inside, and take off my own shoes and socks, then hang up my jacket. Charlie sets his shoes down and tells me he's going to go take a bath. I settle on the sofa with my latest book and wait for him. He comes out about twenty minutes later, wearing sweats and a cropped T-shirt. I can't keep the smile off my face, and I find myself once more wanting to get my mouth on that delectable midriff. He smirks at me when he catches my gaze on him, but I just clear my throat and go back to my book.

He moves closer and shoves my legs aside, taking his place next to me on the sofa, his own book in hand as he curls up in the corner.

"How was your bath?"

He gives me that award-winning smile. "Amazing. My feet still hurt, though." He flexes his toes and it gives me an idea. I set my book aside and reach for his small feet, pulling them onto my lap. His eyes widen slightly.

"Are you giving me a foot massage?" he asks with a smirk.

"Not if you're going to be a brat," I reply. He laughs and leans back, his arm behind his head and his book abandoned on top of the couch.

"Nope, I'm going to be a very good boy." My gaze shoots to his and he fucking winks at me, a one hundred watt smile on his face. Fucking hell, Charlie. His words go straight to my cock and I have to hold back a groan.

I take one foot in my hand and massage it. I'm no expert, but I do my best. I used to give Rachel foot rubs too and she seemed to enjoy them. His feet are so small my hands practically engulf them, and I can't help loving it. He wiggles his toes and I laugh, and yet at the same time feel overcome with an intense desire to kiss them. They're so fucking cute, and they smell amazing after his bath. What-ever he does to keep them so soft is working. Apparently I have a foot kink, or a toe kink. I can't help it, I lean over and press my lips to his toes softly. He giggles, his toes twitching.

"I don't believe that's part of the typical massage package, Papa Bear," he tells me. "But I'll allow it."

I bite my lip and smile at him. I press a few more kisses to his other toes as I continue to work on his foot. Christ this is turning me on. I want to lick and suck on them but I don't let myself. This is already pushing things as it is, and I'm sure I'll be beating myself up for it later.

I switch feet and give his left foot the same treatment, minus the kisses, until Charlie wiggles his toes at me, whining softly. I look at him and he pouts.

"This one feels left out." I smile and take his foot in my hand before pressing tender kisses to all five toes. I look back at him then as I continue to massage it, and he beams at me. "You give the best toe kisses."

"Maybe I should start a business."

"Only if I'm your only customer." My eyes meet his. His gaze is soft and his tone teasing, but I have a feeling he is being very serious. Why do I like that so much? The idea of him wanting to keep me for himself? I press kisses to the toes on his left foot one more time, then again to his right foot, before I move them both aside.

"Snack?" I ask. He looks at me for a second, then nods.

"Thank you."

"You're welcome." I make us a bowl of popcorn and return to the couch. I set it between us and we share it while we read our books. He seems antsy but doesn't say anything. When the popcorn is gone, I move to put it back in the kitchen. When I come back I sit and Charlie shuffles close to me, then drapes the blanket on the back of the couch over us before we turn the tv on. His head rests on my shoulder as we watch an episode of *Queer Eye*, his soft curls tickling my jaw and cheek, his hands gripping my arm. I tilt my head and press a kiss to his hair.

I want so much more. I want to feel him and know him in

every way possible. I want my fingers in his hair and my lips on his neck, his chest, his hips, leaving my marks on his pale skin. I want to mark him as mine and never let him go. I want to know what he sounds like when he comes. I want to finally see if that gorgeous cock has all the freckles I imagine it does. I want to know what it feels like to have it pressed against me while I bury myself inside him, or to have it in my hand, soft and firm, stroking him while he moans my name. I want him to fall apart at my touch. I want to taste his release in my mouth. I want him more than my next breath.

But it's not just his body I want. I want all of him; his past, his scars, his insecurities, and his demons. I want his future, his dreams, his hopes, and his ambitions. I want to be the one he talks to about his struggles, the one he laughs with, the one he comes to when he is hurting. I want to be the one who encourages and comforts him. I want to be his everything because that is what he is to me. And it scares the shit out of me, because I don't have any right to want those things from him, for so many reasons.

How can someone I didn't even know just three weeks ago suddenly be my whole world? How can I care for him this much? I wasn't supposed to fall for someone again. I wasn't supposed to risk that.

A moment later I hear his soft snores, so I turn the tv off and carry him to bed, tucking him in. I press another kiss to his hair and run my fingers through it. "Goodnight, beautiful boy," I whisper, before leaving the room and closing the door behind me.

That night, sleep won't come to me. I try to ignore my aching cock, but after an hour of lying in bed with a frustratingly painful hard on, I give up and slide my hand into my pajama pants, gripping myself through my boxers. I snap open the fly and moan as soon as my hand comes in contact with my bare length. It's already leaking obscenely and the precum is the perfect lube. God, it feels so good. I haven't done this in ages. I'm surprised I even remember how, but thankfully it's just like riding a bike.

I close my eyes and moan as I move my hand up and down my thick shaft and circle the head.

I tell myself not to think of Charlie while I do, but it's hopeless. The more I try not to think about him the more I inevitably do. His gorgeous smile and incredible laugh, his thick crimson locks, that breathtaking, lithe body, that tight ass, the way his hips sway when he dances. Heck, when he moves at all. God, I'm so gone on him. I hate myself for what I'm thinking, for the things I'm picturing. For the things I want to do to him, the things I want him to do to me.

What the fuck is wrong with me? I can't think these things, envision these things. But I'm so hard, and he's so perfect, and I want him so badly.

I keep stroking as my chest tightens and tears slide down my cheeks. My balls draw up. I can't stop, no matter how much I want to. No matter how much I fucking hate myself. I tell myself it's just a phase. It's just because I haven't had sex in so long. I won't do it again after this. Just this one time and I'll be done. I'll get him out of my system and I'll be good.

My orgasm crashes over me. I come so hard I almost black out, biting my lip to keep from crying out Charlie's name, as my hand fills with my release and slides down my side and onto the sheets. I breathe heavily and I wipe the tears from my eyes.

I'll be fine. It was just this one time. Just this one.

# CHAPTER
## *Ten*

## PAUL

I'm so fucking ashamed. It's been three days since our date and since I jerked off to thoughts of Charlie for the first time, and even though I told myself it wouldn't happen again, it's happened every day since. I've never had such intense orgasms in all my life. Not even when I was making love to Rachel. What does that say about me? One thing's for sure. This isn't a phase. This isn't something I'm going to 'get over' or 'work out of my system.' He's embedded in me like a drug, addictive, painful and irresistible.

Guilt gnaws at me, keeping me awake once again. I run my fingers through my hair and let out a sigh as I lie in bed.

I start when I hear a scream from down the hall that has my body tensing and my heart slamming against my ribcage. I jump out of bed and race for Charlie's room, flinging the door open. I can barely make out his form in the darkness.

"No!" he cries. "Stop! Please!"

I stumble towards him, stepping on clothes and magazines that are strewn across the floor, my hands reaching for the cord on the bedside lamp before I find it and flick it on.

He's whimpering as he tosses and turns, his arms thrashing, sweat beading his brow. "Stop!" he cries again. "I'm sorry!"

I climb onto the bed and reach for him. "Charlie," I say loudly, trying to wake him. He doesn't stop, and his cries make my chest ache. I reach out and grip his arm. He thrashes wildly. "Let go!"

"Charlie, wake up," I urge. "It's me, sweetheart." I shake him, and his eyes fly open, darting around, panicked, before his green irises meet mine in the dim light, his cheeks streaked with tears.

"Papa Bear," he says, his lower lip trembling. The next thing I know, he's scrambling up and into my lap, wrapping his arms around my neck as he settles into me, his body shaking and wracked with sobs. I cradle him, his nose pressed to my neck, his knees bent and his small feet resting on my thigh.

"Shh," I soothe. "You're okay. You're safe, Charlie. I promise." I rub his back and press kisses to his sweat-slicked hair. I stroke the nape of his neck as he nuzzles me with his nose, sending shivers down my spine. "Do you want to talk about it?" I ask. He shakes his head.

I nod and rock back and forth slightly with him in my arms until his trembling lessens.

His chest heaves and he wipes his nose. "S...stay with me?" He stutters. "P...please. I don't want to be alone." Fresh tears fall, and I cradle him closer, my hand gripping the side of his head as it rests against my shoulder.

My poor boy. I can sense how hard it is for him to ask this of me, and I wish it wasn't. I wish he knew he didn't have to face his fears alone and that when I said I wanted him to tell me if he needed anything, I meant anything, including someone to talk to about whatever keeps him up at night. I wish I'd known he was fighting night terrors all along. I'm so thankful I heard him. No wonder he's been so run down and exhausted since he got here. "Of course," I tell him. I press a kiss to his head. I expect him to extract himself from my embrace but he doesn't move, so instead, I lower us both to the bed and he stays wrapped around me, his arm across my torso, his head resting on my chest, his leg slotted in between mine and his nose pressed against my neck. I feel his warm breath on my skin and his tears sliding under the collar of my shirt as I stroke his back and arm simultaneously. His chest rises and falls against me, and with each breath I can feel him relaxing into me. I reach over and grab a tissue from the nightstand and rub his nose and he buries his face in my neck afterwards, flushing. I hold him more tightly and stroke my fingers through his hair once more. My heart aches for him. How could anyone hurt this beautiful boy, this incredible human being with such a compassionate tender soul?

After a moment he does pull away. "I think I'd like to shower," he tells me. "I feel gross."

I nod. "I'll be right here," I promise, and squeeze his hand as he slides out of bed, still a little shaky. He grabs a change of clothes from his dresser before disappearing down the hall, and I take the opportunity to change the sheets so he can come back to a clean, comfortable bed that isn't drenched in sweat.

He's back in the room ten minutes later, wearing pajama pants and a cropped T-shirt, and my heart stutters in my chest as he runs his fingers through his damp red curls. He looks worn, and slightly pale, but when his eyes meet mine, he smiles, and it's so genuine it makes my chest ache. And yet my heart is pounding, knowing he'll be in my arms tonight, his warm body pressed against mine in that adorable outfit, my hands on his bare skin. How am I supposed to keep myself from reacting to that?

He climbs into bed and positions himself just as before, and I wonder if I'll sleep a wink tonight as my arm wraps around him.

"Thank you," I hear him whisper, his breath tickling my ear. The soft snores I hear only moments later are the best sound in the world, and I don't let go because if he wakes again I will be here, right where he needs me.

―――――

When I wake, we're in exactly the same position we fell asleep in the night before. Charlie slept soundly the rest of the night, thank goodness, and honestly I can't remember sleeping better myself. It's been a long time since I shared a bed with someone, and having a warm body wrapped around me, holding someone I care about close, it felt good, right. Why does everything feel so fucking right with him?

He stirs, and I realize I've been carding my fingers through his hair absentmindedly. Then he tilts his head up to look at me and my heart starts pounding because his lips are so full, and pink and—

"Morning, Papa Bear," he says, and gives me that gorgeous smile, his eyelashes fluttering. God, he's so pretty.

"Morning. You sleep okay, after…?"

He nods. His gaze lowers but then his eyes meet mine again. "Thank you, for coming, and for staying."

I stroke his cheek. "Of course. I only wish you had told me sooner what was going on, Charlie. I'm so sorry you're struggling."

He shrugs. "I'm used to it."

"But you don't have to handle it alone. Not anymore. I'm here, okay? And I want to help you. Remember? You were going to tell me if you need something. This counts. Thank you for asking me to stay last night. I want to be here for you. It's okay to ask for help. It's okay to need people. Handling things alone doesn't make you strong, Charlie. And asking for help doesn't make you weak."

Tears fill his eyes again and he nods. I press a kiss to his head and when I look back at him his gaze lowers to my mouth. I suck in a breath and swallow before I pull away and sit up. My cock is hard, my heart is racing, and I'm so fucking scared of what will happen if I stay. What I will do. He can't look at me like that. Shit, I'm shaking. I have to get out of here.

"I'm going to shower," I tell him, my voice sounding anything but steady, though I try. Then I stand and leave the room.

When I get out of the shower I dress and head to the kitchen. Charlie isn't there, or in the living room. I head back to his room, assuming he's still in bed, but he's not there either. Where did he go? I check the backyard but it's void of any sign of him. What the hell?

"Charlie?" I call. There's no answer and the house isn't exactly big. The keys are still on the hook by the door. I pull my phone out and text him.

**Me: where are you?**

*Please be okay.* If anything happened to him I'd never forgive myself.

There's no reply, and after several minutes I start to worry. That's when the front door opens and he steps inside, dressed in his black skater skirt with the roses on it and his black cropped hoodie with the mesh sleeves. His hair is tousled and his cheeks flushed, but I don't think it's from the weather. I tense when he slams the door hard enough the mirror on the wall rattles. His shoes come off next, landing with a thud, and then he's turning and glaring at me.

"Charlie—" I start, moving towards him, but I stop in my tracks, stunned by the words that come out of his mouth.

"Why won't you kiss me?"

"What?" I say after several long seconds. His gaze hasn't wavered and it's unnerving. I'm shaking as he steps closer. My blood is rushing to my ears and my heart pounds against my rib cage.

"Why won't you kiss me?" he repeats, his voice stern. "I know you want to. You've come close half a dozen times but then you don't do it. What are you afraid of?"

"I'm not afraid." My voice is barely a whisper as he steps

118

closer, only inches from me now. How can he not hear how erratic my heartbeat is?

He narrows his eyes and steps closer still, until our chests are almost pressed together. "Yes, you are."

"No, I'm not," I growl back, my voice more steady this time, more firm, though my heart is still racing.

He clenches his fists, his gaze steely, and stomps his foot on the floor like a fucking child. "Then for the love of god, kiss me, damn it!"

His back is against the door seconds later, and he's moaning into my mouth as I pin him in place. He grunts as his fingers card through my hair and I devour him, my tongue sliding down his throat. Oh, Charlie. My Charlie. I can't get enough of him. He's everything. How did I go so long without tasting him? His lips are soft and his hands are everywhere. He's intoxicating. He tastes like strawberries and sunshine and all things sweet. My body is on fire as his hands roam over me, and the most delicious sounds pour from his thick, beautiful lips. I'm drunk on his moans and whimpers.

Fuck. I pull away, breathing heavily, and stare down at him. His pupils are blown wide and his chest rises and falls as he stares at me. His cheeks are flushed and his hair is wild. I fucking love it. He looks amazing like this.

"Wow," he breathes, like he can't believe what just happened. Like he's stunned that I actually did what he told me to. Honestly I'm not sure I can believe it either. I don't know what we're doing, but I do know that now that I've tasted him, I can't stop.

"Satisfied?" I ask, my cock throbbing. Thankfully, he shakes his head.

"Not at all." Then he's pulling me back to him and jumping up, wrapping his legs around me. Fuck yes. I grip his ass with one hand and his neck with the other, my arm around his back as I press him against the door again. Our tongues tangle violently as we suck and moan. I'm so fucking hard. I feel his erection pressed against me and it's fucking delicious. I want him so badly. I need him. I've tried to be good but I just can't do it anymore. And when he speaks again, that's all I need to hear. My lips find his neck and he gasps as I suck on the tender flesh, his head tilted back to grant me access.

"I need you." It's a plea, his eyes so earnest as they meet mine. I pull him away from the door, my cock pulsing with need and my heart pounding, as I carry him down the hall and to my bedroom. Our mouths stay locked on each other's as I lower him to the bed. His legs are still wrapped around me, his skirt falling up around his hips. Why is that so fucking sexy? I don't know, but I do know that I want him in this outfit while I take him.

I lower myself and grind against him and he lets out the sweetest sound. Something between a whine and whimper. It's fucking music to my ears.

His head falls back and his moans and whimpers fill the room as I rut against him, pressing kisses to his neck and jaw. "Papa Bear," he whispers, making me shiver, "yes, oh god, yes, please, more, I need more."

I stand and slide out of my jeans and underwear while he lifts his hips and slides his briefs down and off, tossing them to the floor. His gaze lands on me and it's so intense it makes me shiver. My cock is red and angry and leaking obscenely. I'm almost embarrassed, but when I look back at him I'm utterly speechless. His skirt is pooled around his hips and his gorgeous hard cock is on display for me. He's utterly sinful this way.

He reaches for me, and even though I still have my shirt on, I go to him and kneel between his legs. His dick is perfection. Long, slender, and pale, with a prominent vein running up the center and nestled in a thatch of ginger-colored pubes. He's cut, unlike me. But the best part is the dozens of freckles scattered about. My mouth waters and I want to get it on every single one of them. I want to lick them, suck on them, kiss them. They're so fucking cute. I'm especially fond of the one on the very tip near his slit. The purple and pink head is so pretty, precum leaking out the side and sliding down his shaft. It twitches as I stare at it, and goddamn if that's not the sexiest thing in the entire fucking world. His chest rises and falls, his stomach sinking in.

I surge forward and press my lips to his, kissing him fiercely. He grunts, but kisses me back just as eagerly. I make my way down his neck, to his collarbone, moving his shirt aside, sucking and licking on his skin. He throws his head back and moans.

"Oh, god, yes, please, more," he cries. I lift his shirt and slide my tongue over his taut nipple and he cries out, his back arching. "Fuck, Papa Bear." My body shakes and my cock throbs. Every part of me wants to get my mouth on his cock. I want to press my lips to his bare length, but I can't. I can't have my mouth on him. Not for two and half more months. Not without a condom between us anyway. We have to be extra careful until he gets retested. God this is frustrating. I growl at the thought and suck hard on his nub, making him grip my back and shout.

"Fuck!" He's writhing under me and I can't get enough. That smooth, pale skin that I've wanted to get my mouth on for so long is finally mine. I nip and suck and bite my way down his torso, leaving my marks on him as I go. I blow on his cock when I reach it and he trembles.

"Condom." I don't recognize my own voice when I say it. Charlie's pupils dilate and his cock twitches. Fuck. I've never been this hard in my life, so full of desire for someone else. I reach into the bedside table and pull out two. One for him now, and one for me later. I hand it to him and he tears it open, sliding it down his shaft. The moment he's covered I bury my nose in his groin and inhale. Fuck, his scent is so heady. He gasps and I feel his fingers curling into my hair as I breathe him in, nuzzling his cock, pressing kisses to his hard length and then licking along his shaft as he whimpers and moans, his belly rising and falling. He tries to plant his feet against the bed but it doesn't work. He's falling apart, babbling senselessly as I pleasure him.

"Nggg," is all he manages, and it's so fucking hot, my cock is leaking like crazy. My comforter is going to be a fucking mess when we're done, and I must be losing my mind because I don't fucking care.

I press my lips to his and he melts underneath me.

Then I take him in my hand and stroke him. I've never touched another man's dick, but this feels so right. His cock twitches in my hand and his eyes roll back in his head as he moans for me.

"Yes," he mutters. "Oh, god, yes. Just like that, Papa Bear, so good." I groan as I continue to stroke him, the feel of his rock hard cock in my bare palm is euphoric. The idea of him ejaculating for me, seeing him reach the peak of his pleasure, watching as he comes and his cock pulses, his spunk shooting out of him, watching him lose control, god I want that so much.

I slide my thumb over the slit because I know how much I like it, and he shakes. I press kisses to his jaw and neck, leaving marks there as well.

"More," he begs. "Please. I need you inside me." His brow glistens with sweat and his thighs are trembling. I can't help but have a sense of pride at that, knowing he's falling apart because of me. I plant a few more kisses to his lips, biting down slightly on his plump bottom lip and tugging. He whimpers, and I lick it before giving it another short peck. Then I kiss along his chin, and down his throat, until I reach his Adam's apple. I lick it and he jerks, sucking in a breath. I lick it again, and he trembles. I growl and start to suck and nibble on it, and fuck, he comes undone. His moans and whimpers echo throughout the room as he tilts his head back, whining desperately, his hands gripping the sheets and then my shoulders, his feet pressing against the mattress and then rising, his legs spread, his body shaking uncontrollably. "Shit,

shit, shit," he manages in between his panting and gasping. "Oh god, please, please, please."

Fuck, I have to get inside him. He's driving me insane with want, and need, and lust. I need to feel that tight hole and watch as I give him everything he's asking me for and more. I work my way down his neck, lifting his shirt as I kiss down his chest and abdomen. I press a kiss to his balls and then lick a stripe up his cock. He wines and bucks his hips. I tug on his sack and tears fall down his cheeks. Shit.

"Are you okay?" I ask. He nods.

"Don't stop," he tells me. He shakes his head. "Don't you dare stop."

I take the lube bottle and pop it open. "This is where you'll have to guide me, sweetheart. I really don't know what I'm doing." I know I need to go slow, and I need to stretch him, but I've never been near another guy's hole before. The fact that I want so badly to be buried in his, is telling me I am most definitely not straight. I kind of figured that out when I couldn't stop checking out his ass and wanting to suck on his freckles, though.

He's trembling as he speaks. "Um, just put a fair amount on your fingers and rub it on and around my hole at first, and then slide in slowly, one finger first and then work your way up. I'll let you know if it doesn't feel right, but I have a feeling you'll do fine."

I nod. I squirt the lube on my fingers, probably more than I need, but I figure that's better than not having enough. When I look back at Charlie he's got his legs already spread for me, his hands gripping behind his knees, his chest rising and falling so beautifully, his cheeks flushed. The fact that he's still fully clothed is so fucking hot, and I love seeing his skirt falling over his stomach where I left it after I covered him in my marks.

I let out a breath because he's so eager for me it's amazing. I can't believe he's letting me do this, giving me this precious gift.

"You're sure?" I ask as I grip his knee and slide forward. My knee aches but I do my best to ignore it. I won't let it ruin this moment with him. He nods furiously and spreads his legs wider. His hole flutters and I suck in a breath. So eager. So pretty.

"Please," he begs. My fingers move around the outside of his hole, circling it, and that beautiful little pucker flutters even more wildly, begging for me. I spread the lube around the rim before pressing my finger against it and he throws his head back, moaning. He's absolute perfection. I move my finger in tight, slow circles along the outside of his hole, driving him wild before I slick my fingers up again and then insert one digit slowly into him.

He lets out a slow breath and brings his arms up, one on each side of his head, his eyes closed. "Oh, god, yes," he whines, reveling in the pleasure I'm giving him. "Papa Bear, more, I need more." He's taking it all with no shame, no guilt, just complete and utter abandon. He loves this. My fingers fucking him. And the more sounds he makes, the more I want to give him. I want to hear everything. I want him so desperate for me he can't remember his own name.

I remove my finger and he whines. "Just getting more lube, sweetheart," I tell him. I take a moment to slide a pillow under his hips for better access, then slide my shirt off and toss it to the floor before I squirt more lube on my fingers. Then I'm between his legs again. I lift one leg and drape it over my shoulder, before sliding my lube-slicked fingers inside him, two this time, stretching him wider. I scissor my fingers a couple of times. I slip a third finger in and he jolts, his mouth opening on a silent scream. I panic until he says two words, his head falling back against the pillow, his neck tilted as his eyes close.

"Fuck, yes!" I smile and keep finger-fucking him. His hole is so tight, and so hot around me. His hands are fisted in his sweat-slicked curls and his mouth is parted. Fuck, he comes alive in bed. My finger hits a soft, rubbery area and his body practically convulses with pleasure, his cock twitching like crazy. The amount of precum leaking out of that gorgeous mushroom head is obscene. I know he's close. I have to get inside him.

"Charlie, I—"

"Now," he says. I tear open the second condom and slide it on, then slick my shaft up with lube before positioning myself at his entrance. I breathe out and slowly slide in. Fuck, nothing has ever felt like this before. This intense, this incredible, this fucking good. My eyes roll back into my head as he encases me in his heat. "Oh, god," I groan as I bottom out, my hands gripping his knees. My eyes open in time to see his eyes closed and his mouth parted, a look of absolute bliss on his perfect face.

"Charlie." My voice is unrecognizable, it's so rough. His eyelashes flutter as his eyes open. "I need to move, sweetheart. I'm so hard. You feel so good around me, baby."

He pulls me to him and kisses me languidly as I support myself with my hands on either side of him. His legs wrap around me and I fucking love it. I thrust and he moans. I pull out almost all the way and slide back in. Then pull out a little and back in again. Each time he gives me exactly what I want. A beautiful whimper or soft moan that tells me I'm bringing him pleasure. I thrust again and hit that soft rubbery spot and he cries out.

"Fuck! Yes, Papa Bear, more, please," he begs. His body is sweat-slicked and his lips are swollen and puffy from our kisses. He looks utterly debauched. He moves his legs up and drapes his knees over my shoulders so that he's practically bent in half. The new position gives me such an incredible view of my cock in his hole that I almost come on the spot.

"Fuck," I growl, and thrust harder. "Fuck, Charlie."

He grabs me and pulls me down for another kiss and I fucking let loose. I hit his prostate again and again and he unravels beneath me. Everything about this feels so right. Like this is where he's supposed to be. My precious boy.

"Oh, god," he whimpers, and I know he's close. I'm right there with him. "Yes, yes, please, please, yes, so good."

"Charlie!" I cry and my back arches as cum shoots out of me and fills the condom deep inside him. His hole clenches not a moment later and his condom fills with his release as he throws his neck back on a silent scream. It's so damn sexy I almost cry. Then I'm peppering his face with kisses before I collapse on him, both of us breathing heavily.

I wait for the guilt to overtake me, the shame, the *I just had sex with a man* freak-out. But it never comes. Any of it. He feels right underneath me, around me, in my arms. It feels right to be inside him.

What I do feel is fear. Fear that we don't belong together. That we can never make this work. That whatever this is, it can't last. Fear that I will ruin him like I ruined the other two people I loved most in the world, and in the end I will lose him anyway. Fear that I don't deserve him, and that at some point, sooner or later, he'll wake up and realize that, too.

## CHARLIE

Holy shit. That was amazing. He fucked me so good I saw stars. I have never experienced sex like that before. And to see him unraveled, slamming into me over and over, his muscles taut and his pupils blown wide, sweat beading his brow, it was the fucking hottest thing in the world. He wanted me. I knew he did, and watching him take what he wanted, it was glorious. This man is everything. He's also significantly bigger than me, though, and I'm finding it difficult to breathe with him lying on top of me now.

"Papa Bear," I gasp, "I know I look all tough and muscular but it's just an act. I'm actually quite frail and dainty."

He chuckles and picks himself up. His gaze rakes down my body before his eyes meet mine. "You are perfect," he says. "But I have a feeling that was code for 'get off me.'"

I grin and he slides out of me, lying on his side. I miss the feeling of fullness immediately and want him back. Even in his roughness he was tender and sweet and just as I imagined he would be in bed. He was everything I needed. I knew sex could be good and he proved me right. He wanted me to feel good. Despite his own need, I was his priority and I've never felt so seen.

We dispose of our condoms in the trash can beside us. I slide out of bed and head to the bathroom. Returning with two warm, wet washcloths, I hand him one. We wipe ourselves clean and toss them onto the pile of Paul's clothes. I grin and slide my underwear back on, then climb back onto the bed and roll onto my side, gazing at him. He really is so handsome. I love his flat stomach, and chiseled abs, that adorable outie belly button. I'm gonna get my mouth on it sooner or later and make him moan the way he made me moan. My gaze tracks over his thick gorgeous thighs and the gray hair that dusts his legs and arms. He looks so distinguished, even naked, his thick cock resting against his thigh.

"You okay?" I ask, and his eyes meet mine.

"What are we doing, Charlie?" he asks. His voice is so earnest it makes my chest ache. I swallow.

"Do you regret it?" I'm not sure I want to know the answer but it's too late. He reaches over and strokes my cheek. I rest my hand on top of his. *Please don't take this away from me.*

"No," he tells me, and I believe him. A breath of relief leaves me and I can't help but smile. "Maybe I should," he continues, "but I don't. I don't know what's going on, but I can't stay away from you no matter how hard I try."

I smile wider. "Stop trying." He chuckles.

Despite his words and the fact that we just made love, I sense his hesitancy, and I can't really blame him. We're almost thirty years apart, and we will be judged for it, for what we're doing, for whatever this is. But I've never felt more sure of anything in my life. He makes me feel safe and whole and wanted. He drives away my anxiety and fears like nothing

127

ever has before. I need him. I want him. And I know he wants me. I know we can be good. "We're not wrong." His eyes meet mine. I sit up and throw my leg over him, straddling his hips. "We are not wrong," I repeat as his hands grip my legs and he stares at me, fully naked while I sit astride him. His cock twitches against my thigh.

"All my life I've been told that the things I liked and wanted were wrong. That what made me happy was wrong. Dancing, makeup, nail polish, feminine clothes, boys, and then you came along, and for the first time in my life I had someone tell me that it was okay to like those things, and that I was free to be me. To like the things I liked no matter what anyone else thought or said. To take joy in the things that make me happy. And you, you are the thing in the world that makes me the most happy, makes me feel the most alive. I know this is unconventional, okay? I know you're old enough to be my dad, but I don't fucking care, because you and me, we're right together, somehow, and nothing and nobody will ever convince me otherwise. We are not wrong, Papa Bear. We're not hurting anyone. And we don't owe anyone an explanation. We work, you and me. Maybe we shouldn't, but we do. I won't feel guilty for wanting you. And I wish you wouldn't feel guilty for wanting me."

His chest heaves and his large hand comes around to grip the back of my neck before he's pulling me down and slotting our lips together again. There's no hesitation in this kiss. He's devouring me. His fingers card through my curls, his other hand sliding under my shirt again and up my bare back as his tongue delves into my mouth. I grip his cheeks and kiss him back hungrily.

"Fuck," he breathes, pulling away again. His chest rises and falls, his cheeks flushed. "Why can't I get enough of you?"

"I wouldn't overthink it," I tell him, brushing my nose against his.

"Did I tell you how pretty your cock is?" he says.

I grin as his large, rough hands glide up my almost naked thighs. "I can't remember."

"I may have been wondering whether it had freckles or not, like the rest of you." His gaze meets mine as he squeezes my hips. He smiles and so do I.

"You were wondering that, huh?" He nods, his cheeks turning bright pink. I lean down and kiss him.

"It does," I say, and he smiles.

"It does," he replies.

"You like that?"

He nods. "Very much."

"What else were you wondering?" I wiggle a little bit, brushing our cocks together.

He shivers. "What you taste like."

I grin because the idea of him taking me in his mouth bare is everything. I wish we didn't have to wait so long before we could explore each other without barriers. But there's a chance the chlamydia could come back so we can't take the chance until I'm retested. "You want to taste me?"

"Of course I do." He brushes my cheek with his finger.

I smile and brush my cheek against his. "You'll have to wait a couple of months before you get to do that," I whisper in his ear, and then nibble on it. His breath hitches and I grind against him. "But I promise it'll be worth the wait. I'll let you do whatever you want when the time comes. You can suck, and kiss, and lick to your heart's content. It'll be all yours."

"Charlie," he groans, gripping my ass cheeks and squeezing. I can feel him twitching against me and it's delicious, but if this keeps going we're going to be in trouble. I'm getting harder by the second.

I grin and sit up. I press another kiss to his swollen lips and then slide off of him. He frowns and I laugh. "I have to get ready for work."

"You little brat," he grumbles. I kiss him again before sliding out of bed, but not before he slaps my ass, making me shriek, looking back at him with wide eyes. He grins broadly. "Serves you right."

I stick my tongue out at him and he shakes his head as he climbs out of bed himself.

"Will you be home for dinner?" he asks. I nod. He steps towards me and presses a kiss to my forehead. "I'll make us something, then."

I can't help the smile that spreads across my face. "Thank you." He taps my ass again as I leave the room, and I don't stop smiling the entire time I'm showering and getting ready for work.

———

"Okay, what happened to you?" Dorine asks as we're tying our aprons on, preparing for our shift.

"What do you mean?" I ask, but I know I'm not fooling anyone. I still can't wipe the smile from my face.

"Come on, I haven't seen a smile that big since my daughter's crush asked her to prom."

I blush fiercely but don't say anything. "Nothing, everything's perfectly normal," I lie, grinning from ear to ear.

Her mouth opens and her eyes go wide. "Holy shit, you fucked him!" she whisper shouts.

I wave my hand and shush her and she winces and then clamps a hand over her mouth. "Sorry."

"I didn't fuck him," I tell her.

She frowns.

I grin wider. "He fucked me."

She practically squeals.

I laugh. "Why don't you tell me what you really think?"

Her face splits into a huge grin. "You two are hot together. I'm totally shipping you."

I bite my lip and flush.

"You guys together, then?" she asks, her eyes sparkling.

I shrug.

130

She frowns again. "Charlie?"

I shuffle my foot. "We haven't really defined what we are, and it's okay. I'm good with things the way they are right now." I know I'm falling for him, but I won't tell her that. And I certainly won't tell him that. Not when I'm so afraid he'll ask me to leave if he's not ready for something more, too. Besides, what we have right now is good. It's better than good, and I don't want to ruin it. I'm happy for the first time in my life, and last night, sharing a bed with him, being in his arms, was the first time in a long time I felt safe and at peace. I can't lose that. I won't.

She nods.

We hear a rowdy group of college students come in as the bell above the door rings, and Dorine narrows her eyes. They've been here before and they are never pleasant. Loud, rude, and demanding. The one time they were seated in my section I was getting ogled and flirted with by both the guys and the girls the entire time. I can't be certain because the restaurant was so crowded that day, but I'm pretty sure one of them grabbed my ass.

"This way please," we hear Monica, the hostess, say as she leads the group to their table. She turns and gives me a grimace on her way back, telling me she's sorry. I know she wouldn't have put them in my section if she had any other choice.

I sigh.

"You want me to take them?" Dorine asks.

"No, I can handle it," I tell her.

"Okay. But don't let them treat you like shit." She squeezes my arm and makes her way to her own section, and I head to the table of hell.

"Good afternoon," I say cheerfully, to the group of eight. "What can I get everyone to drink?"

"Oh, so glad you are working today, cutie," one of the guys says, not even trying to hide the fact that he's checking me out. He reaches out to touch my arm, but I step back.

"To drink?" I repeat. He narrows his eyes at me.

"Coffee," he says. I look down the table at his cohorts and get their orders and then scamper away. I know I'll be getting a lousy tip, if any, and that already has me on edge. Just the fact that that guy thought he had any right to touch me pisses me off. I'm not a fucking toy. There's only one man who's allowed to put his hands on me, and he would never mistreat me.

I'm back with the drinks shortly and Dorine helps me because there are so many. "Ready to order?" I ask as she hurries off to her own section. I pull out my pad of paper and pen.

"I know what I want," another guy at the table says, his gaze raking me over. He winks at me and everyone else laughs. My cheeks flame and my jaw clenches but I hold my tongue.

"Oh, I'll have the same," one of the girls jokes. "You up for a three way?" Everyone cackles and I'm shaking now.

"Food." I try to keep my hand steady. "What food do you want, please?"

"Aww, someone's shy," another girl pipes up. "What's the matter, sweetheart, you a virgin?"

"Excuse me," I say, then turn and walk away. I hope I don't get fired for this but I don't care at this point. If there's anything Paul has taught me in the last few weeks, it's that I deserve to be treated with respect, and these idiots are being nothing if not disrespectful, and in a family restaurant, no less.

"Charlie, what's wrong?" Dorine says when she sees me standing behind the counter, shaking.

"I can't do it." I tell her what they said to me and see her momma bear flame to life. She grabs my hand and leads me to our manager's office. We're not in there for more than a minute before he's storming out to the table and demanding they leave, informing them that anyone who treats one of his employees like that will no longer be welcome at Sunny's.

I'm so relieved that I have to hold back my tears. Don is a great guy, but I didn't know he'd go that far for me.

"Thank you," I tell him. "I'm sorry I walked away—"

He shakes his head and rests his hands on my shoulders. He's several inches taller than me with a beer belly and a bald head, but he has the kindest eyes of anyone I've ever met. Well, anyone except my Papa Bear. "You did the right thing, Charlie," he tells me. "I'm sorry that happened to you. I'd have kicked them out the last time if I'd known. Don't worry, okay?"

I nod.

"You okay, or you wanna take the rest of the day off?"

I shake my head. "I'm fine. Thank you."

He nods and slaps my shoulder, then heads back to his office. Dorine gives me an encouraging smile and we get back to work.

When I get home that evening my feet are aching and I just want to crawl into Paul's lap and cuddle on the couch, but I'm also fucking starving.

"Hey," Paul says when I walk into the kitchen. He's holding a pan of what appears to be some sort of casserole in his hands and it smells amazing. I can see the steam rising off of it from here and my mouth waters. And not just from the casserole. He's dressed in gray sweats slung low on his hips and a white T-shirt that clings to his gorgeous upper body. If I had the energy to drool, I would be. "Perfect timing." He smiles at me and my insides melt to goo. As soon as the pan is on the table, I'm across the room and my arms are around him, my head against his chest.

"Woah." His arms come around me, but then he realizes he still has his oven mitts on and tosses them aside before he embraces me again. "You okay?" he asks.

I nod but don't let go. "I missed you."

He chuckles slightly and presses a kiss to my head. "I missed you, too, sweetheart." I sigh against him and feel his half hard dick against my stomach.

133

"Hungry?" he asks. I pull away and nod. He scoots my chair out for me and I smile. He's so damn sweet. I can't get over how he fusses over me sometimes.

"What did you do besides make dinner and look gorgeous while doing it?" I ask as we dig in. The meal is just as amazing as I thought it would be. It's covered in cheese which is my favorite, and there's broccoli, tater tots, ground beef, and what looks like cream of mushroom soup mixed together. It's delicious.

He flushes but shrugs. "Nothing." Surely he did something, but maybe he just doesn't want to tell me? But what on earth wouldn't he want me to know? Hell if it's something kinky I'm down for learning about that. Somehow I have a feeling that isn't it, though. Pity.

"I promise, if you spent the day in bed I won't judge." I grin at him. He gives me a soft smile but doesn't reply. "Porn?" I ask and his eyes go wide. I laugh. "Okay, not porn. You rob a bank? Work on your pole dance routine?"

His eyes widen again and he swallows. "You know about that?"

It takes me a second to realize he's fucking with me and then my face is flushing. "Very funny," I say, and he chuckles as he wipes his mouth off with his napkin.

"Okay, before you start getting really ridiculous I'll tell you."

"Thank you."

He clears his throat. "I cleaned."

I blink. "Cleaned?"

He sighs. "Yes. I dusted the tops of the cabinets, and above the doors, cleaned out the refrigerator, cleaned the washing machine, cleaned out the air vent, organized the hall closet.Then I iced my knee and back because they were killing me."

"Ooh, you're getting me all hot and heavy talking like that," I tease, fanning my face. "Next time you have that much fun you need to include me."

"Shut up." He smirks. "I know its weird, okay, but it actually relaxes me and makes me feel accomplished and—"

"Hey," I interrupt. Honestly I think it's kind of adorable that he spent the day cleaning. "You don't have to explain yourself to me. I like you just the way you are." I reach over and squeeze his hand. He relaxes and gives me that award winning smile.

"Sorry," he says. "At my age I shouldn't still be defending myself. I'm pretty set in my ways and I know that but I don't want to make you uncomfortable here either, Charlie, or make you feel like you have to live up to my standards of cleanliness. This is your home, too. I've gotten used to doing things my way the last five years. Even before that, Rachel was pretty tolerant of my analness. There were chores that I just did on a regular basis and she left them up to me to handle because I was so picky about how they were done. Or that they were done, period. Things that she told me she never would do, like dusting the tops of the cabinets."

I grin and so does he. "Rachel was your wife?"

His eyes widen slightly and he swallows his food before saying, "Oh, yes, sorry, I can't believe I haven't mentioned her this whole time."

I squeeze his hand. "It's okay. We've had a lot going on."

"We realized the first week we were married that changing the sheets on the bed was going to be my job." He grins and takes another bite of food.

"Oh?"

He nods. "I saw her doing it and tried to correct her so she handed them to me and left the room. It was my job from that day on. I did have to get used to letting her load the dishwasher her own way. That was rough. I just couldn't watch while she did it."

I laugh. That sounds just like my Papa Bear. I squeeze his hand. "How long were you married?"

"Nineteen years," he says, a somber note to his voice. His eyes don't meet mine. I don't ask what happened. Something

135

tells me now isn't the time. But, fuck, don't I feel...young. That's as long as I've been alive.

"She's the one in the picture on the mantle?"

He nods.

"And, the boy?" I hope I'm not prying too much, but it seems like a logical progression in the conversation, and I've had the picture staring at me for weeks.

"Our son," he replies. "He passed away five years ago."

Shit. That might explain the divorce. I can't imagine how painful that must have been for both of them. "Fuck, I'm sorry."

"Me, too," he says, and I see the pain in his eyes, even as he attempts a smile.

"I want to hear about your day," he changes the subject. "How was work?"

I tell him about the elderly couple who gave me the amazing tip because I was a "sweetheart and reminded them of their grandson," and he beams at me. His mood sours immediately when I get to the part about the rowdy college students who harassed me.

His nostrils flare and his jaw clenches. I can practically see the veins in his forehead bulging. "Down, Papa Bear."

"Sorry." He visibly relaxes as I stroke his hand with my thumb. I smile.

"I like knowing you disapprove of their behavior," I tell him. "I knew you would. I'm fine, though. It's been taken care of. I have a very good boss."

"I don't like to think of anyone treating you that way."

I bring his large hand up to my lips and brush a kiss over his knuckles. "I know. And that's why these are the only hands I want on me."

His pupils dilate and he sucks in a breath. He wipes his face on his napkin. Then he's scooting out of his chair and pulling me to my feet in one swift motion, taking me in his arms and kissing me like he's starving for my lips.

I grunt and pull back. "Can I take a fifteen minute

raincheck?" I ask. I laugh as he chases my lips. He's so fucking adorable when he's horny. I love that he needs me, wants me.

He growls and fists his cock through his sweats, his eyes flaring. "You're teasing me again."

I smile. "I just want to shower. I feel gross. It'll be worth it. I promise."

He reaches around me and grips my ass cheeks, giving them both a squeeze. I moan as I brush my cheek against his rough stubble. We're both quivering with the need to be near each other. But I can't make out with him when I smell like home fries and BO.

"Fifteen minutes, no more," he tells me. I nod and scurry off. I can't lie, I'm a little disappointed when he doesn't swat me on the ass. I shower and dress in my sweats and a crop top that reads *Woke up gay again*. I don't bother with underwear because I have a feeling I won't need them. I grab two condoms and shove them in the pocket of my sweats before making my way back to the living room. Paul sits on the couch with his legs across the cushions. His glasses are on and there's a book in his hands. I grin when I see that he's already tenting in his pants quite prominently.

My cock twitches in my sweats when his blue eyes lock on me from behind those sexy as fuck frames, and his gaze rakes over me. He lets out a low guttural groan from the back of his throat as he sits up and sets his book aside as I move closer. I can't wipe the smile off my face.

"Come here," he says, his voice sounding like gravel. I stand between his legs and his hands grip my hips as his lips press to my midsection. The second his mouth comes in contact with my bare skin I'm hard. My fingers card through his hair as he lavishes me with kisses, sucking and licking. My eyes roll back in my head as he grips my ass cheeks and squeezes, leaving his marks on me. Fuck, this is hot. Why does the idea of walking around with evidence of his touch on me turn me on so much? My body shakes and a shiver runs down my spine as he pulls me closer to him, running his tongue along my abdomen, moaning as he does, his fingers kneading my bum. He's devouring me. I love it. I grip his hair, my head thrown back, and let him have his way with me. His hands trail up my back, along my sides. My cock is leaking and twitching like crazy.

"Papa Bear," I moan, and he hums. I jerk when I feel his hand gripping my balls through my sweats. He kneads them gently and then he's brushing his cheeks against them like they're silk against his skin. Holy fuck that's hot. Why is that so hot? I squirm as if I'm trying to get away even though I don't want to. It feels so fucking good. I've never had anyone do that before. It's a strange sensation, but I fucking love it. He presses a hand to my ass and holds me to him. His nose nuzzles my groin as he breathes me in. Then he's growling and pressing his lips to my cock in sweet tender kisses that have my knees almost buckling.

"Condom," he says, his voice deep and raspy. When his eyes meet mine they're darker than I've ever seen them before. "I need my mouth on you now."

Shit. I reach in my pocket and pull out the condom. He pulls my sweats down and my cock bobs against my stomach, hard and angry, precum leaking down the sides. I rip the package open and slide the condom down my shaft, my fingers shaking. He doesn't waste a second. He's on his knees in front of me and has my cock in his mouth before I know what's happening. I gasp. The heat and suction is insane. He's not taking me all the way down, but it still feels incredible. I don't have much to go on. I've never actually had a blow job before, though I've given them a million times. But god, this feels good. Maybe it's the sight of him on his knees for me. Maybe it's the sounds he's making, moaning around my cock like he can't get enough of me, or the way he's gripping my ass as he devours me. I just know I fucking love it. He takes the tip in his mouth and sucks, and I shake. His tongue slides around the head, and I groan as my fingers bury themselves in his hair. Then I'm trembling when his tongue finds its way into the sensitive slit.

"Fuck," I whine. He pops off and stands, pulling me to him in a fierce kiss. My cock is aching and I want his mouth back on it right fucking now. I whimper into his mouth and reach down to stroke myself but he bats my hand away.

"No," he tells me. Then he's sliding his pants and briefs down. He steps out of them, and since I never did, I do the same. He slides his shirt up and off and I watch as it lands on the floor. He's buck ass naked in the middle of the living room, his cock standing at attention just for me. Then he's wrapping his arm around me and pulling me to him. I gasp as our bodies collide. The friction of our cocks coming together is enough to drive me wild, even with the barrier of the condom. "I want to feel you against me as much as possible, sweetheart." His mouth descends on mine again and his large hand grips us both. Once he realizes that I'm having to stand on tip toe to keep us both level, he stoops and picks me up. I wrap my legs around him, and he presses me against the wall as he strokes us both in tandem. His hand grips my neck as his mouth plunders mine and his body keeps me firmly against the wall.

I try to speak. To tell him how incredible it feels to have his hand on me, his cock rubbing against mine, but all I manage is whimpering and whining into his mouth as his tongue delves inside me, his hand gripping us both and stroking as I come apart at his touch.

I try to tell him I'm close, but I can't get the words out. My whines and whimpers grow louder. I grip his hair, kissing him harder. He moans in my mouth and I spasm as my release fills the condom, my body shaking. I almost cry when I feel his warmth through the condom and against my stomach, the way his body tenses, the way he presses closer to me as he climaxes. He breathes heavily against my neck and I hold him close, pressing kisses to his jaw and ear, and cheek.

He steps back, and I land on my feet as a trail of his cum

follows him, dripping to the floor, the rest stuck to both of our stomachs. I grin and he frowns.

"Damn it," he says.

"That's hot," I say at the same time. He smirks at me. "I'll clean it," I tell him, then step forward and press a kiss to his lips. "You get cleaned up."

He smiles at me and heads to the bathroom. I take off the condom and wash myself off in the kitchen and slide my pants back on, then clean up the cum on the floor, not without a smile on my face. I'd rather plant a flag there and label it, but oh well.

He's back out in the living room a moment later and grinning, his cheeks pink. He sits on the couch and pats the spot next to him. I hurry over and sit down, raising my feet and planting them on his lap. He laughs when I wiggle my toes.

"Want something?"

I grin. "They miss you. Especially your kisses."

He takes my foot in his hand and massages it. It feels divine, just like it did the first time. He presses soft kisses to my toes and I can't help smiling. Why do I love that so much? I don't know, but it gives me butterflies every damn time.

After rubbing my feet, he lies down on the floor and I rub his back. Then he's back on the couch and I lie on top of him as he holds me, carding his fingers through my hair.

"Was I okay?" he asks, and it takes me a moment to process that he's talking at all because I'm so close to falling asleep, safe and comfortable with the blanket draped over us and his warm, firm body underneath me, the sound of his heartbeat lulling me to sleep.

"Hmm?"

"Was I okay?" he asks again. I tilt my head up so that my gaze meets his. I'm surprised by the genuine concern in his eyes, but I do my best to alleviate his fears. I press a soft kiss to his lips and brush my fingers through his hair. God, I love his hair. So fucking thick. And honestly, the gray is stinking hot. At least on him it is.

"Perfect," I tell him, my eyes half lidded. Then my head is back on his chest. He chuckles slightly.

"Either I was good enough I wore you out, or you're tired enough you don't know the difference."

I laugh slightly. "You were wonderful, old man," I say. "I've never had a blow job before, so that was my first."

"What?" he says, and I can tell he's surprised. I lift my head again and rest my chin on my hands.

"I had a boyfriend in high school," I tell him. "Well, sort of boyfriend. I thought that's what he was. We fooled around a lot. I blew him all the time, and for some reason it never really occurred to me that he didn't reciprocate, maybe because I actually liked doing it so much I didn't ask him to, or question it. He was my first everything really, first kiss, first…" I trail off and Paul nods in understanding.

"Anyway, that experience was…unpleasant, to say the least. I didn't really know what to expect, but I guess I thought I would enjoy it, and I didn't, at all. It hurt, a lot, and when I told him, he said it was supposed to hurt the first time, so I sucked it up. The pain let up, but I could just tell he wasn't in it for me, or even for both of us. It was about him. He didn't care how I felt, physically or emotionally. It put me off sex for a long time and I didn't want to bottom again, especially. But then when I ended up on the streets, there were times I didn't have a choice." I sigh. "Anyway, he kept pressuring me. I told him no, and when he wouldn't leave me alone I broke it off with him. That's when he told me we were never dating in the first place and he was just using me to figure things out. Then he ratted me out to my parents to get back at me. After that I spent two years living under their roof with them knowing I was gay and being mistreated for it. They made my life a living hell from that moment on, and there wasn't a day that went by that they didn't look at me like I disgusted them." I sit up now, my chest heaving as tears slide down my cheeks. Fuck, I didn't mean to say all that, but it just came tumbling out of me.

"Charlie," Paul says, bringing me back down to him. He holds me tightly as I sob. "I'm so sorry, baby. It's okay to cry. It's okay to be sad and angry. Whatever you feel, it's okay. I'm here, and you can tell me anything. I promise, I'm not going anywhere."

"You didn't sign up for all of this," I blubber.

"I'm not afraid of your pain, Charlie," he tells me. "I can handle your hurt, sweetheart. Whatever you want to tell me, whatever you need to tell me. I will listen. I can't promise to have the answers, but I'll do my best to just be here. I told you to tell me what you need. If you need to cry, or scream, or rage, or talk, I'm here. I'm so sorry I didn't realize you were having nightmares sooner. I knew you were tired, I just, I don't know, I didn't ask about it because I wanted to give you your privacy. But if you're hurting, or scared, I want you to come to me, baby."

Can he be real? No one is this perfect, this good, this wonderful. No one could see all this and ask to keep it. I nod but then my gaze lowers and I ask, "You don't think I'm a fucking whore?"

"What?" he says, his voice stern. "Hey, look at me." I do but it's incredibly hard. My lower lip trembles and my chest heaves as tears slide down my cheeks.

"I think you are one of the bravest people I have ever met, and you did what you had to do to survive, Charlie. I will never think less of you for the choices you had to make." He takes my chin in his thumb and forefinger. "Hear me?" I sniffle and nod. "Good."

I lie back down with my head against his chest and he cards his fingers through my hair. "The nightmares, are they about your parents?" he asks. I nod.

"And my time on the streets," I admit, "but mostly my parents. If you can believe it, that was actually worse." He squeezes me tightly and presses a kiss to my hair.

"Can I ask you something?" he says, and I nod again. "What made you trust me enough to bottom with me?"

142

I tell him the truth. "You've done everything to show me that you care about me. I've never doubted that from the moment I walked through your door. My wellbeing was always your top priority. I knew you would be different. I wanted you. I needed you." My eyes flick over his face.

"It was my pleasure," he tells me. And I believe him. "You're an amazing person, Charlie Morrison. Everything about you is incredible. Your heart, and your courage, your strength, and resilience. The amount of love and light you have left in your soul after everything you've been through. I'm in awe of who you are."

Tears slide down my cheeks as I press my lips to his and kiss him tenderly. He has no idea what those words mean to me. I'm not sure I believe them, but they still matter. Especially coming from him. If someone as incredible as him can find something amazing in me, then I must be loveable and worthy. I must be good, despite what my parents told me.

# CHAPTER
*Eleven*

## PAUL

A week later, I wake before Charlie so that I can surprise him with breakfast in bed. I make coffee, waffles with all the fixings like I know he loves, pour him some orange juice and set everything on a tray along with an envelope with his name on it and a single red rose. Today is no special day for the rest of the world. It happens to be mid October. But for Charlie and I, it's a month since he first moved in, and I guess this is my way of celebrating.

He hasn't slept in his own bed since the morning we fucked. I couldn't let him sleep alone after knowing about his nightmares, or after the intimate moments we'd shared. He's so much more to me than a casual fuck and I even though I can't understand it, he wants me close to him. He needs me. And fuck, I need him.

He's had a few more nightmares since then. I've woken up to his cries, his screams, him drenched in sweat, tears sliding down his cheeks. I take him into my arms each time. I hold him, kiss him, offer him my assurances of safety. I ask if he wants to talk about it. Sometimes he does, and we lie awake for minutes, or hours, while he tells me with tears sliding down his cheeks, his body trembling, about the physical, verbal and emotional abuse both of his parents put him through for years, just for being him. And I can't believe he survived in that house for as long as he did. My beautiful boy. Every part of me wants to drive over there and wring their fucking necks for the things he's telling me they said and did to him. I listen, and wipe his tears away. Sometimes I hold him and he drifts back to sleep. Sometimes I kiss him until I hear his soft snores again. Sometimes I pleasure him in whatever way he asks me to. But always, always I'm there.

I enter the room and place the tray on the nightstand next to his side of the bed. He has the blankets pulled up over his shoulders and chin as he sleeps, and the only part of him I can see is his nose, eyes, and unruly red waves. I can't wait to see those gorgeous green irises looking back at me and hear that snarky sass that is so very Charlie. I can't wait to see that bright smile that has become so very quickly my favorite part of being alive.

My heart swells with affection and fondness for this beautiful young man. I can't believe how lucky I am to have him in my life. I know I don't deserve him, but for some crazy reason, for this moment in time at least, he's chosen me.

I lean over and press a kiss to his head and then whisper in his ear. "Rise and shine, beautiful."

He groans and burrows under the covers. It's not exactly the romantic wake up call I envisioned but I guess that's real life for you. I sit on the side of the bed and sigh. "I guess I'll just have to eat all this delicious food myself then. It's too bad, really. This waffle looks amazing."

He stirs and his head peeks out from under the covers, one eye opening. He glares at me as I move to put a bite in my mouth. "If that touches your tongue my cock won't be for a week," he threatens, sitting up. I laugh.

"I think that would punish you, too," I point out.

"Shut up, I'm not thinking clearly. I'm tired." His eyes light up when he sees the rose and envelope. "Oooh, presents." I laugh again as he snatches the fork from me and shoves the waffle in his mouth, then reaches for the envelope, tearing it open. He swallows too soon and I don't know if the tears filling his eyes are actual tears or because he's choking.

"You...you got us mani/pedis?" he says, staring at me in shock. I nod. The next thing I know I'm on my back and Charlie is on top of me, planting kisses on my face. I can't stop laughing.

"You're amazing," he tells me, then sits up, kneeling on the bed next to me. "What's this for?"

I flush and rub the back of my neck. I hope I'm not making a bigger deal out of this than I should be. "It's been a month."

His eyes widen. "It has. Oh, are we celebrating?"

"I kinda figured we could. Unless you don't plan to stay." My heart starts to beat frantically. I guess I kind of assumed that after everything, he would be staying, but maybe I shouldn't have?

"I might have to think about it." His eyes twinkle.

I frown and he laughs. Then he's on his back as I tickle him, and he squirms and shrieks. I press kisses to his jaw and neck and then blow raspberries on his belly button as he cackles.

"Okay, okay, I'm staying," he tells me. "I promise."

"There now, was that so hard?" I ask, smiling at him. God, I'm so captivated by him as he smiles up at me, his chest rising and falling, his stomach sinking in as he catches his breath. He's so pretty and vibrant and wonderful. I feel like I not only have a lover, but a best friend again, someone who understands me and cares for me, someone I can laugh with, and it's the best medicine. My chest constricts and I have to keep myself from being overcome by my emotions. Shit. I'm so fucking crazy about him, and I want to keep him so badly, but what will happen when he finds out the truth about me?

"Waffle," I say, gesturing to the food. "Eat before it gets cold."

"Yes, sir," he says, and salutes me, a mock serious expression on his face. I kiss him and then we eat together, after which I take our trays and return them to the kitchen.

"Shower with me?" I ask him, poking my head in the bedroom door. He smiles and jumps off the bed. We make our way to the bathroom and strip. We decided to keep condoms and lube in the bathroom to make things easier and we've used them a few times already. The other day we had a bath together and it was wonderful. We lit candles and had bubbles, and soft music playing. I sat with Charlie resting between my legs. It was intimate and relaxing, and absolutely perfect. It ended with my giving him a handjob that was out of this world. I still can't get the image or the sounds he made out of my head. The way he reached back and gripped my neck, the way he moaned "Papa Bear", the bruises his fingers left on my thigh. I love pleasuring him, and finding new ways to do it is one of my favorite things.

It seems like we've fucked in every possible way this past week. I've taken him on the kitchen table, which I never thought I would do, given my penchant for cleanliness, but Charlie makes me crazy and I can't help myself when it comes to him. I did wipe it down thoroughly afterwards while Charlie laughed. I've blown him in the hallway, the kitchen, and fucked him countless times in bed, and I've loved it every single time. Sex with Charlie is my new favorite hobby. To say I crave him is an understatement.

I grab the bottle of lube once we've stepped under the water. His eyes widen and his cock perks up. "May I?" I ask.

He nods and turns around, jutting his perfect little ass out for me. Fuck, yes. I love it when he presents himself to me, like I fucking own him. He's mine. All mine. I slick my fingers up with lube and slide one digit into his tight hole, moaning as I do. Heat surrounds my finger as I move inside him, stretching him, his hands resting against the shower wall. He moans so loudly I almost wish there were someone else in the house to hear him, to know what I do to him.

"Love the sounds you make, sweetheart," I croon, and he comes alive. I've learned pretty quickly how much Charlie thrives on praise, in and out of the bedroom. And I love praising my boy. His cries become even louder as I insert a second finger and he shoves his ass back against me, his head bowed, the water cascading down his back. I press kisses to his spine and watch as he shivers under my touch, his legs spread. I reach lower and grip his balls, giving them a tug. He mewls and I scissor my fingers, making him gasp and cry out, his body shaking.

"Oh, god," he whimpers. I press my cock against his backside and it's fucking glorious. No condom. Just skin on fucking skin.

"Lube," I tell him. He's so far gone he barely registers my words but he grabs it and then gazes at me, his head resting against the shower wall and his eyes half lidded. "Touch yourself, sweetheart." He squirts the lube into his hand and begins to stroke himself while I insert yet another finger inside his hole.

He spreads even wider, one hand braced against the shower wall, the other gripping his cock as I peg his prostate over and over with my fingers. "Fuck, yes, Papa Bear," he whines.

"You're so pretty, Charlie," I tell him. "You feel amazing sweetheart. I love this hole, baby. Love your ass. Love hearing you fall apart for me."

"Fuck, that feels so good," he whines. "Right there. Right there. Don't stop. Yes. Yes. I'm so close."

"That's it, baby," I tell him, pressing my erection against his ass so he can feel what he does to me, my hand wrapped around him and resting against his abdomen to keep him steady. I move my hand up and grip his throat gently, then whisper in his ear, "Come pretty for me, sweetheart." He explodes, his head falling back against my shoulder as his orgasm races through him, his hole clenching beautifully around my fingers. I reach up and cover his mouth to keep the water from falling into it as he howls. I growl in approval as he shakes with the aftershocks of his release.

He stays in my arms as I wash him, planting gentle kisses against his bare skin and reviving him. Then he turns me around and strokes me from behind until I'm spraying all over his hand and my stomach before he does the same for me.

We dress and head to the salon. Charlie is so fucking cute in his white skinny jeans with holes in the knees and a cropped T-shirt that reads *I'm A Delight* across the front. He's been experimenting more with his makeup. He went simple today, just eye makeup and lip gloss, but it's amazing. He wears a deep green eyeshadow, and the mascara and eyeliner around his eyes make them pop. On his lips is a red shimmering gloss. God he's gorgeous. His hair has gotten slightly longer too, which makes him look even more stunning.

I'm not going to lie, the salon experience is a new one for me. I've never stepped foot in a salon before, other than when I went to get the gift card. But it seemed like something Charlie would love, and I wanted to share the experience with him. I guess it shouldn't surprise me when he tells me he's never done this before either. He says he tried nail polish once after the incident in the second grade, and it didn't go well when he forgot to take it off before he got home. I don't ask for details but I have a pretty good idea of what "not well" means.

Well, today my precious boy gets to indulge and have his nails done however he wants, with no one telling him he's wrong or making him worry that he'll get abused for it later, because he's mine, and I will always keep him safe. I will always let him be himself.

When we get inside, the woman behind the counter smiles at us and gestures for us to sit in the chairs for the pedicures. While I'm a little nervous, Charlie is practically beaming. He's taking in this whole experience and it's making any amount of anxiety I'm feeling absolutely worth it.

We take seats next to each other and I can't help relaxing into mine. It's insanely comfortable, and I get even more excited when I realize I can get a massage while they do my toes. Charlie starts pressing all the buttons and lets out a little "ooh" sound when it starts massaging his ass. I can't help laughing.

"Thought you got enough of that before we got here," I tell him, and he gapes at me. I flush but can't help smiling.

"Please choose your colors," the woman says as she comes over with samples of polish. There's another lady with her, this one quite a bit younger. The younger one sits in front of Charlie as he peruses his options.

"Is it okay if I don't get a color?" I ask.

"Of course," the older lady replies. "We can do just the treatment." I nod. That sounds perfect.

Charlie lets out another "oooh" when he finds a color he likes and shows the young lady. "That one," he says. He shows it to me and I smile. It's a deep green with silver sparkles that matches his eyeshadow. It's perfect. I smile at him and he beams at me. There's a part of me that wants to kiss him, but we're too far apart.

The young woman smiles and nods. "Good choice. It will be lovely on you. Same for your fingers?"

"Yes, please," Charlie says. He turns back to me. "Thank you."

"My pleasure," I say, reaching over to take his hand.

———

I'm lying on my back on the couch and Charlie is on top of me. We haven't stopped kissing since we got home. After our mani/pedis we went out for lunch. Then we did a little bit of window shopping. We held hands the entire time. He was bummed about the fact that his Keds hide his newly painted toes, but at least he got to show off his fingernails.

He's been smiling all day and I can't get enough of it. My

hands rest on his bare back as his lips slide against mine over and over. My jaw is sore but I can't stop kissing him. He's fucking addictive. We're both hard but we're not taking things further right now. This is enough.

I hum as his fingers run through my hair. He smiles down at me as he pulls away, his hands resting on either side of my head.

"Thank you for today. It was perfect."

"You're perfect," I tell him, and he shakes his head at me fondly before sitting up and straddling me.

"You know there's a couple of things we need to talk about now that you're staying for sure," I tell him, my hands resting on his thighs.

He grins. "Getting my GED, and what was the other one again?" He puts his perfectly manicured finger to his lips and gives a mock quizzical expression, but I know damn well he knows what I mean. Little shit. I slap his ass and he chuckles, then leans down and presses a tender kiss to my lips again, humming into my mouth.

"Is there something you want to see me in?" he asks, brushing his cheek against mine.

I slide my hands inside his pants and under his briefs so that I come in contact with his bare ass cheeks. I stroke them with my thumbs and my cock thickens. "You know what I want, you little brat." I nibble on his ear and he chuckles.

"I want to hear you say it." He sits up, his back arched and his ass jutting out to fill my palms. I squeeze it. Damn, it feels good. A pair of silk panties against the back of my hands would feel even better.

"I want to buy you some panties," I tell him, and he grins so big he looks like the fucking cheshire cat. I knead his ass cheeks even more, and he pushes his ass back into my hands, chasing the feeling. "You'd be so gorgeous in lace, Charlie, or satin, or silk. I want to see it all on you, and feel it, on my hands, against my thighs, and my balls, and my cock. I want

151

it against my lips when I kiss your cock and feel you hard against me."

His eyes darken and his pupils dilate. "Fuck, Papa Bear, you've got a dirty mouth." He grips his cock through his jeans and squeezes and I suck in a breath.

"Wanna do some shopping?" I ask. He nods and slides off of me. After he asks me where I got the lacy thong he wore on our dinner date, I admit rather sheepishly that it came from Amazon, and while it wasn't my first choice, I was on a bit of a time constraint. Prime shipping for the win. However, this time I'd rather find a site that is tailored to men's lingerie, even if it means we have to wait. He grins and kisses my cheek, and we navigate to a site that excites us both.

After browsing for some gorgeous panties in different styles, fabrics, and colors, and adding several to our cart, we're both so fucking horny that we end up trading blow jobs.

I can't wait for the panties to get here. It'll be a week, since it's not Amazon, but I'll survive. Until then I'll just have to picture Charlie in them. My favorites were a deep purple pair with sheer lace in the back that will showcase his gorgeous buttcheeks, and satin in the front with a cute bow at the top. God, he'll be so sexy. The hardest part will be wanting to leave them on and rip them off at the same time. He's also getting a black satin string bikini, a deep blue silk thong, and a couple of floral designs that will look amazing on him as well.

After exchanging blow jobs, we look more into the GED. Charlie seems pretty excited about it, and he has saved up almost all of the money he's earned since he started his job. I've insisted that he spend some on himself and he's tried to pay me back for the phone bill, clothes and medical expenses but I've had none of it.

We sign him up for online classes that he can do on his own time, and he can start whenever he's ready. It shouldn't take more than a few months, so hopefully by the end of

January he'll have his certificate. I know he can do it. He's smart and determined.

"One more thing," I tell him once we've gotten that accomplished. "I still want to get you a car. It's getting colder out and I don't like the idea of you on that bike."

He smiles at me. "I'm okay with that, if you let me pay for the gas and the upkeep as much as I can. I want to share in the expenses around here."

"Then let's go car shopping together after I get off work tomorrow, and hopefully we can find you something."

He smiles at me and we head into the kitchen to make dinner together.

Car shopping the next day is interesting. After the first two dealerships make comments about us being father and son and we have to correct them, even though we walked in holding hands, we decide to forgo the hand-holding. We still haven't discussed exactly what it is we're doing or what we are to each other. I know we should. He deserves to know what he means to me, but I'm terrified of what defining our relationship will entail. I've stayed single this long for a reason, and I can't bear to let Charlie down.

At least at the end of the day we come home successful. We found a decent used Honda Civic in a deep blue color that Charlie loves. It's got around seventy thousand miles on it, but it'll work for taking him back and forth to work, and I won't have to wait up until midnight to pick him up when he has the later shift and then be up for work at six am. It's really a win-win.

After dinner, we settle on the sofa, and Charlie props his feet up on my lap again. It's become a nightly thing for him to ask for foot rubs (and kisses). Who knew that when I started doing it spontaneously it would become one of his favorite things. I love that we can trade massages. His back rubs are heaven and always make me feel better. And not just because half the time now they lead to more.

I take his foot in my hand as *You've Got Mail* plays in the background, and rub it. He's stretched out with his arm behind his head, dressed in what appear to be puffy harem pants, though he tells me they are yoga pants, and a white cotton, cropped camisole. I don't care what the fuck you call them as long as I get to see him in them, cuz they're sexy as fuck. He laughs at the movie. I press a kiss to his toes, partly because I know he's waiting for it and partly because I love hearing his laugh and seeing him happy, and I want to shower him with affection. I watch his face and he grins at me, wiggling his toes, his way of asking for more. I press more kisses to his toes before I do something I haven't done yet, but have been dying to do. I take his toes in my mouth and suck on them. His foot jerks, but he makes a pleased sound. I look at him and his eyes are lidded, his cheeks flushed. His cock is half hard and getting harder as I continue to suck and lick. It's not his cock, but it's still fucking addictive. I love having his toes in my mouth just like I knew I would.

"Fuck, Papa Bear," he groans, his back arching. I see his dick twitch in his pants. "Why does that feel so good?"

I take his other foot in my hands and press kisses to his toes as I massage it, then suck them into my mouth, and his eyes close as he moans. He's fully hard now, and the sight of his gorgeous hard cock in those pants is driving me insane.

"Fuck, that's good," he moans. I watch as he slides his hand down his abdomen, under the ruched waistband of his pants, and begins to stroke himself. Fuck, this is hot. I can't believe I'm turning him on this much. My own cock is throbbing, and I slide off the sofa and onto my knees as I continue to work his toes into my mouth, moaning around them. He's stroking himself harder, his hips undulating and his back arching, desperate whines pouring from his lips now.

"Charlie," I growl around his toes. I slide my tongue between two of them and he lets out a sound that is somewhere between a wail and a gasp. It's fucking everything, and my cock goes crazy, precum leaking down the shaft as it twitches obscenely. He opens his eyes in time to see me on my knees, my zipper undone and my hand working my length. My head is red and angry and I'm so damn hard.

"Fuck, yes," he breathes, and jerks his pants down so that only his underwear covers his cock. His head falls back again, his eyes closing once more, and we jack ourselves as I lick and suck on his adorable, precious toes. I keep sliding my tongue between his toes because he goes insane when I do, his body jerking and spasming like crazy. I have to grip his foot to keep him from pulling away. He's whining and his chest is rising and falling as sweat beads his forehead, his stomach sinking in.

"Shit," he cries. I let go of my aching dick so I can take both of his feet in my hands, and when I've got them in my mouth at the same time he falls apart. His body shakes as his head falls back, his mouth open, and I watch as a glorious pool of cum floods his underwear.

"Roll over," I rasp, and he does without question. I know I'll regret the cum stains later but right now I'm too fucking horny to care. I kneel over him and jack myself until I'm crying out and spraying all over his back. Then I reach over and grab a tissue, wiping my release from him, before I collapse back on the couch.

He turns and climbs on top of me and I wrap my arms around him.

"What the fuck was that?" he asks, as I run my fingers through his curls.

"I don't know," I say. "But I liked it. A lot. Apparently I have a toe kink."

"Apparently we both do." He chuckles.

———

That night, Charlie wakes up to another nightmare. It takes me so long to wake him, and he's so beside himself, trembling and tears streaking his cheeks, that I'm crying while I hold

155

him. I keep telling him to breathe in and out because he's having a panic attack, and his arms are wrapped around me so tightly I can barely breathe.

Tears slide down my cheeks as I hold him close and rock him, my cheek pressed to his head. "I'm so sorry, sweetheart," I tell him. "You deserved so much better. They failed you, Charlie. It was their job to love you, and they didn't. I'm so sorry. You are exquisite, just the way you are, and there is nothing about you that needs to change, or isn't good enough."

"I had to leave," he sobs. "I couldn't stay. They hurt me. I couldn't stay." He shakes his head furiously, his curls slapping me in the face.

"Shh, I know," I tell him. "I know. You're safe, Charlie. It's okay. I will never hurt you."

He cries himself to sleep in my arms and I don't let go for the rest of the night.

————

The following week is my monthly get together with Rachel. Charlie's staying at home. I don't think it's time for them to meet, but I'd like to talk to her about bringing him to the wedding.

I let out a deep breath when I see her through the window of our regular restaurant. Her hair is down today and falling over her shoulders. She wears a light gray jacket over a green sweater, and jeans. Silver earrings dangle from her ears. I see her fiancé, Colin, get up from across the booth and kiss her, then walk away.

"Hey," I say, once I reach her. She stands and presses a kiss to my cheek, smiling at me.

"It's good to see you." She holds my hands, her eyes studying me. "You look different," she says. "Happier."

I can't help my smile.

She gasps and covers her mouth with her hand. "Did you

meet someone?" Her eyes go wide and her face lights up. She wraps her arms around me in a hug before I can even answer. "Tell me everything." She sits down and gestures for me to do the same, her elbows resting on the table. She leans forward in anticipation. "What's her name? Where did you guys meet? And when do I get to meet her?" Her smile is endless but I shake my head.

"Listen, it's not what you think." I look at her and she frowns. "I wanted to talk to you about something else. You remember I was telling you last month about the young man I was trying to help?"

She raises her eyebrow. "The homeless kid?"

I nod, my skin prickling. For some reason it unsettles me to hear someone refer to Charlie that way. Like he's nothing more than a piece of street trash. Like being homeless defines him. I know she doesn't mean it like that, but it ruffles my feathers nonetheless. "His name is Charlie," I tell her. "And he's been living with me for the last month." Her eyes widen. She sets her coffee down and stares at me.

"How's that going?"

"Good," I say, a smile on my face. I can't help it, talking about Charlie. "Actually, I was wondering if I could bring him to the wedding."

She blinks.

"Look, Rach, I know it's a bit of an inconvenience, but I can't leave him home alone. He's honestly the sweetest person you'll ever meet and he's had a rough time of it. His parents were assholes and I think he'd love it. Please think about it."

Her gaze softens and she studies me for a moment. "Seems like you really care about him."

"Yeah, I guess you could say that." I can't stop smiling as I run a hand through my hair, and I realize what a mistake I've made when her face pales.

"Shit," she whispers. "Tell me you're not fucking him."

My face heats and I open my mouth to reply, but then close it again, because I have nothing to say.

"Jesus Christ, Paul," she hisses, leaning closer to me, her gaze fierce. "He's a kid."

"He's not a kid." I glare at her. "He's nineteen."

Her eyes get even bigger. "Fuck, Paul, that's younger than Trey would be if he was alive. Do you have any idea how that looks? How messed up that is?" Her eyes start to fill with tears. "What's gotten into you? I understand that you're hurting, but this is—"

"I don't give a shit how it looks," I snarl. "He's not some form of messed up therapy, Rachel. He's the best thing that has happened to me since I lost you two. We aren't doing anything wrong by being together." I glare at her and move to stand. "You know what I love about this whole thing? You're excited and happy for me to be in a relationship again as long as it fits your heteronormative standards of what that relationship should look like. A five-four curvy brunette who probably works at a bank and has a teenage kid or two. And you're judging Charlie without having even met him yet. What is acceptable to you? A three year age difference? Six? Twelve? How many years is too many? What number is acceptable until I have to tell the man I want to be with that I can't be because of our ages, even though he's my best friend and he's made me feel like life is actually worth living again?"

I take a breath and then say slightly more calmly but just as firmly, "You know the hardest part of all of this is trying to convince myself that I have any right to care for him the way that I do, especially after all the bullshit we put Trey through. Yet for some crazy mixed up reason, he wants me, too. And I've been miserable long enough, so yeah, I'm fucking a nineteen-year-old, because he makes me happy. And for the first time in a long ass time I'm letting myself be happy, and I don't need your approval or your permission."

"Paul," she calls, but I ignore her and make my way out of

the restaurant. I want to be at home right now, with Charlie. I want his arms around me and his body against mine. I need him right now. The longer I have to wait to have him the more my body aches for him.

## CHARLIE

I worked until midnight last night, and thank god I have today off and so does Paul. So as soon as he gets back from his lunch date with Rachel we can spend the day together. He explained that they have lunch together every month, and not only that but that she's getting re-married soon and he's the one walking her down the aisle. I guess our current situation isn't the only thing in his life that's a bit unusual. I'd rather he have an ex-wife that's a friend, though, than one he can't stand. It's good for him. He needs friends. I'm hoping their get-together goes well.

I showered this morning and dressed in my skater skirt with the black and white stripes on it and my cropped black hoodie with the mesh sleeves. The best part, though, is that my panties came yesterday, and underneath my skirt are the dark purple ones that Paul wanted me to get so badly he practically came on the spot while we were shopping. I can't fucking wait until he sees me in them. My ass has never looked better, if I do say so myself.

I start from my spot on the couch when I hear the front door opening, and then Paul's deep voice saying my name.

I stand as he enters the room. He gives me a soft smile, but the fact that he's home so early, and the way his shoulders are slumped tells me his date didn't go so well.

"Is everything okay?" I ask. He reaches me and presses a kiss to my forehead. Then he takes my hand and pulls me to the couch. He sits and I straddle him.

"It is now. Missed you." He nuzzles my neck with his nose and breathes me in.

I chuckle. "It was less than an hour." I sift my fingers through his hair. "How was it?"

He sighs. "It could have gone better."

"I'm sorry."

He tightens his arms around me and I rest my forehead against his. "I just want to hold you."

"Here I am." I give him a soft smile.

He smiles back at me and presses his lips to mine in a gentle kiss before looking me over just like he did before he left. He hums. "God, I like this outfit."

I grin. "You like all of my outfits." He flushes adorably and I kiss him. "I made a little adjustment to it. You wanna see?" He raises an eyebrow at me and I stand, then I lower the zipper on my skirt. It falls to the floor, pooling at my feet. His eyes go wide and he scoots forward on the couch, sucking in a breath. I'm rock hard already and the panties barely contain my erection.

"Charlie," he half growls, half whispers. Then his hands are on my hips, and he's pulling me back onto his lap. I straddle him once more and we kiss fiercely, our mouths exploring each other, our tongues tangling. His hands find their way into the back of my panties, and I feel his rough palms against my bare skin. I moan at the sensation and push myself up on my knees, gripping his cheeks in my hands and angling his head just right. I suck on his tongue and he moans. I feel his cock hard against me from behind the confines of his jeans.

"Oh, Charlie," he grunts in between kisses. "You feel so good."

"Shut up and kiss me." He falls back on the couch and I lie on top of him, our cocks grinding together. I run my fingers through his hair and his moans get louder. There's still layers of clothes between us, but this feels so damn good. His hands knead my ass cheeks as we dry hump each other, the friction absolutely delicious. I'm shaking against him as I feel a wave of pleasure race down my spine, and I start to whimper, my mouth still melded to his.

He pulls away from the kiss and I sit up. His hand slides into my panties and he begins to stroke me. I arch my back, drinking in the pleasure. "Don't stop," I beg, my eyes closed as I thrust into his hand shamelessly. I fist my hands in my hair and let him play with my cock and balls until the pleasure is so overwhelming I think I might black out. "Oh god, yes," I whine. "Papa Bear."

"You're so beautiful on top of me, Charlie," I hear him tell me, and it makes me want to weep at the same time that I feel my balls drawing up. I'm so fucking close. "Come for me, sweet boy. Come hard for me. Fill my hand with your gorgeous spunk, sweetheart."

I cry out, and my body shakes as I do exactly what he told me to. My release fills his hand and I feel it soaking through my panties and dripping down my leg.

"Beautiful," he says, and pulls me down for a kiss. He grabs a tissue and uses it to wipe off his hand, then tosses it to the floor. I crash on top of him, feeling his still very hard cock underneath me. I'm jello right now, but I desperately want to reciprocate.

"Give me a second and I'll blow you," I tell him, trying to catch my breath.

"You're fine," he says. "I don't need anything more. This was gift enough. You were incredible, Charlie."

I flush. Can he really mean that? Can he really find pleasure in getting me off, and be satisfied in that? I lift my head and look at him.

"You wanna come to Rachel's wedding with me?" he asks, sifting his fingers through my hair.

"Am I invited?" I've never been to a wedding before, but I've always wanted to go to one. They sound so elegant, and I love the idea of dancing with Paul and getting dressed up, maybe even meeting some of his friends.

He nods. "I'm not going without you."

I gaze at him for a moment, then nod. He smiles then presses a kiss to my nose.

"We should get cleaned up."

"Can we cuddle?"

"Of course." We shower and change into our lounge clothes before making some lunch and snuggling on the couch. I suggest *Die Hard* because I know he could use a pick me up after his lunch with Rachel not going so well, and he kisses me, a wide smile on his face.

"Oh, I do have one more thing for you," I tell him, and jump off the couch. I come back and hand him a small package. He raises an eyebrow at me and takes it. He tears it open and pulls out a small box and then smirks at me. I grin.

"It's either this or I have to sleep in my own room again." Not really. I'm not going back to my own room no matter how badly he snores but this little clip is supposed to help if he wears it on his nose and I figured it was worth a shot.

"Fine," he says, with a sigh, and a small smile playing at the corners of his mouth. "I'll try it. Has it been keeping you up?"

I shrug.

He grabs my hand and pulls me to him. I sit on his lap and he kisses my cheek. "I'm sorry."

"It's not your fault," I tell him.

He breathes me in. "I don't want to keep you up. You have enough trouble sleeping without my snoring causing problems."

"Well, that's what this is for. We'll see if it works."

He nods. "I'll try anything."

I kiss him and we turn on the movie.

# CHAPTER
## *Twelve*

**PAUL**

"Holy fuck," I say, walking into Charlie's room to see him dressed in skin tight black pants, and a black cropped long-sleeved shirt. A black headband with cat ears adorns his head, and attached to the back of his pants is a long black tail with a white tip. Shit, he looks good. That's the sexiest kitty I've ever seen.

"You like it?" he asks, stepping away from the mirror. I smile when I see his face paint. He's got the kitty nose and whiskers too, and they're perfect.

"That depends. Are you a sweet, docile kitty or a stubborn, naughty kitty?"

He flushes and grins. "Depends on if I need to get your attention or not."

My eyes rake over him. "Oh, you have my attention."

He grins wider and kisses me as I wrap my arms around him. "You excited?" I ask.

He nods. "It's been years since I was at a Halloween party."

I smile and have to keep myself from brushing the tip of his nose with mine so that I don't mess up his face paint.

"You'll be the cutest kitty there. And maybe if you are very good I'll play with you when we get home."

He chuckles. "And if I'm not?"

I reach around and slap his ass and he squeaks, but grins at me. "No toe kisses for a week," I tease. He gasps and I laugh. He pulls back and looks at me.

"What are you going as? You aren't dressed up."

I glance down at myself, dressed in my regular jeans and T-shirt. "I'm going as the kitty's owner who will murder anyone who touches him."

Charlie smirks at me. "I'll be fine, Papa Bear. We'll be with friends, right?"

I nod. My coworker Aaron and his girlfriend are hosting at her place, and Aaron invited us to come. It meant a lot to me that he included Charlie in the invitation because I wouldn't have gone without him, and Charlie was thrilled at the idea. It will be good for us both to get out. Charlie hasn't met my coworkers yet, and as long as he's staying I want him to feel like he's a part of my life, and he deserves to be involved in whatever events I have taking place. Besides that, I want him to get to know my friends. He's important to me and I want them to know that.

"Ready?" I say. He nods.

We arrive twenty minutes later at Aaron's girlfriend's apartment, who I've learned is named Stephanie. It's dark outside as we make our way up the stairs. The outside of the door is decorated in skeletons and pumpkins and the music is loud enough you can hear it from the hallway. Voices come from the other side of the door and I recognize Aaron's before I see his face.

"Hey, you made it," he says, a wide smile on his face. He's dressed as a cop and I smile. It suits him. He looks me over and frowns. "Nice costume."

"He's going for the grumpy old man with a cat look," Charlie pipes up, then holds his hand out for Aaron to shake. "I'm Charlie."

164

Aaron smiles and takes Charlie's hand. "And you would be the cat?"

Charlie smiles widely and nods. "Don't be too jealous, darling. We can't all be this magnificent."

Aaron laughs and I smile as he waves us inside. "Come on, you have to officially meet Stephanie. And Carlos is here with his wife and son. You should introduce them to Charlie."

Stephanie blushes when she meets me and apologizes for ogling me in the bar, but I smile and wave it off. She's clearly got heart eyes for Aaron and it makes me happy to see. They look good together. I tell her I like her costume and she gives me a big grin. I never would have pegged her for a geek but she's dressed as Princess Leia and she's the spitting image of her, bun head and all.

My gaze moves around the apartment and can't help but be reminded of Rachel with all the decorations. She loved switching out the decor in our house for the different holidays. Stephanie's place looks amazing. There's paper ghosts, witches, skeletons, and pumpkins hanging from the ceiling and attached to the walls, and window clings on the sliding glass door. Halloween themed candy dishes sit on the counter tops and side tables. They really went all out. There's even a pot of "witch's brew" which is actually punch, on the counter in a cauldron. All the snacks and treats are Halloween themed. There's spider cookies, ghost pretzels, and eyeball cake pops. Damn, this girl can throw a party.

I turn to see that Charlie is nowhere in sight, but then I spot him across the room talking to Carlos's son, Diego, who is dressed as a ninja. They're laughing and seem to have hit it off already. I smile. Diego is a senior in high school and I'm hoping he and Charlie can be friends. He's a good kid.

"Paul?" I hear and turn to see the last person I expected to see here tonight.

"Rachel?" I don't hold in my surprise. "What are you doing here?" She's dressed as an angel, complete with the halo and wings. I'm sure Colin is the devil, but I can't find him.

"Stephanie was a recent client of mine. We got to be friends."

"Where's Colin?"

"Getting a drink."

I nod. "Well, I think I'll go find something to drink myself." I take a step away but she grabs my arm.

"Wait, Paul, please." My gaze meets hers and I shove my hands in my pockets. "I wanted to apologize for how I behaved at the restaurant last week. I didn't mean to upset you. I was caught off guard. It wasn't just the age difference that threw me, it was hearing that you were with a man, period, and I know I should be more accepting of that, and I'm trying. I've come a long way after everything that happened with Trey, you know that. In general I am okay with it, but I think it was so much more of a shock because it was you. Hearing that the man I was married to for almost twenty years is suddenly with a guy was kind of a lot to process, and then hearing two seconds later that the guy he's with is nineteen, just kind of..." she takes a deep breath and lets it out. "I'm sorry, though, Paul. It doesn't matter who you are with. Only that you are happy. It's your life and your choices and I have to respect that. And you don't owe me an explanation. And you were right, about what you said about Charlie. I should never have passed judgment on the two of you without having even met him. I'm still learning and growing but I'm trying to be better and do better."

A knot that I hadn't realized I'd been carrying in my stomach unfurls and I wrap my arms round her in a tight embrace. "Thank you," I say. "I understand how that news could have been hard for you." I pull away and she's smiling. "To be perfectly honest, I'm still trying to process it myself. It was never something I was keeping from you, I want you to know that, Rach. Charlie is the first man I have ever found myself being attracted to, and I can't explain it, I just know it's real."

She rests her hand on my arm. "I'd really love to meet him, if that's okay?"

I raise an eyebrow. "Be nice?"

"I'll be the perfect angel." She grins at me. I take her hand and lead her across the room to where Charlie is laughing with Diego still.

"Hey, Diego," I say. "Good to see you again."

"You, too, Paul," he says.

"I see you've met Charlie."

"Yeah, he's been telling me about living with you. Sounds like torture." He grins at me and I shake my head.

"You know my ex-wife, Rachel," I say, and he nods and shakes her hand. I see Charlie's eyes widen, and he swallows, standing up straighter. I chuckle. Somehow it amuses me that he and Rachel are the same height.

"Charlie, sweetheart, this is Rachel. She wanted to meet you."

"Hello," he says, holding out his hand. She takes it and smiles warmly.

"It's nice to meet you, Charlie. I'm glad you could come tonight."

"Thank you. It's nice to meet you, too." He glances at me and I give him an assuring smile. Diego excuses himself and I press a kiss to Charlie's cheek before doing the same. I want him and Rachel to have some time to talk on their own.

Half an hour later she plops herself down next to me at the bar looking over the kitchen sink. "I invited him to the wedding. He's doing my makeup."

I almost spit my drink out. "What?"

She laughs. "That boy is amazing, Paul. He's intelligent, and funny, and sweet as hell, and he knows how to work a brush and do eyeliner better than anyone I've ever seen. I can tell that by looking at him. I asked who did his make up tonight and he said it was him. I've been scared to death about finding someone to do my makeup for the wedding. I don't trust myself. He clearly has an eye for it and he was thrilled at the idea. So now we're besties."

I can't help laughing.

Her voice softens. "I've been wondering, you think it's possible that you've been bi or maybe pan this whole time, but you repressed it because of how we were raised?" She gazes at me, her eyes soft.

"I don't know," I tell her honestly. "It's possible, I guess." I run a hand across the back of my neck and let out a breath. Neither of us like to talk about our religious backgrounds. It's a sore subject, and painful to think about what we went through because of our faith and how it let us down. Our therapist referred to it as religious trauma, and it sounded pretty spot on. "Sexuality is fluid, too, though, right, so…" I shrug.

"Well, whatever the reason, don't you dare screw this up," she tells me, pointing a finger in my direction. She gives me a smile.

I sigh. "I don't even know what this is."

"Maybe you should figure that out. What do you want it to be?"

I run a finger over my cup.

"Paul, does he know about Trey?"

I bite my lip.

"You have to tell him," she says softly.

My stomach tightens and my chest constricts. I feel tears stinging at the corners of my eyes. "I could lose him." My gaze meets hers. "If I say anything, I could lose whatever chance I have of anything more serious happening between us. I'm scared, Rach. He's the best thing that's happened to me in a long time. I don't want him to hate me. I don't want him to leave me."

She reaches over and takes my hand. "That's his choice to make, Paul. You have to respect him enough to let him decide that. And the longer you wait the more painful it will be."

I nod because I know she's right. But I just don't know if I can do it. Telling Charlie what I've done, who I am, seeing the look on his face. It would destroy me.

## CHARLIE

Paul has been super affectionate ever since we left the party. Not that I mind. He hasn't stopped touching me since we got home. Hell, since we stepped outside the apartment door. He held my hand the entire way to the parking lot and in the truck on the way home. Now he's standing with his arms around my waist in the bathroom as I remove my makeup, planting kisses on my neck and shoulders and nibbling on my ears, making me squirm.

I don't know if I've ever sensed his need for me as much as I do now. Not a need for fucking per say, but a need for closeness and connection, like he's reaching out to me, begging for me to see him. These touches are tender and filled with longing and affection, rather than just lust and passion. Like he misses me, not just my body. Like he's afraid I'll disappear at any moment and he can't let go. It makes me wonder what happened at the party. He needs me, that I know.

I feel his nose nuzzling in my neck as his arms tighten around me and his palms rest on my chest. "Are you okay?" I ask him. He nods.

I turn and take his hand in mine, pulling him towards the bed. I lie down and pull him with me. He hovers over me and we kiss tenderly. Our clothes come off little by little. We're not hurried or rushed. He grabs a condom and lube from the nightstand and stretches me slowly. His eyes stay fixed on me the entire time he's thrusting, and I can't help but feel like that means something. Like he's trying to tell me something with his body instead of his words. Whatever it is, I wish he would just say it. The look in his eyes is so earnest, like he's aching to say something but he's so afraid. How can he not know he doesn't have to be afraid with me? After everything, I would never care for him less no matter what he told me.

He thrusts harder, sweat dripping down his forehead as he nails my prostate. "Toes," I gasp. I start to stroke myself, desperate for release. "Please, Papa Bear."

He takes my foot from where it's resting over his shoulder. The second I feel his warm, wet tongue on my bare skin I'm gone. "Yes!" I cry. "Fuck, yes! Papa Bear!" My back arches and my neck muscles strain as I throw my head back, my eyes closing and my mouth falling open as my orgasm crashes into me, my release coating my hand. He's right behind me, and I shake as I feel the warmth of his release through the condom before he buries his face in my neck and collapses on top of me.

I stroke my fingers through his sweat-slicked hair, feeling his chest rising and falling against me. "You sure you're okay?" I ask. He seems distant somehow, even though he's as close as he can possibly be. Sadness emanates from him in waves. What the hell happened at that party?

"Just tired," he tells me. I know he's not telling me the whole truth, but I don't push it. He lifts himself up, presses a kiss to my lips and pulls out of me, before heading to the bathroom. We stay in my bed that night, and he clings to me like he never has before.

I wake that night to him crying out a name in his sleep. It's a name I've never heard before, but I have a feeling I know who it belongs to. His voice is laced with grief and turmoil, and he tosses and turns as he repeats the name over and over. I turn on the bedside lamp and shake him. He starts and his eyes fly open. His breathing is heavy and tears slide down his cheeks.

"I'm sorry," he says, as he sits and rests his back against the headboard, his knees pulled up to his chest. He's shaking and I go to him, taking his large frame in my arms and resting my head on his shoulder, trying to calm him.

"You don't have anything to be sorry for," I assure him.

"You're allowed to have your demons, too." He sobs, and I cling to him before I say, "Was Trey your son?"

He looks up, startled. "What?" Tears streak his cheeks and it guts me.

"The name you were saying, it was Trey. Was he your son?" He nods but doesn't say any more, and I don't ask him to. I just rest my head back on his shoulder and rub his back, trying to soothe him. My poor Papa Bear. I hate that he's hurting.

"You don't have to tell me if you don't want to," I say eventually, as his tears subside. "But I'm here if you do." He wipes away his tears and nods.

"I just want to go back to sleep right now," he says. I lie down and he holds me, but I can't help feeling like he's more broken than I ever thought he was. And I hope that he knows I won't leave him either, and that I can handle his pain, too.

———

I wake before him the next morning, which is odd. He never sleeps past eight o'clock. I slide out from his arms and take a shower before dressing and making my way into the kitchen for some breakfast and coffee. I curl up on the sofa and find myself staring at the pictures on the mantle once again. My gaze lingers on the ones of him, Rachel and Trey. I still can't imagine what it would be like to lose a child. Though my own parents don't seem to be too heartsick over having lost me. As much as I tell myself I'm better off without them, and I know I am, I'm still grieving over the fact that they were never who I wanted or needed them to be. It took me a long time, in fact, to realize that all the anger I dealt with while I was at home and on the streets was actually grief. Grief that didn't have anywhere to go, that had been bottled up for years. But at least now I have a name for it, and that helps. It helps with the acceptance, knowing that they don't love me, that they never will. The love that Paul had for his son is evident and I hate that he doesn't have him in his life anymore. No amount of time can heal a wound that deep.

I hear Paul's heavy footsteps coming down the hall. He leans over and presses a kiss to my hair. His breath doesn't smell the best but I don't say anything. I've craved touch that is genuine and real for so long, that there's no way I'll dismiss it now. And after the rough night he's had, there's no way I'm giving him a hard time.

I wait for him to grab his coffee and take a seat next to me before I shift over and curl up beside him. "Can I ask you something?"

He hums and I take that as a yes. "How did Trey die?" I know it's a big question but I can't sit on it anymore. And if he really isn't ready to tell me, he doesn't have to. It's silent for a long moment and he rests his cheek on top of my head before he takes a deep breath and lets it out.

"He overdosed on drugs."

Shit. I lift my head and stare into his eyes. "I'm so sorry." His gaze is pained. He rests his forehead against mine and closes his eyes.

"Charlie." He trembles. Shit, what's wrong?

My phone rings then, and I see that it's work. Damn.

"You should get it," Paul tells me, backing away.

I shake my head. "I can call them back. It's not an emergency. I'm not supposed to work til later."

"Answer it, Charlie," he tells me gently, then places a kiss on my forehead before resting his hand on my leg and standing.

I sigh but grab my phone. "Hello?"

"Hey, Charlie, it's Don, can you come in a few hours early today? We could really use the help, son."

"Yeah." I rub my thumb and forefinger over my eyes, squeezing them shut. I hate to leave Paul alone right now, but honestly, part of me feels like that's maybe what he wants, and I know I can't leave my boss and my coworkers hanging. "I'll be there as soon as I can."

"You're the best," he says, and we hang up.

"Going to work early?" Paul asks from the kitchen as he plugs the blender in. He's got a small smile on his face now. I have a feeling our previous conversation is over. But I can't shake the feeling that he had more he needed to say.

I nod. "I'm gonna go get dressed."

I'm back out in the kitchen a few minutes later, and he's washing the blender now. I plant a kiss on his cheek. "What will you do?" I ask.

"Oh, I don't know. I might get wild and mop." He smiles at me and I grin back.

"See you later." I kiss his lips and head out the door.

I'm exhausted when I get home twelve hours later, and Paul must have been too, because he's already in bed. Damn. I don't need to talk more about Trey. I think that ship has sailed for now, but I wish I could see his face and snuggle with him for a minute or two, get him to rub my aching feet. He did leave me dinner, which I devour before soaking in the tub and then climbing into bed next to him. I take his arm and drape it over me. He stirs, pressing even closer.

I'm hoping that neither of us wake to nightmares tonight.

# CHAPTER
## *Thirteen*

TWO WEEKS LATER

## PAUL

It's getting colder out, now that it's mid November. Of course, colder for Georgia means it's in the sixties. We're making progress on the firestation. Today we're working on the bathroom, which is probably my least favorite part of the process. It's cramped and there's not as much creativity involved, but we do our best to make it look nice.

My back is aching and my knee is sore. I'm finding it's bothering me more and more lately, and I'm having to ice it and take meds on a daily basis. I hate that I feel so fucking old. And I've had to tell Charlie that there's certain...um, positions, I can't get into sometimes because of it. Especially if I've been doing a lot of kneeling and crouching at work already. I'm always embarrassed, but he never seems to mind, just goes with the flow. He's good at that, which I appreciate. I get more frustrated with my broken body than he ever does. I've fucked him from behind while we're both on our sides more often than not because kneeling is painful, which also means we've had to come up with new and interesting ways for me to blow him. Lately, instead of me kneeling, he's been on top of me when I take him down my throat, and it works, it's just not ideal. And honestly I miss kneeling for him. I think he likes the idea of me on my knees, and so do I. I know it's not my fault and he doesn't blame me for it. We have to work with what we've got, and we still get to be close, but I can't help resenting my own body, and being angry that it won't do what I want it to so that I can give Charlie all of myself. There's a huge part of me that still wonders why on earth he wants to be with someone so much older than him, dealing with all of this when he could have anyone he wants. Someone whose body isn't falling apart. Someone who isn't sporting gray hair and using ice packs every night. Someone who doesn't groan every time he stands or use antacids on a daily basis. Someone who can go two rounds in a night like he occasionally wants to.

I hate when I have to turn him down because I can't get it back up like he can. But he never pressures me. And sometimes I do jerk him off if he's especially horny and I'm not ready to go again. Honestly, those moments are special too, because I get lost in him completely when I'm not focused at all on my own pleasure, and I get to see the look on his face, hear his whimpers and moans and feel his warm length in my palm. I get to watch him fall apart for me without a single thought for myself, and it's overwhelming sometimes to know that my touch affects him the way it does, that he craves it the way he does, and that his body responds to me so strongly. Having my full attention on the way he moves and breathes, the way his mouth falls open and sweat clings to his skin, the way his hands grip the sheets, the way he says "Papa Bear," like no one could ever give him what I do. I find myself overcome by the fact that he wants this from me, that I get to be his lover.

I still haven't said anything more about Trey to Charlie. I've decided not to until after the wedding, just to be safe. I don't want anything to ruin Rachel and Colin's day, and if Charlie doesn't respond well, it just might. At least that's what I'm telling myself. Maybe I'm just scared out of my fucking mind.

I don't realize how much I'm in my own head until I hear Carlos saying Charlie's name, and I turn to see my favorite person walking towards us, hips swaying as he carries a to-go container full of Starbucks cups. I set down my trowel and stand, grunting once again, but can't hide my smile at the sight of him.

"Charlie!" Aaron shouts, a wide smile on his face.

Another coworker, Melissa, beams as well. She met him at the Halloween party.

"Hi everyone," Charlie says, giving us all an award-winning smile. He winks at me, causing my cheeks to heat. I step forward and kiss his cheek and we hear the "oohs" and "ahhs" from everyone else.

"Shut up," I mumble, then turn back to Charlie. "What are you doing here?" He's dressed in his white skinny jeans and a black sweatshirt that falls off of his shoulder on one side and has a large rainbow-colored heart on the front. It's sexy as hell on him. Today his eyeshadow is bright pink and so is his lipgloss. His cheeks are rosy from the blush he applied, and his foundation makes his face appear almost flawless. On his feet are the boots I bought him at Macy's.

"I just had some time on my hands, and I thought I'd bring you guys some hot chocolate," he tells me.

"Ooh, yummy." Melissa reaches for one and Aaron and Carlos follow.

"Thanks, amigo," Carlos declares. I raise an eyebrow at Charlie.

"You're trying to get out of doing your GED work, aren't you?"

He pouts. "It's giving me a headache."

I chuckle but take the last cup of steaming hot chocolate and press my lips to his. He grins at me, wiping his lipstick from my lips with his thumb.

"It's okay to take breaks," I tell him. "You've been

working hard, Charlie. Besides, I'm always happy to see you. You don't need an excuse to come down here."

He looks around. "This place is amazing."

I smile. Having someone acknowledge our work always makes me feel good and like all the aches and pains are maybe worth it. "Wanna stay for lunch?"

He beams at me. "Can I?"

"Sure. I was just about to take a break."

We eat together, and it's wonderful to share my lunch break with Charlie. I can't believe that in all the time he's lived with me we've never done this. My coworkers join us and we joke and laugh and it feels absolutely amazing. When it's time for him to leave, I give him another quick kiss and he waves at everyone.

"So, you and Charlie, huh?" Carlos says, once Charlie is gone.

My anxiety spikes immediately but I try not to show it. "Yeah," I say, praying I won't have to deal with any more judgment. I'm really not in the mood, especially not from someone I work with and have to see every day.

"I thought you two might be together at the Halloween party but I wasn't sure. Glad to have it confirmed." He claps me on the shoulder. "It's good to see you happy, man."

I smile and my body relaxes, the tension leaving me. "Thank you. That means a lot."

"You guys doing anything for Thanksgiving?"

I blink. "Oh, um, no, I don't think so." I hadn't given it any thought honestly. Last year I was by myself, and honestly, the past several years I haven't really cared to celebrate. Haven't really felt like I had much to be thankful for. This year, though, things seem a little brighter, thanks to a certain red-haired, freckle-faced boy that stumbled into my life.

"You guys should come to our place. We always have more than enough food. And Charlie and Diego hit it off the other night. He's been asking about hanging out with him."

"That sounds great. I'll talk with Charlie about it." I smile and we get back to work.

Turns out Charlie is elated about the idea of Thanksgiving with Carlos's family, and two weeks later we're in their home. Salsa music is playing.The house is packed with people. Carlos warned me it would be, so I'm not surprised. They're all dancing together and I see Charlie's eyes lighting up like a kid at Christmas.

Food covers the kitchen countertops, but it's not the typical American food I'm used to seeing and grew up eating —mashed potatoes and stuffing and turkey. This is Spanish food, and it looks amazing! I don't recognize a lot of it but the churros I do recognize, along with the flan. There's also something that looks similar to stuffing. Carlos tells me it's called "pastelon," and has plantains, onions, and different kinds of ground meat and veggies. There's Spanish deviled eggs which are to die for, and ham and cheese empanadas and carnitas. And that's just the stuff right in front of me. God, I think I've died and gone to heaven. This will totally be worth the Tums I have to take later. I can't believe it when Carlos tells me this is just the beginning and the main meal will be in a few hours. He laughs when my eyes bug out of my head.

"Enjoy yourself," he tells me. "And I hope you don't mind dancing, because you will get pulled into it."

I flush because I do not want to dance. But I resign myself to the fact that it's going to happen and make the best of it. When I look over and see Charlie already in the middle of the living room with the rest of Carlos' family, his hips swaying to the music and his arms in the air, I have to smile. He's so happy it makes my chest ache with fondness for him.

He catches my eye and smiles at me, then gestures for me to join him. I shake my head and motion to my plate full of food. He moves towards me as he continues to dance and I laugh. He takes my hand in one of his and my plate in the other and sets it down.

"Dance with me, Papa Bear," he says. God, I can't resist

him. I go, and he drapes his arms over my shoulders, swaying his hips.

"I don't dance," I whisper, my body stiff as a board. My cheeks are heating and my heart rate is spiking. I feel so out of my element.

"You're doing fine," he tells me, giving me a warm smile. I relax a little. But I notice we're not exactly moving the way everyone else is.

"You're doing great," he tells me again, noticing how my gaze is lingering on the rest of the group. "This is enough. Baby steps."

I nod. We dance for a little bit longer with his arms draped over me before he steps back and sways his hips, his arms jutting out to the sides. I smile as I watch him, then reach out and take his hand. He spins and I pull him into me, then find my own hips moving. The music is quite catchy. He grins.

"There you go," he cheers. A second later, a young girl is grabbing my hand. I think she's Carlos' niece. She has long dark hair and brown eyes and a sweet smile. I think she must be eight or so.

"Like this," she says, and starts to do a few simple steps that I follow. I smile and find myself relaxing to the rhythm. Charlie takes my other hand and all three of us do it together. Then suddenly, there's a circle forming and almost a dozen people are holding hands and dancing together. It's the most fun I've had in a long time, even if I don't know what I'm doing, because these people don't care, they just love that I'm here and that I'm trying. And they are the kindest people on the planet. I've never felt more welcomed.

When it's time for us to go several hours later, I find Charlie in Diego's room. He's showing him his book collection and his video games.

"You should come over some time so we can play," Diego tells him as Charlie fawns over the Nintendo Switch.

"I'd be horrible at it. I've never even touched one," Charlie tells him sheepishly.

"That's okay. I'll teach you."

Charlie smiles. "I'd like that."

"You ready?" I ask him.

He nods. "See you later," he tells Diego, and we head home. It was an amazing day, but we're both exhausted and it doesn't take long for us to fall asleep once we're in each other's arms.

## CHARLIE

*One week later*

"Do I look okay?" Rachel is standing in front of the mirror in her dressing room at the church. I've never seen a bride more radiant. Her dress is absolutely stunning. It's form fitting and hugs her curves, but flares out at the bottom in a mermaid style. It's covered in lace and has thick straps but a deep v-cut that shows off her cleavage tastefully. Her hair is in a partial updo and the rest falls in waves over her shoulders. I finished doing her make-up a while ago, and she was so grateful she almost started crying. Thankfully the mascara is waterproof.

"I've never been to a wedding before, so you're the first bride I've seen, but I can honestly say you are perfect," I tell her. "Colin is very lucky."

She smiles at me. "Oh, it's me that's lucky. But thank you." She squeezes my hand. "You know, I never thought I'd find love again after Paul, and honestly I was a bit of a mess, but Colin saw past all that and loved me in spite of it. He's really quite incredible."

I smile. "I'm happy for you."

"You know, Paul is lucky, too," she tells me. "You guys are good together, Charlie. I can tell. Don't let anyone tell you differently."

I flush. "Thank you. I'll leave now. Would you like me to get Colin?"

"Yes, please." She gives me a wide smile. "Charlie?" she

says as I reach the door. I turn to face her. "I'm really glad you're here."

I nod. "Me, too."

After finding the groom, I make my way to the men's room to get into my own clothes. I didn't want to be helping Rachel with her makeup and risk getting my dress dirty, so I waited. It's a gorgeous one-shoulder maxi dress, black on the top and multi-colored on the bottom, in white, pink, purple and gold. I pair it with pointy gold heels and then stand in front of the mirror to apply my own makeup.

I hear a breathless "Wow," a moment later and turn to see Paul standing in the doorway. He's absolutely breathtaking in his tux and I can't take my eyes away from him. The light pink bowtie and the lily corsage make his attire even more appealing. I've never seen him in a suit or tux before. Jesus, my mouth is going dry. We have to attend formal events more often.

"Oh, Charlie," he whispers as he takes a few long strides towards me. Then he's gripping my bare arms and his gaze is raking over me. "Sweetheart, you're stunning," he says, and it's so heartfelt and sincere I almost melt.

"Thank you. So are you."

He smiles and kisses me. I finish with my makeup and he takes my hand, leading the way to the sanctuary. I take a seat in the front and he makes his way back to find Rachel. I think him walking her down the aisle to her new husband is probably the strangest and sweetest thing on the fucking planet.

My phone buzzes and I see that it's a text from Paul.

**Hot old guy: can you come back to Rachel's room please? We need your help.**

I stand and make my way back to where she was when I left her. I knock on the door, wondering what could possibly be wrong. Is her makeup messed up? Is something wrong with her dress? What could I possibly help with?

"Come in," I hear a male voice say that isn't Paul's. Colin, no doubt. I open the door to see Paul and Colin trying to soothe a clearly panicked Rachel. She's pacing the room and shaking her hands. I have a feeling she'd be running her fingers through her hair if she could be.

"What's going on?" I ask, shutting the door behind me.

"Our flower girl is sick," Colin tells me, and my eyes widen. "She's got some sort of stomach bug and she can't make it."

"Oh, I'm sorry." I feel terrible for them but I'm not sure what—

"Will you do it?" Rachel blurts, her brown eyes pleading as she holds her hands up to her mouth as if in prayer. "Please, Charlie?"

My eyes widen further. "Me?"

She nods and takes a step closer to me, gripping my hand. "I'd be honored."

I don't know what to say. She really wants me walking down the aisle at her wedding, in front of everyone? "Are you sure? I'm not exactly the traditional choice." I laugh a little as I feel tears stinging at the corners of my eyes.

"Fuck tradition. You look amazing in that dress and you deserve to show it off. And I don't care what other people think. What do you say?" She squeezes my hand and I find myself smiling from ear to ear. I nod, and she squeals before giving me a bone crushing hug.

"Okay, we better get out there," Colin says. He squeezes my shoulder and gives me an appreciative nod before leaving the room. I head out with my flower basket shortly after, and wait for the music to start playing before I make my way down the aisle, tossing petals on the gold runner. It's obvious some people are confused to see me instead of an eight year old girl, but there are a lot of smiles as well, and damn it, I enjoy myself.

I find my place at the front as the music starts for Rachel and Paul to come down the aisle. Rachel is beaming the entire time and so is Paul. I look over and see tears in Colin's eyes as he stands with his groomsmen, and my chest starts to ache. I wonder if I will ever have this. Is this in my future? This love, commitment, and trust? This level of devotion? I want it to be, so badly.

My gaze lands on Paul, and I know more than anything that I want all of that with him, and only him. I just wonder if he wants it with me, too. I've been dying to tell him how I feel, how I've felt since the moment he took me into his home, into his life, but I've been so afraid that if I say anything I'll scare him away. Which is also why I haven't brought Trey up again. I can't risk losing him, or pushing him away. I've experienced too much rejection in my life, and being rejected by him would be more than I could bear. It's too soon to tell him that I want us and only us forever, no matter what. That he's the only person for me, and there could never be anyone else. No one sees me the way he does, understands me the way he does, cares for me the way he does, makes me feel worthy and deserving the way he does. I can't imagine my life without him. Being with him the past couple of months has given me so much. Not just a home, a safe place to rest my head, food, and a chance to better my future; it's given me healing. A chance to talk and cry and feel, and things I never gave myself permission to do before, to feel safe not just physically but emotionally as well, knowing he won't judge me for my tears or heartache or grief, or anger. He's been my harbor, and I can't lose that, but I hope that in some way, he's come to need me too.

# CHAPTER
## *Fourteen*

## PAUL

I can't get over how devastating Charlie looks tonight. His dress is exquisite and his make up is flawless as always. His smile is radiant. I can't help myself, I have to have him in my arms. And even though I know I'm not the world's greatest dancer, I scoot out of my chair where we're seated at the reception and hold my hand out to him.

There is live music playing, slow and romantic. I want this moment with him. I need it. His gaze meets mine and he smiles, then scoots out of his chair and picks the hem of his dress up off the floor to keep it from dragging. I don't know what it is about seeing him in a dress that I love so much, but I really do. He holds it in his hand as I take him in my arms.

"Having fun?" I ask him as we sway. He nods, the smile never leaving his face.

"I don't know when I've enjoyed myself more." We dance for a moment longer, gazing into each other's eyes, before I speak again.

"You really do look incredible, Charlie," I tell him, and he blushes beautifully. "I think you might make the bride jealous."

He chuckles then. "Not possible. Rachel is radiant."

"Well, thank you," we hear, and turn to see her standing there. We stop dancing and she gives Charlie a big hug.

"Thank you again for everything today," she tells him.

"Of course."

"Do you mind if I cut in?" she asks, and I'm about to take her into my arms as Charlie steps back when she says, "no, not you, I want to dance with Charlie."

My eyes widen and she laughs. "I won't hurt him, I promise."

"I don't know if the dance floor can handle all the gorgeousness," I say, and wink at Charlie. He shakes his head and I squeeze his hand before making my way to the open bar where Colin is sitting with some of his groomsmen.

"You ready for life with her?" I ask him.

"More than ready," he tells me. In all the time I've known him, I think I've seen him smile twice. Even now he's serious, but I know him well enough to know that doesn't mean he's not happy, or one hundred percent devoted to his new wife. He'd give anything for Rachel, do anything to make her happy, sacrifice anything for her in a heartbeat. I raise my glass to his and we clink.

"You're a good guy, Paul," he tells me. "It means a lot to both of us that you are here, and that you walked her down the aisle."

"It was my pleasure," I tell him.

"You and Charlie," he continues, "you seem good together."

I clear my throat and look in the direction of my two favorite people on the dance floor together. "Yeah, I don't know what it is about him, but I'm not trying to figure it out, honestly."

He laughs. "Why you work doesn't really matter. Only that you do."

———

When we get home that night, I'm aching to make love to Charlie. He's so beautiful, and the magic of the evening is still in the air as we undress. It's taking me far too long to get out of my tux, but Charlie's dress slides off of his slender frame in one fluid motion, pooling at his feet, leaving him standing in front of me in only his lacy, black, floral panties. Fuck, I'm hard in an instant. The panties accentuate his cock so beautifully. He's half hard as he moves towards me in the low light of the bedroom, his hips swaying slightly. He looks so fucking gorgeous. All that pale skin, those adorable freckles, and those crimson curls flopping in front of his eyes. My Charlie. I still don't know what I did to deserve him. I can feel myself trembling as he reaches up and presses his lips to mine, unbuttoning my shirt as he does. It's joining his dress on the floor seconds later and then he's palming my erection through my slacks, and I'm moaning as he stands on his tip toes and presses kisses to my neck.

"Fuck, I want you," I moan. "Charlie, sweetheart. Please."

"I'm fucking you tonight, Papa Bear," he tells me, squeezing my cock harder. "You're mine." My cock twitches and I growl, then grab his face in my hands and slam my mouth against his. Fuck, yes. My pants are on the floor seconds later and I can feel the wet spot forming on my boxer briefs as the cool air hits my skin.

"Lie down," Charlie instructs. I slide my briefs off and do as he says. He grabs the condoms and lube and kneels on the bed. My cock is twitching in anticipation, my body humming with need as beads of precum leak out and slide down my shaft.

I take a condom from him and slide it on, and as soon as I do he's leaning over and pressing kisses to my balls. "Oh, Charlie," I moan, gripping his hair in my hands. He hums and nuzzles my balls this time, breathing me in before licking a stripe from my sac all the way to the tip of my cock. "Fuck!" I shudder and cry out, "Charlie!"

"I've been waiting weeks to do this, old man," he says.

Then he straddles my legs and lowers his face. I'm expecting him to go for my cock again, but I gasp and my stomach sinks in when his warm, wet tongue slides along my belly button. I groan because it feels so much better than I ever expected it to. Fuck, my nerve endings are on fire. And he's loving this. He's eating me out, sucking and licking, and, "Fuck, sweetheart." My cock twitches like crazy and I grip his hair again, my hips bucking. Oh, sweet Jesus, I never knew my belly button was this sensitive. God, this feels good. He flicks his tongue over it and I fucking wail, my back arching. Then his mouth is over it and he's sucking on it again. I'm whimpering and whining, writhing underneath him, my body shaking and my thighs trembling.

"Want me inside you?" he asks, lifting his head. There's spit sliding down his chin and his face is flushed. His red curls fall in front of his eyes. He looks absolutely gorgeous. I nod my head furiously and he slides off of me, shimmying out of his panties before reaching for the lube. Then he's between my legs and I'm spreading for him, and even though I've never done it before, it feels like the most natural thing in the world. My hole flutters and I can't wait to be filled by him.

He works me open slowly, carefully, and I enjoy every moment of it, the way his eyes gaze at me with so much fondness and adoration, the way his fingers move inside me, gentle at first but then harder and faster when I ask for more, the way he plants kisses to my knees as he stretches me to be filled by him.

When I'm ready, he slides on the condom, then positions himself at my entrance and pushes his way slowly into me. I breathe out as I take him. Every inch feels so good. I moan at the feeling of fullness as he bottoms out, his cock buried deep inside me.

Tears fill my eyes, because I've never in my life experienced this feeling of completeness, wholeness, of absolute rightness at being taken, being owned, belonging to another person, our bodies being joined together, being one. I never felt this deep of a connection with Rachel, even after nineteen years of marriage and all the times we made love. But with Charlie, it's so profound my chest aches with it. Every time we do it, it becomes more special. And having him inside me for the first time, giving myself to him, I know it's something I want to do again. Over and over. I want everything with him.

He rests his forehead against mine and I feel his warm breath on my face, his hands on either side of my head as he supports himself. "You okay, Papa Bear?"

I nod, and stroke his cheek. "Just overwhelmed at how good you feel," I tell him. He smiles.

"Want me to move?" I nod and kiss him as he begins to thrust. Our lips never leave each other's. He reaches down to stroke me in tandem with his thrusts, and it doesn't take long at all before I'm coming with a whimper, and he's not far behind. Our lips part and we're breathing heavily, our bodies slicked with sweat, our chests rising and falling. He pulls out of me and collapses on his side.

We lie with our legs intertwined and our noses nuzzling each other's, our fingers running down each other's sides or gliding through each other's hair.

"It's getting close to Christmas," I tell him. "What do you say tomorrow we go tree shopping and get some decorations?" His eyes light up and he nods enthusiastically. I can't help but laugh. Oh, my Charlie.

## CHARLIE

Paul lets me sleep in the next day, and when I wake up he has my favorite breakfast waiting for me again. I shovel down two waffles and a cup of coffee before showering and dressing in dark wash jeans and my off the shoulder sweater with the heart on it. Then we pile into the truck and make our way to the store to hunt down a Christmas tree and trimmings. We find a gorgeous seven foot tall one that's extra fat, with fake snow, pine cones, berries, and just a tiny bit of glitter on it that I love, and he doesn't hesitate to put it in the kart when he sees the way my eyes light up.

I love seeing all the holiday decorations around and hearing the Christmas music through the store speakers.

After we've picked out some funky ornaments and a gold star, he turns down another aisle and I follow him. This one is full of stockings and he turns to me with the biggest smile. "Which one?" he asks.

"Huh?" I say, confused.

"Pick one," he says.

Tears start to fill my eyes. "Really?"

His smile widens and he pulls me close, planting a kiss on my forehead. "Of course. It's your home now, Charlie. And I don't want my stocking hanging on the mantle looking sad and pathetic all by itself. Go on."

I smile and grab a pink one in the shape of a mermaid tail, making him laugh and kiss me. We grab some reindeer stocking holders next, and some blue and gold ribbon for garland. Then he lets me pick out a tree skirt. I choose a blue one with gold stars scattered across it.

"Okay, that's it or we'll go broke," he says, and we head to the check out.

We spend the afternoon putting up the tree and then make hot chocolate and settle back on the sofa admiring our handiwork, the fireplace crackling and *The Santa Clause* playing in the background. It's cozy and perfect. I'm so excited to celebrate Christmas with him in a few weeks. I haven't had a good Christmas in ages. I have to think of something to get him. It has to be good, too, after everything he's given me.

Paul's phone rings, and he reaches forward to pick it up off of the coffee table. "Hey, Carlos, what's up?" There's a pause and then he says, "Oh, yeah, he's right here, let me ask him." He turns to me. "You interested in going out tonight with Carlos, Aaron and Diego?"

"Where? And yes," I say, grinning. He smiles and tells Carlos we'll be there, wherever there is, then hangs up the phone.

"There's a club nearby he's been to a couple of times with his wife. Planning to meet there at eight. And Diego is looking forward to seeing you again."

I smile. I like Diego. He's fun, and really nice, and having someone else there who won't be able to drink will make me feel better.

The place is lively as ever when we arrive, and Carlos and Aaron are already at the bar when we walk in. I don't see Diego yet but Carlos tells me he'll be there soon. He's driving separately because he was hanging out with his girlfriend.

True to his word, Diego arrives only minutes later. He gives me a wide smile and a hug when he sees me. I'm not used to other guys being my same height, and I'm not gonna lie, it's kind of nice. He's only a couple of inches taller than me. There's some dancing going on a few feet away from us and he gestures for me to join him. I smile and nod. I get Paul's attention to let him know where I'm going before we head off.

I'm having the time of my life with Diego, sweat dripping down my forehead, my arms raised and my hips swinging to the steady beat around us, when I feel a hand on my shoulder and turn to see Paul there. I smile at him.

"Come to join me?" I ask over the music. Before he can answer, someone runs into him and he in turn runs into me, nearly knocking me over. Diego grabs me and keeps me upright as the stranger turns around, facing Paul.

"Shit, I'm sorry," he starts, but then his eyes widen and his face turns red with rage. His dark eyes narrow as his jaw clenches, and before I know it he's gripping Paul by his shirt and shoving his face in his. "What the fuck are you doing here?" he snarls.

"Hey, take it easy, Dylan." Paul's voice is calm but he's trembling as his hands grip the younger man's forearms. This stranger can't be older than twenty-one and I know I've never seen him before. Who the hell is he and why does he look like he wants to fucking murder my man?

"Let him go," I say, stepping up to them, even though this Dylan character towers over me just like everyone else. His arms are bulging as he keeps his fists clenched in Paul's shirt and I'm certain he could annihilate me with a single punch. But I don't care if I get hurt. No one treats my Papa Bear like this.

"Are you serious?" Dylan says, looking at me and then back to Paul. His face is getting even redder and the veins in his very large forehead are bulging. "Is this your fucking date? Are you fucking kidding me?" His hands only tighten on Paul's shirt, his knuckles turning white. "After what you did to Trey you show up here with a fucking twink on your arm? You're a real piece of work, you son of a bitch!"

I see Paul's face going ashen and my heart rate spikes. "What is he saying?"

Dylan laughs maniacally. "You don't know?" he says. "Oh, that's epic. You don't know you're dating a murderer." His eyes glare daggers at Paul, who is shaking now, and I can't breathe. Surely this must be some kind of a joke.

"You're wrong." I shake my head. "He wouldn't hurt anyone. You're wrong."

This Dylan character looks back at Paul, studies his face for a moment, then says, "What do you call a man who kicks his son out of his house for being gay and leaves him in an alleyway to die with a fucking needle in his arm?" He shoves Paul back, causing him to stumble, then glances between us. A look of glee crosses his harsh features when he sees the horrified expression on my face. "You're a fucking monster," he snarls, pointing an accusatory finger at Paul. "I hope you rot in hell." Then he's gone, making his way through the crowd.

## PAUL

It takes every ounce of courage I have to turn and face Charlie. And when I do, I wish I hadn't. His face is ghostly pale and he's shaking. Tears are filling his eyes and his lower lip trembles. His hands are clenched in fists, gripping the sleeves of his cropped sweatshirt. He swallows.

"Is it true?" he asks. I can barely hear him over the noise around us.

"Charlie, can we go somewhere else, please?" I reach for him, but he jerks away.

"No!" he shouts, tears sliding down his cheeks. "Tell me now!" We're attracting quite the crowd now and I'm more humiliated than I've been in my entire life. This is not how I wanted him to find out. Why didn't I tell him sooner?

My stomach clenches as bile rises in my throat, my temples heating. I can't do anything but nod.

He takes off through the crowd before I can even blink. "Charlie!" I call and go after him as fast as my legs will carry me. It's hard to find him in the throng of people dancing and gyrating, especially since he's so small. I spot him outside the double glass doors. Diego is with him, and Charlie whispers something in his ear. Diego nods and hurries off, and I crash through the door.

"Charlie, please," I beg. "I can explain."

"I want to believe you, Paul," he says, and I flinch at the sound of my own name. He's never called me that before. "But how do you explain what I heard in there?" He gestures inside. "Maybe you aren't the man I thought you were. Maybe this was all too good to be true. Maybe I don't deserve to be happy."

"No, Charlie, that's not true." I take a step towards him but he backs away, holding a hand up, and god, it stings like nothing ever has before.

He shakes his head and turns away before facing me once more. "Just tell me something," he says, as tears slide down his cheeks. "Is that why you took me in? Because you were trying to make up for what happened to your son? Is that what I was to you? Some sort of project? A way for you to redeem yourself? Is that what all of this has been?"

I shake my head as my chest heaves. It's taking everything in me not to move closer to him again. I swallow. "No." It comes out as barely a whisper. "No, Charlie. It might have started out as me wanting to help you because of what happened to Trey and maybe I felt obligated, but I genuinely cared about you, and it became so much more than that so quickly. You are so much more to me than that. You have to know that." I'm sobbing now. "And nothing can or ever will make up for what I did to my son. There is no redemption for me."

Diego's car pulls up to the curb then, and Charlie moves to get inside. My breath catches. NO. No, no, no. My feet stay planted on the sidewalk even though everything in me is screaming to reach out and pull him back, beg him not to leave. *Please.* I gasp when I feel the familiar ache of grief radiating through me, filling me, becoming overwhelming, the physical sensation of my heart feeling like a knife is sinking into it. "Where are you going?" I ask as he opens the door.

"Home to get some of my things, and then I'm going to stay at Diego's for a while. I need some time. I can't be with you right now. I'm sorry." He climbs in the passenger side door and the car speeds away.

My chest heaves. I can't imagine walking through my front door knowing he won't be there when I get home. I feel an emptiness settling in my chest already that's so painful I can barely breathe.

———

I barely function over the next several days. I find it difficult to concentrate at work. I woke up the day after Charlie left with the mother of all hangovers. The spot next to me on the

193

bed was empty and cold and I'm reminded everywhere I go in the house now, of Charlie's absence. There's no shoes by the door, no wrappers left out on the coffee table, no music playing. His car is gone. All of his things are missing from the bathroom. My chest constricts, and as much as I try to tell myself it's better this way, I know I'm lying. My arms ache to hold him. I miss his smell, his soft curls against my nose and cheeks, his kisses, his laughter. I miss his snarky comments. I miss the sound of his footsteps in my home. I miss him. And every time I think of what happened in that club and the words that came out of Dylan's mouth, the things Charlie heard, I can't blame him one bit for leaving, for wanting nothing to do with me. I'm so ashamed.

I never intended for any of this to happen. I never intended to run into Charlie that night at the bar almost three months ago. I never intended for him to show up on my doorstep a week later, or to find myself instantly attracted to him. I never thought I'd have to risk telling him about Trey or lose him, because I never expected it to matter that much in the grand scheme of things. I never thought anyone would grab hold of my heart the way he has. I never wanted to give my heart to someone else again, but he never gave me a choice. From the moment I met him, he captivated me, inspired me, enthralled me. He made me want things I've never wanted before, made me laugh and smile again, made me see the world in ways I'd never seen it before. He brought color back into my life. My soul is alive again because of him and I don't want to know what it would be like to live without him.

I'm in love with him. I know that now. I've known it for a while, I think. I just didn't want to admit it, because that meant I had to come clean. I had to be brave enough to give him everything, even the darkest parts of me, and hope he loved me too, enough to not walk away in the end. But I don't have anything left to lose now. I just have to hope that at some point he's willing to listen to what I have to say, and hope that it's enough for him, that he'll find it in himself to forgive me. It's been two weeks and I haven't heard from him, and I don't know what to think. I don't know if he'll ever come back, or if I've hurt him so much he's going to stay gone for good.

"Hey, you okay?" Carlos asks, and I come out of the daze I've been in.

"Yeah," I say as we finish up with our lunches.

"Worried about Charlie?"

I nod slightly. "You sure he's okay?" Carlos and Aaron were far enough away from the incident the other night that they didn't see what happened, but they knew Charlie and I had a falling out. And after I ended up getting wasted, they had to get me home. I told them I could get an Uber, but they insisted on taking me, because they wanted to make sure I was safe inside my home before they left. That was not my finest moment at all, but they didn't judge me for it. In fact they've been nothing but kind and empathetic, which is another thing I feel that I don't deserve, and I'm quickly coming to realize how much I truly need their friendship. But how would they feel if they knew what Dylan had said the other night? Would they look at me the same way Charlie did? I've avoided relationships and friendships for so long for this reason. I honestly thought Diego would have told Carlos what happened, but it doesn't sound like he has, which I am tremendously grateful for. I just hope he doesn't hate me, too.

"He could be better, amigo. He's quiet. Doesn't say much, but he's working on his GED still, making it to the restaurant. He hangs out with Diego mostly, in his room. I didn't ask for details, you know. It's not my business, but I hope you guys can work out whatever went wrong. It's clear he misses you. We told him he could stay as long as he needs to, but it's not home. You are."

I nod again, my chest tightening. "I know. I miss him, too. I messed up, Carlos. Not just now, but a long time ago, and I don't know if he'll be able to see past that."

"We all mess up, man. Sometimes big. But Charlie doesn't seem like the kind of person to judge someone by their worst mistakes."

I bite my lip. "I want to tell him my version, but I don't think he wants to hear it. He left. He was so hurt. And he had every right to be. What I did, it's…" I shake my head and have to keep myself from crying.

Carlos rests his hand on my shoulder. "Look, I don't know your past, and I don't need to, to know that you're a good guy. He wanted space, and time. That doesn't mean he doesn't want to listen, or that he doesn't want you, just that he wasn't ready at that moment. It's been two weeks. Maybe it's time to try again."

## CHARLIE

Diego and I are sitting on his bed playing *Super Smash Bros.* when my phone buzzes. I suck at this game but he's trying to distract me, and if I study for my GED any more today I will go crazy, and thinking about Paul is just making me miserable.

I reach for my phone when he pauses the game, assuming it's work, and am surprised to see that it's Rachel.

"Hello?" I answer.

"Charlie," she says. "How are you?"

I sigh. "I've been better." I try to keep the tears from falling because I've done enough crying over the past two weeks, but nevertheless they come. I feel like such a lousy guest because I'm sure Diego is sick of listening to my sniffles and sobs. But he just stands and squeezes my shoulder before leaving the room and closing the door behind him, to give me privacy.

"Paul told me what happened, sweetie. I'm so sorry you had to find out that way."

"I know I should listen to his side of the story," I say. "I want to. That guy at the club was super pissed and clearly bitter, and I know there has to be more to it then what he said. I know Paul isn't a murderer. I'll never believe that. I just, I feel so hurt, and like I've been lied to and manipulated for months by the one person I thought I could finally trust, you know? And I don't understand why he wouldn't tell me. He told me he would never hurt me." I sniffle and wipe my eyes.

"I know. He never meant to, Charlie. He's not perfect, sweetheart, but he is good, I promise you that."

"I know." No matter what I've heard from some random stranger at a bar and no matter how bad it sounds, I know the kind of man he is, and he is good. He's better than good. He's wonderful. And I miss him so much. I miss his arms around me at night. I miss his laughter and his sparkling blue eyes. I miss the bashful look on his face when I catch him cleaning "for fun." I miss the feel of his stubble against my cheek. I miss his foot massages and his toe kisses. I miss our reading sessions. I miss everything about him. Fuck, I even miss his snoring.

"I don't know if he wants me to come home anymore, after I've ignored him for so long," I say, my chest heaving. "What if he doesn't want me?"

"Oh, honey, he will always want you to come home," she tells me, with absolute assurance in her voice. "Trust me, Charlie. That man is crazy about you. Don't ever doubt that." Her tone changes suddenly.

"Hey, listen, sweetie, I need to get back to Paul but I wanted to tell you first."

My body tenses and my stomach tightens. "Tell me what?" I ask. "Rachel, Is everything okay?"

"Well, mostly," she says, and now I'm super confused, and also a little panicky.

"Is something wrong with Paul?"

"Charlie, don't freak out okay? Because he'll be fine," she starts, and my heart rate skyrockets. "He's in the hospital."

"What?" I shout, jumping off the bed and letting the controller fall to the floor. "Oh my god. What happened?

197

What hospital?" I pace the room, biting my lip and running my fingers through my hair. If something happened to him and I wasn't there, I'll never forgive myself.

"He has a kidney stone." She doesn't sound worried, so I relax a little.

"A what?"

"A kidney stone. Trust me you don't want one. They're painful motherfuckers and he's drugged up on morphine. Son of a bitch drove himself here when he started having side-splitting pain. Apparently he just thought it was some sort of work injury at first, like he'd pulled a muscle or something, but then it got a lot worse. They did a CT scan and it's not super big, so they think he should be able to pass it on his own. If they can get him comfortable with pain meds they can send him home tonight, if not they'll have to admit him, and they may have to do surgery to remove it."

"Oh, no." My poor Papa Bear. I can't believe he went through that alone. It's all my fault. If I'd been there I could have taken care of him. I could have driven him to the hospital. What was he thinking, driving himself instead of calling an ambulance? "Why didn't he tell me? Why am I hearing it from you?"

"He didn't think you would come, Charlie. He's convinced you won't want to see him and he's afraid of being rejected. But I know him. He wants you here."

"He doesn't know you're talking to me, does he?"

"He thinks I'm in the bathroom."

"Idiot," I say, wiping my eyes. "I might be upset, but I wouldn't leave him alone in a hospital."

"I know," she says. "Are you coming?"

"Of course I'm coming. But I might smack him when I get there."

She chuckles. "Not too hard. He's in enough pain as it is."

"Fine," I groan.

———

When I get to the hospital, I get my visitor's sticker and they tell me where to find Paul's room. I told Rachel I'm there but she never told Paul I'm coming, so this should be interesting. He's on drugs and we haven't seen each other in two weeks.

I reach his room and Rachel sees me from the open doorway before Paul does. She smiles and stands.

"I'll give you two a minute," she says, then squeezes my arm and leaves the room.

Paul's eyes widen when he sees me. "Charlie?" He's groggy from the pain meds and he tries to sit up straighter, but it doesn't work. I notice he has more stubble than normal. I wonder if he's been as depressed as I have and that accounts for the lack of shaving, or if he's just going for a new look.

"Yeah, old man, I'm here." I hand him the teddy bear I brought, and he blinks, his cheeks flushing.

"Is this for me?"

"Sure, I don't think the little girl I took it from will miss it that much," I tease.

He hugs it to himself and my chest clenches. God, I've missed him. "Can I sit?" I ask. He nods.

"I take it Rachel called you?" He turns his head to the side so he can see me. I nod.

"Yes, although I would have appreciated it more if you had."

His gaze leaves mine and his fingers play with the creases in the blanket draped across him. He has an IV in his arm and a blood pressure cuff around his left bicep. A pulse oximeter is on his left index finger. I hate seeing him with so much stuff strapped to him, even if he is technically okay. It makes the reality of what could have happened to him hit so much harder, and I hate that I was so stubborn and stayed away for so long. If anything had happened to him while I was gone and I hadn't been there...Hearing that he was in the hospital, that he was sick, that I wasn't there when he needed me. Nothing felt worse than that. And I don't ever want to feel like that again. "I didn't think you'd care."

I sigh. "Just because I'm upset doesn't mean I don't care." *I care more than anything. That's why you keeping things from me hurt so much. I want you to trust me. I want you to be honest with me. I fucking love you.*

He looks at me again. "I'm sorry, Charlie. I should have told you about Trey sooner. I should have told you a lot of things sooner. I was scared. I didn't want to lose you." He takes in a breath and continues, his voice soft. I scoot closer and take his hand and he trembles. "You've changed my world Charlie. I never expected to fall in love again, and then you bulldozed into my life and I fell for you so hard and fast, and it scared the shit out of me. But the idea of losing you scared me more, and I just couldn't tell you. I couldn't have you thinking less of me because of what I'd done. And then I lost you anyway, and I…" Tears are filling his eyes now and sliding down his cheeks as his chest heaves, and I stand, moving to his side.

"Shh," I say, stroking my fingers through his hair. "Rest, Papa Bear. You didn't lose me. I'm here now, and I'm not going anywhere. We can talk later, okay?" I press a kiss to his head and he nods. I squeeze his hand and then I lie down in the bed with him. His breath hitches and I look up at him.

"This okay?" I ask. "Does it hurt?" He shakes his head and drapes his arm over me, closing his eyes.

*I never expected to fall in love again.* His words echo in my mind as I doze off. I wonder if he realizes he just told me that he's in love with me, or if it's the morphine.

# CHAPTER
## *Fifteen*

## PAUL

I wake up, I'm not sure how much later, to the blood pressure cuff on my arm going off for the billionth time, squeezing the daylights out of me. That thing fucking hurts, and I'm tempted to just rip it off. I grunt at the weight on my chest and start to panic a little, before I remember that it's Charlie who is on top of me, his head resting against my chest.

I settle back and breathe normally, running my fingers through his hair. I can't believe he's here. I just wonder how long it will last. I take a deep breath and let it out, but just as I'm about to wake him, the doctor walks into the room and does the job for me.

"How are you feeling?" she says, causing Charlie to stir.

"I'm okay," I say. "Pain has gone down quite a bit. That morphine is pretty good stuff."

She chuckles. "Yes it is, but you can't stay on it forever, I'm afraid. Do you feel like the pain is manageable enough that we can send you home with pain meds and see if you can pass this on your own? We'll give you something to help make that part a little easier and we'll give you a strainer to use as well. You'll need to take it with you each time you use the bathroom, in the hopes of catching the stone so you can take it to the urologist when you see them. We'll have you follow up with them in a couple of weeks. Also, make sure you are drinking lots of water."

I nod. "I think I can do that."

"If you feel worse you can always come back," she tells me. "I'll get your discharge papers and be back soon."

"Thank you."

Charlie sits up and yawns. "Going home?"

I nod.

"Good. I'll drive you."

An hour later, we're home and Charlie is guiding me up the front steps and into the house. He helps me change into sweats and a T-shirt since I'm still a little loopy from the drugs, and then tucks me into bed.

"I'm going to go pick up your meds," he tells me. "I'll be right back."

"Charlie, you don't have to do all of this," I tell him.

"Someone has to do it. You can't be driving right now. Besides, I want to. Now shut up." He kisses me on the forehead and then leaves the room.

I wake to pain in my side a while later and start to regret ever leaving the hospital. It's not as bad as it was, but it's definitely not pleasant. It's gone from "I want to die right fucking now" to "yes, some pain meds would be nice, please, thank you." I climb out of bed, wincing, and slowly make my way to the kitchen for the meds. Charlie sees me from his place on the sofa. I'm a little surprised he's still here. I wasn't honestly expecting him to be. Not because I think he's a jerk, but because I am, and I don't deserve him. But he did say he wasn't going anywhere, and I guess he meant it.

"Shit, are you in pain?" he says as I shuffle through the kitchen gripping the countertop.

I wince. "What gave you that idea?"

"Sit down, dumbass." He jumps off the couch and tosses his book aside.

"I'm already here now," I argue.

"Do I need to manhandle you?" He crosses his arms over his chest, and I can't help laughing.

"Now that would be entertaining."

He smirks at me. "If you sit down, I'll give you a kiss. How's that?"

I grin despite my pain. "Better." I move back towards the couch and sit, gripping my left side and wincing again as the pain increases. Charlie brings me the meds and a glass of water. I take them and swallow as he sits next to me. Then he takes my chin in his small hand and presses his lips to mine softly. It's so gentle it's barely there, but it's everything to me after being away from him for what feels like an eternity and feeling so afraid I'd never have him back.

"Charlie, I'm so sorry." Tears are filling my eyes and I'm shaking but I have to do this. My chest heaves and I grimace at the pain in my side.

"We don't have to do this now, Papa Bear," he tells me. "You should rest."

I shake my head. "I can't. Not until I tell you the whole story. It's driving me crazy. I just don't want you to know the kind of man I really am. You're so good, Charlie, and I'm so ashamed."

He reaches up and rests his hand on my tear-stained cheek. "I know exactly the kind of man you really are. Whatever you are about to tell me is in the past, and that's not who you are. It's who you were. And who you were doesn't matter. Because that's not the man that I know. That's not the man that took me in and cared for me. That's not the man that made me believe in myself. That's not the man that made me laugh and smile again, the man that made me feel seen, and worthy, and deserving, and good for the first time in my life." He pauses, staring into my eyes. "That's not the man I fell in love with."

My breath hitches. I shake my head. "Charlie, don't—"

"Don't you dare," he tells me, his gaze firm. "Don't you

dare negate this. I just told you I'm fucking in love with you, Paul Richards. Don't you tell me not to be. Don't you dismiss it. Don't you do that right now. Don't do that because you don't think you deserve it. I don't care if you deserve it, it's here, in front of you. I'm here, and I'm giving it to you. I love you. Despite your mistakes, however big they are. And I want you to know that before you tell me how wretched of a person you think you are. Because nothing can convince me that you aren't worthy of my love."

I'm sobbing as he takes me into his arms and holds me close. "I'm not going anywhere," he tells me again. "So do your worst."

"I killed him, Charlie," I sob. "I killed my son." My side aches the more I cry, but I can't stop.

"Shh," Charlie soothes. He pulls away and takes my hand, standing. I follow him and he leads the way to the bedroom. We climb into bed and he faces me, scooting close. Taking my hand, he links our fingers, then strokes my hair with his other hand as my tears fall. "Take your time," he says. "It's going to be okay. Nothing you say will change how I feel about you. I'm not going anywhere. Remember that."

I nod and take a deep breath in and let it out. I squeeze his hand. I still have my doubts about him staying, but I continue. I haven't told a single soul my story, outside of therapists, and even that was years ago.

"I already told you Trey died of a drug overdose, and you heard the cliff notes version the other night." Tears slide down my cheeks and Charlie wipes them away.

"Why don't you tell me the non cliff notes version?" he says. I nod.

"So, first of all, you need to know that I grew up in a very conservative, Christian home. I was raised in church and on the Bible, and went to a Christian school all my life. Rachel and I were high school sweethearts. We got married pretty young. Mostly I think because we wanted to have sex and didn't believe we could until we were married. We didn't even kiss until our wedding day because we believed we'd be better people for it, that God would love us more. But if there was one sin that was worse than sex before marriage it was same sex relationships. Being gay was okay because that wasn't a choice, but acting on it was. Which meant if you were gay you had to just accept that you would be single for the rest of your life. No sex, no family, no romance. Which was normal for me and I never saw a problem with it. It was just how things were, a part of life, and of course it wasn't a big deal because it never affected me." Charlie's gaze hasn't left my face and I have no idea what he's thinking, but I keep going.

"We raised Trey in church just like we were. It was our life. Every Sunday, every Wednesday night. Rachel was on the worship team. I was a Sunday school teacher. Our closest friends were our church friends. Our faith was everything. Our family was everything." I take a deep breath before I continue.

"Trey was sixteen when he told us he was attracted to boys. Our world imploded. We didn't know what to do. We were scared. We prayed about it. We asked our pastor for advice." I'm starting to shake now, and having a hard time breathing, and Charlie scoots closer, taking me in his arms and holding me close. He rubs my back as I take deep breaths in and out. "We were stunned, but we did our best to be supportive, or at least what we thought was supportive at the time. Now I know we were anything but."

More tears slide down my cheeks as I continue. "We told him we loved him and that we always would, no matter what, but that he knew he couldn't act on these desires if he wanted to follow Jesus. That he ultimately would have to choose between his faith and his sexuality. When he started struggling with that and arguing with us, telling us that wasn't true, we got even more scared. We had raised him to believe a certain way and he wasn't following that, and it terrified us. We didn't want him to fall away from the faith we desperately believed would save his soul. But he insisted he could be gay and in a relationship, and love Jesus. We didn't see that and we argued about it all the time. Our close family unit began to fray. I didn't understand how the faith that had been such a source of strength and unity and peace for us was suddenly an area of contention and causing so much strife and pain, and I really wrestled with that. Why was my son going through this and why wasn't God helping us? Our pastor convinced us that Trey needed counseling, and when he refused to go, we gave him an ultimatum, believing we were doing it out of love, that if we gave him the choice, he would choose to get the help he needed."

"What did you tell him?" Charlie asks. I can tell he's trembling, and I hate it. I know this story is hard for him. I knew it would be. I hate that he's hearing these words come out of my mouth.

I squeeze my eyes shut as tears fall. I feel sick to my stomach, but I choke the words out. "We told him that if he didn't talk to the pastor he had to leave."

I'm so ashamed of my own words and my own behavior that I'm pulling away, but Charlie tightens his grip on me. A choked sob leaves me and I cling to him. "We destroyed him, Charlie. We thought we were loving him, but we were killing him. We taught him that he had to choose between God's love and his sexuality. That he couldn't have both. We taught him to hate his sexuality, and himself as a result. And the boy that was so lively and spirited and beautiful turned into nothing but a shell. We taught him that not only does God not love and accept him for who he is, but that we didn't either. He told us so many times that it was who he was and he couldn't change, that he didn't have to change, but we wouldn't listen. He just wanted us to listen."

"I'm so sorry," Charlie says, and I can tell he's crying too.

"I was so confused, Charlie," I say. "I wrestled with my faith even more after Trey left. I never expected him to actually choose homelessness over counseling. But he did. He said he wasn't going to change no matter who tried to make him, and that the fact that we refused to listen just proved that we didn't love him, so he was better off without us. We were convinced that once he realized how bad it was out there he would be back. But he never was. And we grew more and more uneasy about our decision as the weeks went by. But our pastor and the elders at our church told us if Trey was supposed to come home he would, that it was all a part of God's plan to redeem him, and that we were teaching him a lesson he needed to learn, that we couldn't let him walk in sin. But I felt sick over it, so after a few more weeks we started to look for him. Months went by, and Rachel and I tried calling him and texting him, but he ignored us. All the while we were reading different books and articles and watching podcasts, everything we could get our hands on that was written by gay Christians, so we could hear their stories. We watched films. We found a church that was lgbtq inclusive and talked to the pastor there about Trey and found he had a very different take on our son's sexuality than our previous church members and pastor did, and our viewpoints started to shift. We realized just how wrong we were, and how desperately we needed to ask his forgiveness. We searched even harder after that, trying to find him and bring him home."

"What happened?" Charlie asks, pulling back and peering into my eyes. His eyes are filled with tears now too.

"We had cops show up at our doorstep about six months after he left, telling us he'd died of a drug overdose. We went to identify his body. That was the last time we saw him. He died believing we hated him, Charlie. He was addicted to drugs because of us. He was so desperate for an escape because he wanted to feel something. Because he didn't have the parents he deserved. He didn't have our unconditional love. We failed him. He was alone and scared and hurting because we wouldn't take ten minutes to sit down and listen to him. Because we were so focused on rules and regulations and not who he was as a person and what he was going through. We listened to the spiritual advice of others instead of our guts and our son, and insisted we were right, and we weren't willing to wrestle with our faith until it was too late. And it cost us everything. And in the end, Rachel and I couldn't handle it, and we had to separate too."

"I'm so sorry, Papa Bear," Charlie says, wiping the tears from my cheeks, and sniffling. "It must have been really hard for you, feeling like your faith betrayed you."

I nod. "I haven't stepped foot inside a church since then. I started to question so many other aspects of my faith and what the Bible had to say after all of that, and feeling like I'd been led astray my entire life. And after my own parents told me it was "part of God's plan", I was so upset I haven't talked to them, either. Rachel has actually deconstructed. She's an atheist now. I'm not an atheist, but I don't really know what I am. I believe in God, but I don't know exactly what I believe about him."

"I can't imagine going through all of that." Charlie cards his fingers through my hair. "Losing your family, your faith, everything. I'm so sorry." He rests his forehead against mine. "You're an amazing person, Paul Richards. You loved your son very much, I can see that. If you didn't, you wouldn't care about what happened to him. And you wouldn't be trying to be a better person because of it. It took a lot of courage for you to question what you had been taught your whole life. That isn't easy. I think religion can be really beautiful. It's not all bad. But I hate how often it's used to spread hatred and animosity instead of love and hope. I think if your faith causes you to exclude anyone you're doing it wrong."

I nod and sniffle. " I just wish I'd seen that sooner."

"I know," he tells me, hugging me to him.

"Can I ask you one more question?" he says. I nod. "Who was Dylan? Was he a friend of Trey's?"

I nod again. "He tried to help him after he left, I think, and he did for a little while, but Trey got so addicted to drugs

Dylan couldn't save him, and he blames us. Rightly so." I sob quietly as Charlie holds me.

"Don't ever leave me," I say, gripping him tightly. "Please. I need you." He lies on his back and pulls me to him. I rest my head on his chest and drape my leg across him, pinning him in place.

"Sleep," he tells me, and I feel his arms closing around me.

"Charlie?" I manage before I doze off.

"Hmm?"

"I love you, too."

"I know," he says. "You told me in the hospital."

"What? When?"

"When you were drugged up, you told me you were in love with me."

"Oh, sorry." I want to move my head and look at him, but I can't. I'm so exhausted.

He laughs. "Don't apologize for it."

"No, I'm sorry I'm telling you I'm in love with you twice now when I'm drugged up. I was planning on it being more romantic than that."

"I don't know what you're talking about," he says, pressing another kiss to my hair. "This is romantic as hell, old man."

## CHARLIE

"Rise and shine, sleepy head." I stroke Paul's stubbled cheek and he stirs, blinking his eyes open. Normally I would let him sleep in on his day off, but I can't wait any longer. It's Christmas morning and I want to give him his present. He's had a rough few days. It's been a week since he came home from the hospital. He's doing better physically after passing the kidney stone, but his anxiety has been through the roof since our conversation about Trey, and he still looks at me every day like he can't believe I'm still here. Despite my assurance, he seems convinced I'll change my mind any moment and bolt. I wish he could see himself the way I see him, as the strong, beautiful, amazing man he is. Someone who messed up and grew and learned from his mistakes, who continues to learn and wants to do better. Someone who changed my life and made me better. I will always love him for that. He's the best person I know.

"Happy Christmas," I say and press a kiss to his nose, trying to cheer him up. He smiles, but it doesn't reach his eyes. "I love you," I add, and stroke his cheek. I think it's still hard for him to hear those words, but I won't stop telling him.

His eyes are filled with so much grief and anguish still, so much self-hatred, it breaks my heart. "Are you sure this is what you want, Charlie?" he asks me. "You could have anyone. Someone who isn't broken mentally or physically. Someone who can keep up with you in bed. Someone who doesn't need you to bring them ice packs and ibuprofen every night and give them massages all the time. Someone who didn't lie to you for months."

I press my finger to his lips to silence him as his eyes fill with tears.

"Let me show you how sure I am. I'll be right back." I press a kiss to his head and then slide out of bed, moving out to the living room where his gift is waiting under the tree in the early morning light. I grab the white envelope with his name on it and bring it back to him, kneeling on the bed. He sits up, blinking at me, and I hand it to him. He sniffles and wipes his eyes.

"What's this?"

"Your present. Open it."

He tears it open and pulls out the paper. He unfolds it and his eyes rake over it. I bite my lip as I try to keep the smile from forming on my face. His eyes meet mine and he's crying all over again, but I'm hoping these are happy tears.

"These are your test results?" He's shaking. Oh, god, Papa Bear. I nod. "You're STI free? For sure?" I nod again, barely able to contain my excitement. I shuffle closer on my knees and take his face in my hands.

"This is how sure I am," I tell him. "I want this. I want us, making love, without any barriers, because there's no one else I will ever want besides you. You are my everything, Paul Richards. You are my savior. You are my world. And I will never not love you. I will never not want you."

He tosses the paper aside and takes me in his arms, falling onto his back as our lips meet.

He is my everything, and I know I've found my forever, my home, the place where I belong, and it's right here, with him. No matter where life takes us, no matter where the road leads, we will walk it together, two imperfect, broken souls who are slowly but surely putting each other back together. And I can't imagine anyone else I'd rather be on this journey with than him.

"Charlie," he whimpers, as we undress each other. Moments later he's thrusting into me, my knees hooked over his broad shoulders, his bare cock deep inside me as I stroke myself, whining his name.

"Oh my god, Charlie," he tells me. "Fuck, I never knew it could be this good. You feel amazing, sweetheart." Tears fill his eyes as he gazes at me, and I'm a goner. I take his face in my hands and bring his mouth to mine, kissing him tenderly, our tears mingling with each other's as his thrusting slows and we rest our foreheads together for a moment, just breathing each other in, savoring this sweet connection, our oneness, our unity, our love.

"Okay, I need to move," he says, and I nod. He kisses me as he begins to thrust again, and we both moan, our heads thrown back, each other's names on our lips.

"Fuck," he growls, and I shake at the pleasure radiating through my body as he nails my prostate again and again, his body arching and his toned muscles strained and on display for me. I run my hands up his torso and grip onto his powerful shoulders as his body tenses and he cries out my name. I feel his warmth deep inside me as he releases and I almost cry again at the sensation of him filling me. It's everything I thought it would be and more.

He slides out and I whimper at the loss and sensation of fullness, but not a second later he's sliding his fingers inside me and I'm gasping and writhing as he nails my sweet spot again.

"Oh, shit," I groan. "Papa Bear." My hips buck but he holds me down with his other hand and leans over to take my very hard cock in his mouth as his fingers continue to fuck me. Holy fuck, I'm shaking so hard as he swallows me down, and my cock is twitching like crazy. He's never had me in his mouth before without a condom between us, and this is insane! I'm going to come in t-minus two seconds, especially with him moaning around my cock like that.

"Oh, oh, fuck," I whimper, "so good, I'm so close, Papa Bear," I warn him, just in case he wants to back off. He only moans louder around my shaft and then buries his tongue in my slit at the same time that he probes my prostate with his fingers, and I fucking lose it. "Paul!" I shout, coming hard, my release shooting down his throat and my ass clenching around his fingers at the same time. It feels so damn good, nothing between us. Absolute perfection.

He pops off of my cock and licks every last drop of cum from my shaft and head, humming as he does. "So fucking good, Charlie," he tells me, then buries his face in my groin and inhales before planting kisses on my cock and sliding his fingers out of my hole. He kisses his way up my abdomen, my chest, to my neck, and then his lips meet mine, and we kiss lazily for several moments, me tasting my own spunk on his tongue and reveling in our closeness before he pulls back.

"I like hearing you say my name when you come," he says, a twinkle in his eyes. I grin.

"More than 'Papa Bear?'" I ask. He shrugs.

"We can switch it up." His eyes soften and then he says,

"Thank you for this. For showing me I don't have to be perfect to be loveable."

"You do the same for me every day," I reply. He kisses my forehead.

"Wanna open presents?" I ask.

He smiles at me. "Do you?"

I nod.

"Then yes."

We shower first and then head out to the living room. The tree we decorated is beautiful in the early morning light, and there are a handful of gifts underneath it. I didn't have a lot of money, but I wanted to get Paul a few things. And I know he got me some things too.

I make us some coffee and we each grab the presents we got for each other and sit curled up on the couch.

I beam when I open a set of salon grade nail polish from Paul, some very high quality makeup and some more sexy panties.

I grin widely when he opens his gifts from me; a new blender to make smoothies with, because his old one was constantly glitching, and he refused to replace it even though it drove him crazy, a new mop that he'd been eyeing for a while now, and a tumbler for his coffee with a brown bear on it and the words "Papa Bear" on the front.

He tells me it's too much, and I tell him to shut up and then I kiss him, tell him he better damn well use the tumbler all the freaking time, and then inform him that we have one more thing on the agenda for today before we come back home and relax, preferably in the nude.

He eyes me and informs me that it is Christmas so no place is open, but I tell him to get dressed and that I'm sure this place is open. He seems hesitant, but does as I ask.

Fifteen minutes later, we're in the truck and I'm stopping off at the gas station on the corner to pick up some flowers before turning down the main road and heading in the direction Rachel told me to go. I would have stopped at a nicer place to get flowers, but this was the only place open on Christmas, and I figure this is better than nothing.

"Charlie," Paul says, his voice hoarse when he realizes where we're going. It's within sight now, and tears are sliding down his cheeks as I pull into the parking lot of the cemetery.

"We don't have to," I tell him, reaching over and resting a hand on his thigh. He shakes his head.

"No, I, I want to. Thank you." He squeezes my hand and we climb out of the truck. Paul leads the way to the tombstone and stops in front of it, trembling slightly, his hands in his pockets. I squeeze his forearm and take a step forward, reading the inscription: *Trey Richards, 2002-2018, Beloved Son, Forever In Our Hearts.*

I kneel and place the flowers on the tombstone, then take a deep breath. I press my fingers to my lips and then touch them to the place where Paul's son rests. "Merry Christmas, Trey. I hope you know how much your dad loves you and misses you. I just wanted you to know that you aren't forgotten."

I stand and wrap my arms around Paul as he sobs, my head resting on his chest as he envelops me. "Thank you," he whispers, then plants a kiss on my hair.

"He's my family, too," I tell him. We hold each other for a moment longer before walking back to the truck arm in arm.

## PAUL

*6 months later*

"Happy birthday to you, happy birthday to you, happy birthday dear Charlie, happy birthday to you."

There's cheering and clapping as the song finishes and Charlie blows out all twenty candles on his ridiculous unicorn cake, splayed out on the table in front of us. I kiss his cheek as he grins down at me from his place on my lap, his arms wrapped around my neck.

We're crammed around a booth at the bar I frequent with my coworkers (the same one where Charlie and I met) and this time, several of Charlie's coworkers are here too, along with Rachel and Colin, and Diego. There's not nearly enough room for everyone to sit, so several of our guests are standing, but they don't seem to mind, and having too many friends and family is always a problem I feel blessed to have.

We're all wearing birthday hats, except for Charlie who has a tiara perched on top of his head and an "It's my birthday, bitches" sash draped across his torso that Dorine surprised him with. He's dressed in a black leather mini skirt and a long-sleeved, leopard print, off the shoulder crop top, complete with his strappy black heels. HIs smile is endless as he takes us all in. I don't know when the last time was when he had a birthday celebration. Next to the cake are the giant ass balloons that Rachel and Colin brought, and beside them are the endless amounts of gifts from everyone, in all different shapes and sizes. Charlie is squirming on my lap now, and I laugh. I know he's eager to get to his gifts.

"Don't you want cake first?" I ask him.

"Okay, but just a little bit," he tells me.

"Why don't I get us some drinks," Carlos says, and glances around, waiting for everyone's orders. Almost everyone asks for a beer but there's a few requests for margaritas or mai tais. Charlie and Diego share commiserating looks at the fact that they still can't drink, and Carlos and I tell them they can have sips of ours. I'm shocked when Rachel asks for water instead of her usual drink. Carlos doesn't think anything of it and walks away to fill our orders, but I know my ex-wife. That's strange.

"You're not getting a margarita? On a Friday night? Who are you and what have you done with Rachel?" I ask as we dig into our cake.

She chuckles as her cheeks pinken. "I'm fine," she says. Her smile widens and Colin kisses her temple.

"Holy fuck," I whisper, and drop my fork. I swallow.

"Rach?" She's biting her lip and I can tell she's trying not to tell me something. Her eyes light up.

"Oh my god," Charlie says, catching on. "Are you pregnant?"

Rachel exchanges a glance with Colin and he smiles wider than I've ever seen him smile before. He nods. She turns back to us and nods. I have tears in my eyes as Charlie shrieks and jumps off my lap. Colin stands so that Rachel can escape and Charlie gives her the world's biggest hug. She laughs with tears in her eyes. "I wasn't planning on saying anything until after the party. I didn't want to ruin your special night, Charlie."

"Are you kidding?" he says. "This is the best birthday present ever." He squeezes her again and she laughs.

"Thank you."

I stand and give Colin a hug. "Congratulations," I tell him. He's beaming at me and I just know he's going to make an amazing dad.

"Thank you," he says, letting out a breath, his hands shoved in his pockets. "It was kind of a surprise, but we're rolling with it. I'm going back and forth between being excited and panicked."

I laugh and squeeze his shoulder. "Sounds about right."

I turn to Rachel. She has tears in her eyes as I hug her to me tightly. Pulling away, I take her face in my hands. "You're going to be amazing," I tell her. "This baby will be so blessed to have you for their momma, Rachel. You and Colin together, you've got this. And they'll have Charlie and me, too. They'll be surrounded by so much love."

"I know," she says. "That means a lot. I'm really glad we still have each other, Paul. After everything that's happened. I still need you."

I smile. "I still need you, too, Rach." I squeeze her hand.

"Hey, what did I miss?" Carlos says, returning with our drinks.

Charlie looks at Rachel and she nods, so he blurts out so the whole table can hear. "Rachel's pregnant!"

———

5 months later Rachel gives birth to a beautiful baby girl, and I have tears streaming down my cheeks when she announces her name. Tracy Gabriella Ford.

"We wanted to honor Trey," Colin tells me, as I take her in my arms and stare down at her beautiful round face, her tiny body swaddled in the hospital blanket and the little pink hat on her perfect little head. She yawns and it makes my heart clench. God, I'm so in love. Charlie stands next to me, wiping tears from his eyes and rubbing my back.

"Thank you," I whisper, looking to Colin and then Rachel. I plant a kiss on Rachel's forehead and then sit with my niece. This beautiful gift of life that I can't wait to get to know and love and spoil with everything in me.

"Okay, my turn," Charlie says, squirming, and I laugh. He reaches for Tracy and I hand her over. Charlie's face lights up as he takes her in his arms and holds her close.

"Hey there, princess," he says in such a sweet voice it makes my heart melt. "We're gonna have lots of fun together you and me. We're gonna have dance parties and tea parties and nail parties and if you want to play in the dirt I guess I can do that too because I love you, even though it's not really my thing." We all laugh, and Tracy sneezes. It's the cutest thing ever.

"Actually, Charlie," Rachel says, "we were wondering if you would like to be Tracy's nanny."

Charlie's head snaps up, his mouth falling open. He seems to be at a loss for words.

"You don't have to give us an answer now," Colin says. "We know you have a job already, and you're in school, and might want to take some time—"

"I'll do it," he says, his eyes filling with tears once again. "You really want me to watch her?"

Rachel nods. "More than anything. You would be amazing, Charlie. There's no one else we'd rather have."

"Holy shit," he says, wiping his eyes, then gasps and covers his mouth. "Sorry."

We all laugh.

*Epilogue*

5 YEARS LATER

"Big day for you guys," Carlos remarks as we work on painting the inside of the barbecue restaurant we've been building for the past several months. We've got the doors and windows open to help air the place out, and a lovely breeze is blowing through. I'm still sweaty and disgusting, though, and my back and neck are aching, as is my knee. I've been on prescription medication for it for a while now as it's been getting worse, and I've done quite a bit of physical therapy. It's helped, but it's still an ongoing problem. Fortunately I have Charlie to soothe my aches and pains in the best ways.

I smile widely in spite of my discomfort. "Yeah, it is." He has no idea how big.

Charlie has worked so hard over the past five years, earning his GED and then attending night classes to get his degree in elementary education, all while being nanny to his favorite little girl. Tracy keeps him on his toes, but he adores her. She's sweet as pie, but an absolute spitfire as well, and just as full of snark and sass as he is.

It was only a few days after she was born that he came to me and told me he wanted to start seeing a therapist to help him "work through his shit" as he put it. He told me it was something that he'd been thinking about for a while, but holding Tracy in his arms was the final push he needed because he wanted to be his best for her, for us, and for himself. He said the idea of spilling his guts to a stranger scared the crap out of him but it was something he wanted to do, for all of the people in his life now that had made it better, offered him a place to call home and family when he'd thought he would never have either of those things again. And though I never would have thought less of him for not going to counseling, I couldn't have been more proud of him for taking that step. He's made so much progress. He only sees his therapist on an as-needed basis now but I can tell how much working with her and talking through his trauma has made a difference. He's even more vibrant and lively than he was when we met and his night terrors have all but vanished. With her help and guidance he is truly becoming the best possible version of himself and it's a beautiful thing to witness.

He did have to quit his job at Sunny's after becoming Tracy's nanny, but we're back often enough he still gets to see his friends there and show off his little niece. Of course she's not so little anymore. She'll be five soon and starting kindergarten. And tomorrow, Charlie will be graduating from college. I couldn't be more proud of him. My beautiful boy. Though, he's grown into quite the young man now. Even more gorgeous than when we met all those years ago, and my heart is still so full of love for him. He's taught me so much about forgiveness and grace and second chances.

"Paul Richards!" I turn and see the object of my affection coming towards me, but he doesn't look as devastatingly handsome as he usually does. Probably because of the scowl on his face. Oh, lord, what have I done this time?

He's dressed in black leather pants that cling to his skin and a cropped pink and black sweater that falls off of one shoulder, showcasing his lovely freckles. I can't help the smile that creases my lips, thinking about how I had my mouth all over those freckles just last night. On his feet are combat boots, and his red curls fall into his eyes. But he's clearly upset and I have no idea why. What did I do?

"Uh oh," Aaron says from across the room. "Angry ginger alert." I glare at him and he goes back to work.

"What are you waiting for?" Charlie asks once he reaches me. He stares up at me with those gorgeous green eyes that still have the power to make me weak in the knees.

I set my paint roller down over the tray and step towards him off the drop cloth, making it crinkle. My coworkers pretend they aren't listening, but I know damn well they are hearing every word. They're right fucking there.

"You wanna tell me what this is about?" I ask. He huffs, crossing his arms over his chest, and I can't help chuckling. It's kind of adorable. Then he reaches into his pocket and pulls out a ring. My eyes widen before I start to laugh.

He frowns. "You've been hiding this in your dresser drawer for weeks. Why haven't you asked me to marry you yet?" He shoves it in my face.

I laugh more now and pull him towards me, kissing his forehead. Oh, my Charlie.

"What's so funny?" he pouts. Now all my coworkers are staring at us and not even trying to hide it. I hear a gasp and a squeal come from Melissa.

I push him back gently and peer at him, brushing the hair away from his eyes. "I was planning to ask you tomorrow night, after your graduation. After we celebrated with everyone. I thought it would be a nice surprise, something romantic, just the two of us." He flushes beautifully and bites his lip.

"Oh."

"But if you hadn't burst in here demanding that I propose to you, you wouldn't be the man that I love." He grins at me. Then I take the ring and kneel, very thankful for the meds and PT that are allowing me to do this right now. Charlie's hands go over his mouth and tears fill his eyes. He starts to squirm.

"Charlie, you've changed my whole world," I tell him.

"From the moment you showed up on my doorstep and threw up on my very clean floor, my life hasn't been the same." He chuckles and wipes tears from his eyes. "You've made me happier than I ever thought I could be or ever would be again. You are the sunshine in my life, my greatest joy. I want to spend the rest of my life with you. Charlie—"

"Yes!" he shouts, grabbing the ring and sliding it on his finger. Then he's pulling me to my feet and jumping up, wrapping his legs around me and pressing his mouth to mine. My coworkers are clapping and whistling, and I'm kissing him as he clings to me.

"There now," he says, pulling away and beaming at me. "Was that so hard?" I laugh and kiss him again and again.

"I hope you realize you probably have paint on your outfit now," I tell him.

He shrugs. "It was worth it."

We have our own little celebration that night, and I can't deny that as he struts across the stage the following morning in his cap and gown (and bright pink heels), the only thing sexier than seeing him get his diploma, is my ring on his finger.

The End

# Thank You

Thank you for reading Until You. If you enjoyed Paul and Charlie's story please take a moment to leave a review on your favourite review site or wherever you purchased it from. It would mean a great deal to me.

Do you want to read Paul and Charlie's wedding story? You can get it for free by signing up for my newsletter at felicitys-now.substack.com. The newsletter goes out once a month and the link to the story will be included in each publication

You can listen to my playlist for Until You at tinyurl.com/UntilYouPlaylist. These are songs that really spoke to me while I was writing this story and that I feel reflect Paul and Charlie so well.

# About the Author

I live in sunny Florida with my husband, three children, and our Maltese. I love rainy days and sunshine, curling up with a blanket and a good book, and watching my favorite tv shows. I love creativity in all its forms, which is why writing is such a passion for me. I'm a big fan of the tv show Supernatural, and believe that Starbucks is a form of self-care :)

# More Books by Felicity Snow

Chasing You

Come Fly With Me

Best Friends (Free Download)

payhip.com/b/SrEMC

You can follow me on social media, join my Facebook group, see my Pinterest storyboards and more at linktr.ee/felsnowauthor.

Milton Keynes UK
Ingram Content Group UK Ltd.
UKHW041828310823
427750UK00004B/102

9 798223 605362